Predetermined Bonds

THE HIGH COUNCIL WITCH CHRONICLES

JULIE CATHERINE

PREDETERMINED BONDS

THE HIGH COUNCIL WITCH CHRONICLES

JULIE CATHERINE

Edited by
KATIE WOLF

For Bub and Little Bub

ONE

A SPECIAL INVITATION

"WHAT ABOUT THIS ONE?" Aunt Abeline lifted a shirt adorned with a thousand shimmering sequins over the top of my dressing room curtain. I dragged the drapery open, completely ignoring her latest offering.

"I'm just gonna get this," I told her.

She looked down at my selection and frowned. "A gray T-shirt."

"It goes with everything."

"Black cords and a gray T-shirt. That's your look?"

"I look nice." I smoothed the simple style over my shape, looking back in the mirror. I was right, the neutral color was working for me. It matched my eyes. My grandmother's moon charm necklace peeked out at the collar. I tucked it safely back under my tee. Ever since I'd recovered the delicate chain from the rooster's perch of Kate's barn, I'd taken to wearing it all the time. Aunt Abeline wore her matching star charm jewelry too.

1

"Did you even read it?" Aunt Abeline wiggled her sequined choice again.

"And sew it begins," I read. "Punny."

"It's word play! You like word play."

I raised an eyebrow in her direction. "*You* like word play."

There was always a game of Scrabble going between us at the house. I had yet to win a match.

"I do love a good pun," Aunt Abeline agreed. "A fun pun?" She pondered the words aloud, but she could see she was losing me. "Well, what about this?" With her other hand, she held up a pale green tee with embroidered summer fruit bursting out of the breast pocket.

"Too pineapple-y."

"This?" Next came a red tee with tiny black flowers.

"I don't think so."

"This." Aunt Abeline was quickly becoming a shop-happy octopus, grabbing clothing off multiple racks at once. She revealed another flower number.

"Do I really seem floral?"

"Well, you don't seem drab and gray. Your clothes should reflect you, Mae. Take a chance. Don't be afraid to be your true self," Aunt Abeline encouraged.

"This shirt is me," I said. "I look okay." I retreated to the changing room and tugged the curtain closed again. I don't know why I even agreed to go shopping in the first place.

"It'll be fun," Aunt Abeline had told me. "You need some new clothes," she had claimed with a nod.

I didn't know then that she meant my whole wardrobe.

It was hard to choose even one new piece. I had no idea what to buy. What does one wear on their first day at a secret witch school?

It was the very definition of unknown.

Plus, it didn't help that I had only two days to decide.

The introductory letter inviting me to the Judicial Studies of the High Council had arrived shortly before our official induction was to begin, and I had wasted the first day of that window in total moonfaced shock over the whole thing. The letter they sent was maddeningly sparse.

It is with great pleasure we wish to extend to you a cordial invitation to the Judicial Studies of the High Council.

While the circumstances of your entry were not the typical mode of welcome, by a vote of six to one, the High Council has agreed to include you in this year's class. Studies commence on the 17th of the month. Entrance to the school can be found at 128 Wiltonshire Road.

Please be packed and ready to begin your semester abroad.

. . .

That was it.

Five sentences to welcome me to the biggest invitation of my life.

What their secret society really needed was an orientation pamphlet to put their new inductees at ease.

So the magical powers of fate have decided you're worthy...

(Or, a little worthy. You got in with a vote of six to one.)

Welcome to the Judicial Studies of the High Council.

See shopping list on page five.

Magical wizards in the movies got a shopping list. Why couldn't I?

I quickly redressed in my former clothes before Aunt Abeline could recommend any more sparkling, fruit-covered items. Plain, muted colors seemed like a safe, simple choice.

I should call Josie, I thought, pulling on my shoes. She'd know what to wear.

Maybe when I got home.

We left the store with only one T-shirt in my shopping bag. I thought I'd made a smart decision, but once I arrived home, I wasn't so sure. Aunt Abeline was right. There was an awful lot of gray in my wardrobe.

And there was still no word from Josie.

I checked my phone for the millionth time. If I got my letter yesterday, it seemed reasonable that she would have got hers too. We would, after all, be inducted into the same Judicial Studies class at the High Council together. Wouldn't we?

I looked at the wording of my letter once more.

The members of the High Council have agreed to include you by a vote of six to one.

One person said no.

Was it possible Josie's induction score had been even worse than mine? Could she have not gotten in? There was only one way to find out. On my cell phone, I flicked to the message app and stared at the digital keyboard. How to tactfully open the conversation?

So... will I see you at the High Council?

The cursor flashed at the end of the sentence. Ready to go. I squinted at the letters. Not bad. It was playful in tone, but succinct and to the point. I frowned and deleted it.

Good news! I'm in. Are you?

Ugh. I immediately deleted again.

Just checking if... they liked me better...

Delete. Delete. Delete.

I threw my phone on the bed.

This was why I was hoping Josie would have opened the conversation. She must have gotten in. Right? I couldn't think of a single way to ask without sounding like a jerk. I'd be stuck with my foot in my mouth if the answer was no.

But the silence was unnerving.

If she was admitted, she would have texted...

wouldn't she? I pretended not to notice the double standard I had built in my head.

The rest of the afternoon and evening went by without a word. Finally, Aunt Abeline poked her head in the doorway of my bedroom.

"Well, did you pack all your gray shirts and black pants?"

"Not yet." I shook my head.

I looked at the stacks of clothing on my dresser, on the floor, on my bed, all laid out. I sighed. Aunt Abeline was right. There were an awful lot of neutrals in each pile.

"Is it too monotone?"

"Well, at least take this one." She scooped up a bright blue shirt off my designated "no" pile. She held it up to my face. "No sparkles, no text, no style at all. But look, it lights up your eyes."

"It practically screams in my face." I pushed it away.

Aunt Abeline cocked her head to one side and raised an eyebrow.

"Fine," I agreed.

I tossed it into the "yes" group and sighed. The shudder came from deep within my soul.

"Your shirts are fine." She eased up on the teasing at the sight of my distress. "You'll look nice in whatever you wear."

"You have to say that," I complained.

"True... that's the role of a devoted aunt. But luckily, my side of the family gave you good genes. Among other stuff." She winked. When I didn't crack a smile, she shook her head. "You're worrying too much, Mae. Think of it like summer camp."

"Ugh." I dramatically flopped down on the bed. "Summer camp is notoriously hard to pack for! Everyone's trying to reinvent themselves..."

"How would you know?"

"I've seen movies."

"And movies are an accurate source?" Aunt Abeline rolled her eyes. "Well then, I guess to be a witch... you need a long black robe and a big pointy hat. Maybe some green skin?"

"They don't have green skin at the Judicial Studies of the High Council," I corrected in my poshest, most playful accent.

"Family or not, I've got tough news. You don't have the bone structure to pull off a big, pointy hat." Aunt Abeline laughed.

I swatted at her with a pillow. "You're not helping," I said, edging her out of the room.

"Now I would have looked great in a pointy little number... but I wasn't invited."

The smile dropped off my face. Right. That.

Of course Aunt Abeline was happy for me, and proud that I was accepted to the exclusive High Council witches' coven, but it had to be bittersweet knowing I was invited into the secret society when she never got in.

"Oh, Mae." Aunt Abeline saw how her joke had fallen flat. "I was kidding. The world's opened up to you, as it should. Sierra's little girl... following her mama's example. She loved it. Right from day one. She was where she belonged, and you will be too. You remind me of her more and more. I think this little adventure will be really good for you."

"It would be nice to know more about Mom," I murmured. "All we have are her photos..."

There was a time when my aunt and I barely said my mom's name. She died when I was little and although my aunt took full guardianship after her passing, talking about that loss was still a sore spot and tough between us. There was still so much more that I could learn.

"Well, that's it!" Aunt Abeline realized. "You can decipher a proper wardrobe from looking at Sierra's photos!"

"You think?" I sat straight up on the bed.

"Sure."

Aunt Abeline was right. My mom had inadvertently left a visual guide of what to expect at the High Council in her old photo album. Sure, the styles had changed, but the expectations of the students had not. By now, I knew those images backwards and forwards, but it couldn't hurt to look again.

"Aunt Abby, you're a genius."

"I really am," she teased.

"This will help me blend in perfectly." I got off the bed to go dig out the album, but Aunt Abeline stopped me.

"You know, it's okay to be special," she told me in

all seriousness. "You have unique gifts and talents that are yours and yours alone. It's okay to embrace them. Being the best version of yourself will never take away the sparkle from anyone else."

Easy for you to say, I thought. You never got in.

TWO

128 WILTONSHIRE ROAD

"WELL, THIS IS IT..." I said. We stood awkwardly beside the taxi, my suitcase and backpack already safely in the trunk.

"Call, or write, or text, or just come back. Any time, day or night," Aunt Abeline said. She had hired the car service so we could make a clean break from each other in the safety of our own home. Neither of us were sure if it would be okay for a non-witch relative to make the drop off at the High Council, so when she suggested a cab, I jumped at the chance. But now that it was real and we were saying our goodbyes, I wished she were coming with me.

We relocated so many times when I was a kid, I thought I could handle any situation, but this was the first time in my whole life that I was making a move all on my own.

"I'll miss you," I told her.

Words could never express how much my aunt meant to me. I stepped in for an awkward hug. Our family didn't really embrace each other much, but she welcomed me in.

"I'll miss you too," she said.

We gave each other a few stiff pats, then pulled back again.

"I played my final word," I added.

"Oh?"

"Grit."

"Fitting."

"I thought so. You still won. 347 to 291," I admitted.

"Well, some things change, some stay the same. Guess for me, it's back to playing my Scrabble alone or..." she said, then sighed. "Against a stranger on the computer."

"At least then you might not always win."

"Oh, I'll win. The trouble comes when I beat them so badly, they don't bother to finish the game. Such a funny thing, pride."

"I was a glutton for punishment," I agreed.

"Sometimes..." She laughed. "Now, quit stalling. Go. Knock 'em dead." She flicked a stray tear from her cheek.

"I'll see you soon." I nodded.

My aunt agreed.

I slumped into the car's backseat and Aunt Abeline waved from the driveway as the taxi pulled out of the lane. I offered one final gesture goodbye as the safety of the lake house disappeared from view. As I saw it go, a lump grew in my stomach.

This was it.

It was really happening. I was following in my mother's footsteps. If she could see me now, she would be so proud. Her little angel, all grown up. Ever since I'd heard of the place, I knew the High Council was somewhere that I wanted to be. So why, now that I was on my way, did I feel like puking up the breakfast I ate? I was pretty sure I could hold it in. But I kept my lips tightly closed. Just in case. Luckily, my driver had no desire for conversation with a kid. He was dressed in a leather bomber jacket, far too warm for this balmy early fall. To compensate, he'd turned the air-conditioning on full blast. The whirr from the overheated fans in the dashboard supplemented our silence. In opposite directions, we stared out the windows.

The town passed by.

It wasn't so long ago I had moved to Plumpkin. It felt like a lifetime, but living in the home that my mom grew up in, spending time in her basement, learning bits and pieces of the things she went through, was all still quite new. I felt closer to her now than I had through most of my childhood, but there were still huge caverns of knowledge that were empty. Answers I hoped to discover by enrolling in the High Council. Questions I wasn't yet sure how to word. My mind refused to stick with any one thought for too long.

I looked down at my phone.

Still no call or text from Josie.

Did that mean she really didn't parabond? Or was she just worried, as I was, that we hadn't both made it in? Was it possible she just hadn't thought to call? We hadn't been friends for that long, but I was hoping we'd be partners.

Parabonds.

That's what they called them.

Supernatural partnerships forged by the coven and fate. That's what we were. It made perfect sense. After all, unlike all the boys in our community who had lost the game of paranormal hide-and-seek with our stuff, I had found Josie's watch and returned it to her before fate's final dawn. Technically, we fulfilled the parabond brief requirements. One person loses their offering, and their forever partner locates it and gives it back to them. That's all it took. If you followed those logistics, then we had it down cold. Josie and I should definitely be partners.

But if that was true, why was I so afraid to check in with the girl?

I stuffed my phone into my pocket and pulled out the other things I was carrying: my mom's photo and the letter of introduction from Cornelius Child.

I stared at the photo. Mom was in front, stretching out to hold the camera, her other friends leaning on each other, laughing, smiling. The whole lot seemed to be having a ball of a time.

Maybe at the High Council I'd make some really great friends.

Of course we'd all have to suffer through the

awkward getting-to-know-you phase first, but I was really hopeful. For once, I wouldn't be the only new girl in the gang. I didn't need to read the letter from Cornelius Child again. I'd memorized every word. But I held it close at hand in case I'd need to show it as some sort of proof of entry. Who knew how these secret societies worked?

My cab drove straight through Plumpkin and out into the rolling hills of the countryside. The blocks between the side streets grew longer and the fields and the forests stretched out. Here the sky was so big. It felt blue for miles, with pretty white clouds and the warm, distant sun. I wasn't familiar with the address on the invite, but a quick search of online maps said it was near Alderton, which was, traveling from Plumpkin, a ways out of town. The journey seemed to both take forever and be over in an instant. Suddenly, the cab slowed at a dirt road.

"Is here good?" The driver asked, doubtful.

I could see why.

We were in the middle of nowhere. He'd pulled off the highway at a small wooden sign with a green-painted circle. The emblem boasted two double arrows, one pointing south and one pointing north. It was a crest I'd seen before. I whipped open the invite to confirm what I already knew. That shape was on the masthead from the High Council invitation. It was at the top of the document, and it had been the decorative seal on the envelope as well.

"Do you want me to go in? Or..." He looked at the

overgrown dirt path leading back from the sign. He was seriously dubious of its authenticity as a lane. "Off-road'll be extra," he added, hoping to further sway my choice.

"Here's fine," I agreed. I pulled out enough cash to pay the fare and give him a tip. He took the money, unloaded my suitcase and backpack, and left me on the side of the road. He seemed in a hurry. I doubted there was much more need for a taxi service in Alderton than there was in Plumpkin, but wished him well nonetheless.

This was my new home.

128 Wiltonshire Road.

Not much to look at from the highway. If not for the double-arrow-crested placard, I doubted anyone would even know that this was a road. It didn't look viable. Just overgrown and unkempt.

I slung on my backpack and tilted my suitcase onto its wheels. Together, we bumped along at a fair pace. The driveway was surprisingly long and like its entrance, completely overgrown. It wound through the forest, bending its path around rocks and impressive tree trunks to take us deep in the grounds. The grassy curb on either side of the gravel hadn't seen a lawn mower in years—maybe ever. On its little wheels, my suitcase tossed and turned. These weren't the slick low pile rugs and linoleum tiles for which its base was designed. Rolling suitcases were not built for off-road-ing. But we made progress together.

As I walked, I noticed the fall season had settled

in.

The air was still warm but punctuated by a cool breeze that tickled my elbows. I was dressed in slim, dark khakis, a T-shirt, and sneakers. Since it was still warm, I'd rolled the pants up to the length of capris, giving room to my ankles. But instead of my all-gray picks, to lighten my ensemble and please my aunt, I wore a simple white T-shirt. The slight difference in shade worked, as she hadn't complained. And of course, to finish the outfit off, around my neck hung Grandma Mim's moon charm necklace. The thin chain added just a hint of gold to an ensemble that otherwise might have been described as bland. Of course, that was my intention. My hair was blown out and my makeup perfectly curated to create the polished look of a girl without a care in the world. I looked neutral and unassuming, with just the tiniest bit of glam. In my bag, I had also stuffed a jean jacket for when the nights grew cold.

Farther into the grounds I walked.

Soon I couldn't hear the sporadic passersby as their cars flew past on the highway. How much farther was the building? I was just starting to regret dismissing my cabbie so early when I heard another vehicle bumping along the dirt road. It came up quickly behind me. I moved to the side to let it pass, but instead of blasting by in a cloud of dust and gravel, the car slowed.

"Mae-Mae! What are you doing here? Did you parabond?" Marcy Galvas leaned her whole torso out the window. Her hot pink bra peeked out from beneath a tie-dyed tank, putting her ample bosom on curvy, feminine display.

"Kind of, yeah." I recognized Marcy from my graphic design class. "At least..." I wasn't sure how much detail to give her. "I think so. I'm not really sure. But I got an invite!" I ended on a positive note, waiving Cornelius Child's invitation in the air.

Greg, Marcy's boyfriend, let out a hoot from the driver's seat. He was in that same computer design class too. I remembered it well because they'd actually celebrated their parabond connection in front of me and our other classmates on the school lawn with a heavy-handed make out. I'd had an intimate view of both tongues. They were always doing stuff like that— acting first, thinking about consequences later. But their enthusiasm was infectious.

"Well, whatcha waitin' for?! Hop in!" he called.

Marcy nodded, weaving her slim waist back into the car.

I looked ahead.

The building or the school or wherever it was we were all headed still wasn't in view down the road. It might still be quite a walk. Quickly, I shoved the official invite back in my pocket and jumped into the waiting vehicle. In the back seat, I added my two small bags to an already impressive display of luggage they'd packed.

As soon as my door was closed, Greg stepped down on the gas. Yeehaw!" he hooted.

We skidded forward, his black tires whirring, and

he drove aggressively through the forest, his old car kicking up clouds of dust as he went.

"Woo-hoo! High Council!" Marcy threw her hands in the air and let herself bounce all around. She embraced the dangerous speed like the car was a ride on a roller coaster, cranking up the song on the radio and singing along. Greg used the steering wheel as his percussion instrument to build an extensive drum solo. Giant grins stretched across both their faces. I leaned back in the seat and let this new vibe wash over me. To feel so free and right with the world as they seemed was enchanting. Greg and Marcy didn't have a care in the world. It took an extra bend or two in the road, but soon even I couldn't help myself and sang along at the top of my lungs. My arm stretched out the window and I felt the wind through my fingertips as we soared through the forest.

Suddenly, Greg slammed on the brakes.

Marcy and I laughed as the car careened to a stop. The pea soup cloud of gravel particles rolled over us quickly, but when the car stopped all motion, the dust dispersed. As the smoke cleared, we stared.

"Babe! What is that?" Marcy wondered.

"Yikes." Greg voiced what we were all feeling. He inched forward into the open space. The trees parted to reveal a gravel parking lot. The shabby road led to a broken-down motel. Its neon sign blinked on and off, the letter O in the marquee already dark and blown out.

"*This* is the High Council?" Greg wondered.

Both he and Marcy leaned forward to get a better look. I peered out my backseat window.

"It looks like a horror movie murder house," Marcy murmured.

"Not the kind of place you'd expect to find a headmaster named Cornelius Child," I agreed.

"Cornelius Child." Marcy laughed. I wasn't sure what was so funny, but being nervous, I chuckled along.

Now that the building was in full view, Greg slowed his driving to a crawl. We gaped out the window. The more details we saw, the less impressive it was. There were cracks in the foundation, and shutters clunked at odd angles with more than one screw hanging off. The roofline was made up of a strange shingle patchwork, added bit by bit here and there over the life of the building. The parking lot dividers had faded, crumbled, or disappeared. The doorway to the lobby was propped open with a rock. There was no guarantee, if the stone were removed, that the door would close in its frame completely. Slowly, he brought us to a full stop. He shifted the vehicle into park.

"Nobody goes into the forest alone," he told us with a wicked smile.

"Oh, please." Marcy swatted his arm and hopped out of the car. "Come on!"

Greg and I followed. There were a few other cars in the parking lot, so at least we weren't alone at the murder hotel.

"Hello?" I stepped into the rental office first.

The wallpaper on the reception room walls was faded and worn. There was no one behind the counter. Marcy promptly chimed the little silver bell for service.

"It says go around back." Greg pointed out a hand-written sign.

"If you see a little silver bell, it's just begging to be rung." Marcy shrugged.

Nobody came, so we soon wandered outside. As we left the office to follow the sign's directions, Marcy looked at me for confirmation, but this was all happening too fast for my liking.

"Come on." Greg grabbed her hand and he walked her out the way she had come.

I hurried to follow because blowing in with a tornado was definitely better than arriving alone. We passed the parking lot and rounded the corner of the building to see a small cement courtyard with broken down patio furniture and risky-looking chaise loungers filled with several other kids. The chairs surrounded a small kidney-shaped pool. The liner under the water was chipped and cracked. At first, I wasn't sure it was safe to go in.

"Swimming!" Marcy let go of Greg's hand and raced towards the pool, tossing off unimportant clothing as she went. It was a cool afternoon, but she didn't care. She stripped down to her undies and jumped joyfully into the water. Her boyfriend followed her exuberant and ungraceful lead, narrowly missing landing his cannonball on the top of her head.

I stood firmly on the concrete.

"Come on, Mae! The water's luscious." Marcy tried to coax me but gave up almost immediately to play silly pool games with Greg.

They fit right in.

The other kids sitting around on the patio furniture were also in good spirits. All the trepidation we'd felt upon first view of the motel lobby was gone. In denial of the late season date, most of them had changed into swimwear, and there wasn't another suitcase in sight, so someone was organizing things after all.

"You're Mae Kingsley," a girl with shoulder-length brown hair and enormous doe eyes pointed out. She stood to greet me.

I nodded, racking my brain, trying to place her, but hopelessly falling short.

"I recognized you from the funeral. I'm Nicolette Cobb." She offered a handshake. I shook it. She rolled her bottom lip into a frown. "Sorry about your friend."

My friend.

Kate.

Yes. I suppose that's what she was. At least, there was a time she was my friend.

A lot of the kids around town must know of me and Josie from Kate Hucklebee's funeral After all, her service had been packed. As one of the two people who were actually present when she died, I'd become a minor celebrity of the macabre. Hundreds of teens and parents from neighboring communities flocked to Kate's final celebration. Her death was so tragic. The loss of such potential, snuffed out so young. Everyone wanted to pay their respects.

Of course, if any one of those supposedly heart-broken souls had actually cared about or even spoken to Kate while she was alive, there was a good chance she wouldn't be gone. All she wanted was to feel like she belonged to something. Now she did, I supposed, but this ghoulish form of celebrity wasn't what she had in mind. Her passing was still very fresh. I didn't want to be reminded. Kate was gone. But when I closed my eyes, I could still hear her nails scrabbling, clawing at the boards beneath her body, trying to pull herself to safety in the barn. I could still feel the wind in my hair as I rushed forward to try to grab her, as Josie raced in from the other direction, both of us moving in what felt like slow motion, neither of us arriving in time. I could still hear the horrific scream as her fingers slipped away from the beam that she clung to. I could still see that terrible moment as Kate dropped. As her eyes widened in terror. As her body started to fall. Her face had twisted in fear. And then... that terrible sound. When she crashed to the ground with a thick, final thud.

Poolside, I simply blinked. "Thanks," I told the girl.

Nicolette knew immediately she'd said or done the wrong thing and self-consciously beat herself up so I didn't have to. She bowed her head, stepped away, and sat down on a chaise beside another guy dressed all in black and wearing big clunky boots. A scooter was propped against his chair. He rolled his eyes at the girl.

"Room assignments are over there." He nodded in the direction of a picnic table no one was sitting at.

"Great." I gave them both a parting nod and followed his instructions.

I wandered past a blonde-haired girl who was sunning herself in an elaborately cut out one-piece bathing suit. The curves and weaves of fabric left less to the imagination than a tiny bikini, but she didn't seem to care. And why would she? Her body was spectacular. Every inch of her skin was meticulously buffed and polished. Her fingers and toenails were painted in bright fire engine red.

Beside her was an impossibly attractive boy.

He, too, was in a tiny swimsuit, a navy Speedo that cupped and held his package. At least, I think it did. I only allowed myself vague glimpses in their direction, lest they think I was staring. Like his partner, he had barely an ounce of fat on his body. His arms were heavily defined from lifting weights. The boy lounged with one arm raised, casually cradling his brown, curly hair. His body was on full display for anyone blessed with eyeballs.

They were hot stuff, and they knew it.

The two polished teens were probably used to garnering stares. But they disguised their own eyes with dark sunglasses that hid whether they bothered to observe my approach. Still, I tried not to give in to the visual candy. Their tanned skin glistened in the sun. But neither spoke as I passed by. The boy dressed in black had been correct. There were a few place cards and room keys still on the table, waiting to be claimed. My name, Greg and Marcy's, as well as some others like Tej Mithaali, Sloane Lolant, Rick Lowe, and Hilde Dove. I was pleased to learn that each teen was assigned their own room.

But there was no sign of Josie here.

Had she already arrived?

Or was it possible she really wasn't coming?

I looked around for someone to give confirmation or permission or to check in with or something, but it was clear the only ones here at the patio were other kids like me. And they couldn't care less. There was no one to guide us. I seemed to be the only one bothered by the complete lack of adult guidance.

"Are these our rooms?" Marcy asked over my shoulder, dripping wet in her matching bra and panties. They were high cut, hot pink, and lacy. Nothing gray about her selections. I couldn't help but think of my own underwear collection. There weren't two sexy items or a matching set in the whole company. Maybe that's what Aunt Abeline and I should have bought on our last shopping trip. Marcy squeezed the water out of her hair, letting it splatter on the pavement.

At the sight of another perfectly trim, wet, scantily clad woman, the beefcake guy on the lounge chair tilted his sunglasses up on his face. "Welcome to the High Council, ladies," he greeted us both, but his eyes never left Marcy's body. "Jacob Creek." He offered a handshake but didn't bother to get up.

Marcy moved over to receive his outstretched hand, her wet skin dripping on his chair. "Marcy Galvas."

Jacob broke into a smile like a wolf observing his dinner.

"Mae," I added, offering a small wave, staying right where I was. This time, Jacob's eyes flashed in my direction. Instinctively, I crossed my arms in front of me.

"That's Greg," Marcy added, pointing out her boyfriend's legs, which were the only visible part of him, as he had decided to enter an underwater handstand competition with himself.

"Anita, Nicolette, and Vince." Jacob pointed at everyone.

Both girls gave a gentle wave. Vince didn't bother.

"Well... get your suits on, or, you know, don't." He leered at Marcy again.

She giggled.

"Take a load off." He sat back on his chaise, that giant arm floating back behind his head once more.

"I'm all wet," Marcy complained.

"That's what happens when you jump in the pool," Anita muttered to herself.

I smothered a grin. My thoughts exactly. Of course, I would never have said it.

But Jacob sprung into action. "Here, use mine." He slid his terry cloth towel out from behind his back and offered it to Marcy. She was so trim it nearly wrapped around her twice.

"Thanks." She grinned and sat down at the end of his chaise, ready to chat.

I grabbed my room key off the table and headed back to Greg's car. If this was how the High Council was starting, I wanted to get settled before things really got going. As I turned the corner to the parking lot, I heard a supersized splash from where I'd just come.

"Greg!" Marcy screeched. "I just put on his towel!" But it was easy to tell, even around the corner twenty feet away, she wasn't actually mad.

I shook my head. Their brand of energy was great. Kind of. It was exhausting and overpowering, but it was the sort of zest and stamina I wished I could generate. Instead of feeling excited to talk to more people, I was already ready for a moment to reflect to myself. In fact, stumbling back to the silence, I felt relieved. I sighed and grabbed my two bags from the back of Greg's car. The motel parking lot no longer seemed so ominous. It was run-down, for sure, but kind of quaint now. With the others nearby, it lost its murder-y feel. Still a little murder-y... but no longer full-on run-for-cover. I looked back at the pitted gravel road we'd arrived on and the thick forest surrounding this place. It was so private and isolated. The perfect location to teach a bunch of kids how to harness their paranormal skills, although I wasn't sure I really knew what supernatural powers I'd bring.

Aunt Abeline had been right. This did feel like summer camp.

I thought about texting her to tell her I'd arrived,

but calling out to my family after only twenty minutes on the property seemed like a pretty cheap homesick move. Still, I had pulled out my phone, so now I stared at it. There was no one else to message. I couldn't text Josie. What would I say?

I'm here? Are you? I don't see you...

I should have called the moment I got the invite. Why didn't I?

I still didn't know.

I probably would have sat there in silent revelry for another twenty or thirty minutes just staring at a phone I had no intention of using, but the sound of another vehicle approaching pulled me out of my thoughts. I quickly closed up Greg's car and forced a smile at the incoming vehicle. Greg and Marcy would have stayed and said something in way of greeting to the oncoming arrivals. This place was so remote, and the dirt road was so long, there was no way whoever was in that car was visiting by accident. But what should I say?

I didn't have any real information to pass on. I was trying to figure things out as I went.

Instead, I chickened out and ducked around the corner of the building before the driver had time to cut his or her engine. I made my way back to the rooms by the pool. As I walked back across the courtyard, I stuck to the hallway of doors leading to our motel rooms. Marcy, I could see, had laid out Jacob's now totally soaked towel on the pavement and was chatting with Nicolette, who had obviously also offered up her terry cloth robe. But she was fully dressed. She must also be wearing a swimsuit, I decided of Nicolette, underneath all the clothes. Why else would she be carrying a towel? But the big-eyed girl never stripped down. She stayed fully dressed. The towel sat at the end of her chair, crumpled between them, just waiting to be worn. But Marcy didn't bother. She had no issue hanging about in a wet bra and damp panties. Her body confidence was off the charts. If I looked like her, maybe mine would be too. But not likely.

I checked my room number.

117.

My room was near the end of the row, beside Marcy's. I *click-clacked* my suitcase down the sidewalk in rhythm. At the repetitive sound, most of the teens looked up. I gave a forced nod with my over the shoulder glance, making my way to my new bedroom, on my way to the new land of privacy and safety, when suddenly, doors 106 and 107 sprung open around me. Out of the first motel room door stepped Josie. Her straight black hair fell like a curtain, almost covering one cheek. She looked very serious, but when she saw me, she smiled.

"You're here!" I said, full of joy.

"You made it," she agreed.

"I would have texted, but I didn't know…" I trailed off, unsure how to finish that sentence.

"If we all made it. I know. Me too. It was weird." She let me off the hook. "But we did!" she added. I grinned too, but for a second, my mind whirred.

All.

My eyes narrowed at that small word.

We *all* made it. Did that mean...?

"Hi, Mae." Beck stepped out of the room behind his girlfriend and gave me a soft grin.

"Uh, hey. Hi." I stuttered. "Hi, Beck."

He was a full head taller than either of us and I had to look up to greet him. As he so often did, he raked a hand through his tousled hair. "Good to see you," he said.

Common courtesy said I should have reciprocated the greeting, but if I said it aloud, it still wouldn't be true. How did Beck make it to the High Council? Josie and I had confronted Kate and found our offerings on our own. Just the two of us. Beck hadn't been there. In the losing and finding of things, he hadn't completed any part of his task. He and Josie should never have bonded. They couldn't have. If anyone should have parabonded with Josie, it was me.

I was the one who found her stuff.

I was the one who risked my life.

And I was the one who gave it back to her in just the nick of time.

Possibly thinking all the same thoughts, Beck self-consciously leaned against the wall.

"But that means..."

If Beck had arrived... then...

"Hi, Mae."

I spun around in my tracks and came face-to-face with Spade.

THREE
WON'T THIS BE FUN

THE MOON WAS BRIGHT, *with a huge collection of stars in the clear skies above us. I couldn't see all that well, but I wasn't worried. If we needed flashlights, our cell phones could light the way. Spade offered a hand to help me under the chain, which I readily took. After we'd successfully cleared the sign, he didn't let go. His palm felt warm in mine.*

Our pace slowed.

The path weaved through the forest. We were surrounded by trees. I could see the lookout was probably another forty or fifty feet ahead. Spade brought us to a stop in the middle of the overgrown drive. He curved our bodies in to face one another.

"I've had a really nice time tonight," he said.

"Me too," I agreed, feeling the closeness of his breath.

He let go of my hand and raised his fingers to my face. He cupped my neck in his hand and gently pulled me in for a soft, slow kiss. I felt my whole body move towards him in yearning as our lips touched together. His kiss was so soft at first, then opened deeper, more longingly. I followed his passion, matching his rhythms. Before I knew it, I'd slid my tongue into his mouth and his into mine. He tasted sweet, like raspberries picked straight from the vine on a hot July morning. My internal organs vibrated.

"Mmmm."

We murmured together, then pulled apart, breathless.

He looked at me and I smiled back almost shyly. He reached out and touched a stray strand of hair, then grazed my ear as he tucked it behind. My cartilage tingled. It sent a shockwave of desire through my body. His touch was so innocent and so deeply sexual at the same time. I didn't move or blink for fear of breaking the powerful connection between us.

"You're gonna love this," he whispered.

"We did it!" Spade smiled, stepping out of what I put together quickly must be his designated motel room and wrapped me into a big bear hug. Involuntarily, I noted how delicious he smelled, but I didn't return or even accept his embrace. Instead, I pushed back.

"Did what? How did you..." I didn't know how to tactfully finish that sentence.

How did you get accepted into the High Council without completing your part in the bonding process?

It sounded petty. Instead, I trailed off and let the question hang in the air. Because I didn't have to finish the question. All three knew exactly what I meant.

"When I got home from the funeral, the invite was waiting." Spade shrugged.

I looked to the other two. They nodded as well.

"I guess Kate screwed things up for us so badly, they felt they had to let us in." Spade laughed. His arm remained draped across my shoulders, happy as a clam, but Josie and Beck could see how uncomfortable I was.

"Dude, get your arm off her," Beck told him.

"Why don't you mind your own business," he snapped right back.

I pulled myself away and frowned at Josie's guy. There was no need to fight my battles. Beck seemed about to intercede further, but Josie beat him to it.

"Why don't I show Mae to her room?" she suggested, pulling me away before either guy could speak again. My suitcase and I happily followed. "We'll see you over at the pool," she added, just to make it clear they weren't invited.

My head reeled.

By coming here, by accepting their invitation, did I unknowingly agree to parabond with Spade for the rest of my life? Were we now forever partners at the High Council?

No way.

Josie and I rolled my bag the rest of the way down the sidewalk hallway. Neither of us spoke again until we were in the safety of my motel room and away from the nosey ears and eyes of the others by the pool. They weren't within reach, but those kids already clocked everything we'd said and done, and they were filing it away. Who'd they use the information against was yet to be decided.

That's why I liked her. Like me, Josie was intensely aware of others and the secret motivations they might hold.

When we were tucked inside my motel room, she frowned. "I should have called. Or texted. I should have warned you," she admitted, sitting herself on the edge of my bed.

"No. You didn't..." I tried to muster a reason to forgive the transgression but had to settle for the generic "don't be silly."

We sat in awkward silence.

I looked around my new dingy room. "Nice place."

Josie laughed.

The carpet was worn around the double bed, where dull white linens were tucked under a shabby paisley comforter. Like in the lobby, the wallpaper here had started to droop and fray. The whole place felt like an empty shell. Eight lonely hangers hung in the alcove by the door. Under the only window in the room, there was a water-ringed wood desk and an uncomfortable-looking wooden chair. Probably grabbed from an old dining set. Everything about the little room felt over-worked and sad. That was how I felt too.

Overworked.

Sad.

And ambushed.

How could I have been so foolish?

Of course Spade was here. After I got my invite, I worried they'd only let me in and no others. But since they made an exception for me, they'd accepted every other fence-sitter too. And Josie had known it. She'd known the boys were coming, both Spade and Beck. The guys were a package deal. Once Beck received his invitation, it wasn't a leap to realize that Spade would be next.

For Josie, that meant a parabond with the partner she'd always hoped for.

But for me, it meant a supernatural partner I absolutely did not want. Why didn't she warn me he was coming?

"I thought you'd turn it down," Josie admitted, as if reading my thoughts. "It was chicken, I know. But I thought if I told you what was going on, you'd walk away. And you can't. Even with Spade. You have to give it a chance, Mae. This is an awesome opportunity. You can't bail because you're stuck with the wrong guy."

"I can't partner with Spade." I shook my head.

"He's not that bad."

"He tried to sleep his way into being my parabond."

"He did not."

"What would you call slipping his hand up my shirt?"

"So he thought a little physical intimacy might nudge the direction of fate his way. A guy can ask."

"Oh, well why don't I just spread my legs?" I groused.

Josie sighed. "I get it, it wasn't a love connection, but it was just one lousy date."

"I can't believe you're defending him!"

"I'm not... he's a dumb guy doing what dumb guys do."

It sure sounded like she was defending him.

"If you're so keen, why don't you partner with him?" I said.

"So you can partner with Beck?" Josie crossed her arms.

"That's not... no." I flushed bright red.

"I was kidding," she told me.

"Right." I nodded.

Hilarious.

A silence fell over us.

A silence named Beck.

Josie had always been wary of my friendship with her boyfriend. It was the six-ton gorilla in the room. We found it best not to talk about it or him in each other's company. If he didn't exist, the tension couldn't persist. Because Josie and I really wanted to like each other. It was a concession, sure, but the compromise worked. We wouldn't let an attraction to some guy get in the way of our friendship. Not that I was attracted to Beck.

I mean, I wasn't blind.

He was tall and he was good-looking, and he'd always been nice to me. He had a cute sense of humor, and we got along great, but that was as far as it went. I was not attracted to Beck. And I outright hated Spade.

"You're not gonna get me to like him," I told her, picturing Spade's smug, jovial face.

"No," she agreed. It wasn't a fight worth having. "Well... maybe you don't have to," she conceded.

"Maybe." I doubted that.

The silence between us returned. I tried to think of something new to discuss, but all roads led back to things better left unsaid.

"I should let you unpack," she said, stirring, coming perhaps to the same conclusion.

"Okay. Sounds good. Thanks." I opened the door and she hurried out.

But I didn't unpack. I didn't do anything.

The room was so sad, but that wasn't the reason I didn't settle my things. The truth was, I wasn't staying. Josie could try and brush it off all she liked, but if being at the High Council meant I had to forever partner with Spade as my parabond, I would call my aunt and head home tonight.

I peeked out the motel room curtain. More kids were chatting and lounging by the pool. The teens that arrived when I was by Greg's car had sat themselves down at the picnic table. They all looked happy in their paranormal pairings and fairly well-matched. Everyone except Vince and Nicolette. Their combination looked as strained as my twosome with Spade. Although they sat beside one another, they made no effort to inhabit the same space. It was like there was a canyon between them. They each looked off in opposite directions and steered their bodies to create as much room between them as possible. The perfect embodiment of how I felt about "my guy."

He, I noticed, kept looking over towards my window.

If Spade was waiting for me to return poolside as his adoring partner, he could keep right on waiting. Acting like all was right between us now after our date had ended so sour was a chicken move. He didn't even offer me condolences at the funeral for Kate. My friend died, and he hadn't said a word.

The guy was a tool.

But maybe we weren't so alone in our disharmony. Other cracks in the group began to appear. From this far away, Jacob and Anita also caught my eye. At first glance, they looked like the ideal couple and perfected specimens of muscles and mass, but if you took all that gloss and abdominal definition away, their relationship was cold. They barely acknowledged each other. It wasn't as outwardly hostile as Nicolette and Vince's open distaste for the other's choices, but a darker, more sinister veneer hung over their heads.

I remembered what Aunt Abeline had told me. Parabonding isn't necessarily a romantic coupling, she'd said. It's a bond formed by fate. Sometimes it could be based on attraction, and of course those romantic pairings were the ideal mates, but fate created all sorts of pairings, for all sorts of purposes. That's why I thought, even hoped, that Josie and I might be paired together. But Aunt Abeline had never been to the High Council, so what did she know about fate?

There was no way I was supposed to partner with a sleazy huckster like Spade.

I was about to abandon my sneak peek out the window when the last two teens on the list arrived. I remembered their names from the picnic table check-in: Rick Lowe and Hilde Dove. I peeked out the draped window once more for only just a moment, then couldn't help but stare.

My eyes widened in surprise.

My aunt was right.

If Rick and Hilde were a romantic couple, then someone should call child protective services because he was a giant hulk of a man, and she looked barely ten years old. They went around the group making intro-ductions, shaking hands and making new friends as the High Council's weirdest couple, and here I was, the chicken behind the curtain, watching from my room.

Huh.

So lots of people's partners sucked. It couldn't hurt to say hello. After all, the second anyone mentioned parabonding, I could exit stage right.

In spite of myself, I checked my reflection in the mirror before heading back to the group. I wasn't about to put on a bathing suit or anything like that, but I was willing to swipe a fresh coat of gloss on my lips. No point in having the assembly reject me before I rejected them. Satisfied I looked presentable, I opened the door and rejoined the group. The only seats still open were beside Spade, Josie and Beck, or a skinny blonde girl, so I decided it was time to make a new friend.

"Is this open?" I asked her.

"Sure." The blonde waved me in.

"Mae," I offered.

"Sloane Lolant," she volleyed back. "That's Tej," she added, as if we were obligated to introduce our partners as well.

I didn't mention Spade.

Tej, I could see, was fairly short and slunk back in his chair. Despite his small stature, he seemed comfortable in his own skin. He looked out at me from behind his dark lashes and thick black eyebrows and gave a simple nod. His five o'clock stubble had already grown in for the day.

"I saw you around school," Sloane told me. "Plumpkin High. We go there too, one year ahead."

"Oh, right." She did look familiar.

Maybe she was at the funeral. If she was, I was glad she didn't mention it.

"You must be excited to get in on your first try," she said.

Did others get in after successive years? I was surprised, then dismayed. Just another question to which I didn't know the answer. Feeling a little too honest, I let out a long sigh. "What I'm feeling is... numb."

"Yeah." She nodded.

I looked over at her and she shrugged her shoulders. Neither of us felt the need to expand. We fell into a pleasant silence watching the others around the pool position themselves and flirt in the water. Sloane didn't need to fill the space. It was refreshing. Grateful, I quietly took in the antics of the others. On the other side of the table, the little girl I'd deduced to be Hilde Dove sat between Rick and Tej. Even seated, Rick towered above her. A pleasant smile was plastered on her face as her eyes bounced back and forth between the older boys and their conversation like the audience of a tennis match. Left and right went her eyeline. She seemed like she was doing her best to be approachable, but neither guy bothered to include her in whatever was being said. Vince and Nicolette continued to lounge side by side, doing their best to ignore the other. He couldn't seem to care less what she was doing, but why didn't she leave his side? Why not get up and try to make new friends?

Greg and Marcy had fallen into conversation with Josie and Beck. Both boys carelessly had their hands on their girl's back or leg, subconsciously telling all the other dudes on the veranda that this woman was theirs. In the pool, Greg draped all over Marcy. He took little moments to nibble the wet skin of her shoulders and tug and tease at her body underneath the water as if through the magic barrier of clear liquid, the rest of us couldn't see that he was making the most of standing flush against her hips. She took all the attention in stride and chatted away like she barely noticed her boyfriend's hands as they roamed around her body.

Beck was much more subtle.

He absently traced the outline of Josie's knee. Around and around his middle finger went, circling the patch of her skin. His eyes sometimes wandered to me, probably to avoid staring at Marcy's wet breasts, and we nodded in that familiar, acknowledging way.

Perhaps Nicolette was right to stay put where she was. In that little circle, there was no way to break in. And they weren't even the most intimidating crowd. That honor was held by Anita and Jacob and Spade. After I declined to go over and sit by him, Spade had joined the other ridiculously attractive people on the patio. He had promptly removed his shirt and stretched out to tan his already browned physique. He looked just as model-ready as the others.

I took it all back.

For Nicolette to try to connect with any of the others without a formal invite, she'd have to be the bravest girl in the world. She was stuck where she was.

I liked Sloane and her comfortable silence. Unlike with Josie, the pause between us felt safe and warm. "Do you think we can speak freely now? You know, now that we've... made it?" Ironically, I chose not to make a single direct reference to anything witch related.

"Oh, we're not in." She looked at me, surprised. "Not yet. Did you think this was the High Council?"

When she put it like that, I couldn't help but laugh. "I guess not."

Looking around at the deadbeat motel rooms, the uncomfortable plastic seating, the chain link location... no, this was nothing like I had imagined. But if this wasn't High Council...

"Where are we?" I finished my own thought out loud.

"We're about to find out," Sloane murmured. I looked in the direction she was facing. Two women were walking towards us. The first was a short powerhouse with cropped gray hair and a muscular build. Both her arms were covered in tattoos. She walked with a sense of urgency. Her partner was taller, rounder, like somebody's mother, with frizzy brown hair and one shocking strip of gray hair that tumbled in a tuft at her temple. Both wore white tracksuits with different colored piping on the sleeves and legs. The short one with all the muscles had tied her track jacket around her waist. A tank top, matching her tracksuit's piping color, showed off her body art.

Their arrival silenced all chatter.

The women stopped at the top of the pool stairs between two of the chaises. They looked us all over, then smiled at each other.

"Well," the shorter one said. "Won't this be fun."

FOUR
WELCOME TO LIMBO

"WELCOME TO LIMBO," the stocky woman said. Her spiky gray hairstyle matched the sharp staccato of her rough and tumble voice. "I'm Lady Mauve."

"And I'm Lady Gray." The rounder woman accentuated her color choice by acknowledging her strip of white hair, as if that was the source of her name.

Some of us smiled.

The piping on the women's tracksuits matched their chosen monikers.

"Normally, today we would be introducing you to the world of the High Council. But as you're probably aware, this year things were... a little... messy." Lady Gray chose her words carefully.

Lady Mauve stifled a snort. "That's saying something."

I felt the group's eyes flit to me and Josie. My lips formed a tight line. It was easy to see which of the teens were connected to the gossip grapevine and which weren't. Only Vince, little Hilde, and Rick didn't seem to know what the ladies were referring to. Or maybe Vince did know, and he just didn't care.

"What happened?" Hilde wondered.

"A townie stole their offerings." Tej pointed at Josie and I. "And they killed her trying to get them back."

Hilde's mouth dropped open.

"We didn't kill her," Josie corrected.

"But she is dead," Anita said.

"Her name was Kate," I told them.

Anita shrugged.

"Yes, Katherine Huckabee," Lady Gray agreed. "It's an unusual case. Under normal circumstances, the Council chooses seven potential parabonds and the strongest five get in. When you arrive at our gates, the decision has already been made. With this other girl's subterfuge..."

"Kate," I said her name again.

"When Katherine interfered, the fates were... disrupted." A careful word choice again. "So after several discussions..."

"So many discussions," Lady Mauve felt compelled to add, her eyes rolling back in her head.

"We've brought you all here." Lady Grey finished with a overly enthusiastic smile.

"I don't understand," Sloane said, much braver than the rest of us. "If you've opened this year's class, why are we in limbo? Why not simply begin?"

The women looked at each other. Lady Gray hesitated. Again she seemed lost for words. "Well..."

"You missed the point." Lady Mauve took over. "We haven't opened this year's class. The High Council witches' coven will only be accepting ten new members."

"But there's fourteen of us," Nicolette stammered. The rest of us quickly counted.

"Yes," the women agreed.

"By the end of your time in limbo, there will be only ten." Lady Mauve said. But she could see she would have to spell it out. "We've decided to let fate make its selections... again."

FIVE

TIME WILL TELL

ALL AROUND THE pool the teens burst into questions, peppering each other and lobbing queries at the ladies. The women held their hands up to bring quiet to the group again.

"Why not just kick out the bottom couples? No offense." Tej offered a conciliatory gesture to Josie, Beck, Spade, and me at this suggestion.

"How do you know that it's us?" Spade asked.

"They never even bonded," Anita added with a snarl.

"We did... kind of. I found my own object," I confessed. Spade raised an eyebrow. "And I returned Josie's to her."

"Well, that's not parabonding," Anita told me. She shrugged again.

I was getting pretty sick of those shoulders. "I found our missing items and returned them to their proper owners," I countered.

"That's exactly parabonding," Sloane agreed.

"Doesn't matter. It was too late." Anita wouldn't be deterred. "Too bad."

"It *does* matter," Lady Gray corrected the flaxen-haired girl.

"Maybe technically they both bonded with Kate," Vince offered, his voice quietly cutting through the crowd.

"But Kate's not here," Marcy noted from the pool.

Greg sliced his finger across his neck.

"That's gross." Sloane frowned.

Greg shrugged. "True, though."

"The truth hurts," Jacob agreed.

"It hurt Kate." Greg laughed.

Several of the girls, two of the guys, and both of the ladies frowned. I was pleased to see I wasn't the only one disgusted by this exchange. Seeing they were outnumbered, Greg and Jacob dropped it. But I doubted that either felt the least bit of shame.

Again, the ladies held up their hands to silence the group.

"First of all, you're wrong, Mod Squad. No one bonded with Kate," Lady Mauve clarified. I thought Vince might be annoyed by the nickname, but his lips registered the start of a grin. "She took the offerings but never tried to return them, making it impossible for Muscles or Flop Hat to fulfill their fates."

Spade and Beck grimaced at their own nicknames, happy they'd been able thus far to hide from the limelight.

"And you and Josie didn't parabond because the retrieval of a missing item must be uninterrupted," Lady Gray told me. "No third party intervention is permitted."

"Lord knows we don't want a bunch of helicopter parents nosing around, trying to find their kid's stuff and bring it back." Lady Mauve laughed. "Talk about a nightmare."

"Fine. But you just said yourself they didn't parabond." Anita frowned. "So why are they here?" Even behind the black sunglasses, she shot me an especially cold look.

"I *said*," Lady Gray corrected, displeasure creeping into her tone, "things became messy..." She searched her vocabulary again. "The word I used was *disrupted*." The word hung in the air.

Lady Mauve nodded. Her eyes narrowed. One sharp look from her kept us all silent.

It was clear she was not a woman to cross.

"The normal mechanisms were upset by both primary intrusions and secondary impacts. Unfortunately, the impacts and reactions were felt throughout the entire process," Lady Gray said. "Our Council doesn't let anyone in by accident. There's a reason we cull each class from seven potential couples to five. Only the strongest bonds survive. That's how it's meant to happen."

But didn't that mean that Anita was right? If we didn't bond, shouldn't we be kicked out of the process? The women could see we were still unsure.

"It's like this," Lady Mauve frowned. "Kate stuck her nose in and messed it all up. Her screwing around gave a weaker tie a free pass." She crossed her arms. "Simple as that."

Our whole group sat back.

"May have given..." Lady Gray softened the message. "Time will tell."

"We won't let some crap pair in by default." Lady Mauve stared us all down, making it plain that in her eyes, we were all on the chopping block.

"But isn't that the point? Isn't that fate?" I wondered meekly. I wasn't sure whether I wanted to argue for or against us entering the High Council, but the whole mess of the process that they were discussing... wasn't that actually the predetermined choices of fate? "One could argue, by Kate interfering, fate was doing its job and keeping us out."

Lady Mauve let out a long sigh. "Hence all the talks."

"You're right," Lady Gray said. "Or you could be."

"The real question is, where do you draw the line?" Lady Mauve shrugged. "At the moonlight deadline? Then you failed in your task. That is as fate intended. However, that failure caused other ripples. Would the others have fared so well had Kate not intervened? Maybe. Maybe not. We'll never know. We can't go back. But frankly, no one gives a raw damn. It's irrelevant because *after* those moments it was *also* fate that Little Katie-Cat caused the High Council to reconvene and discuss all these questions. And we talked about it.

A lot. It was *also* fate that they decided, in an unprecedented vote, to create this limbo, put on this little show, and introduce Lady Gray and myself to you now. So that's what we got. We'll run the selection process through the hands of fate again. All those repercussions are from the same cause and effect. It just depends how close or wide you turn your lens. Far as I'm concerned, the line in the sand is here now. So put your big girl pants on."

"But that's not fair." Anita pouted.

"Why do they get a second chance?" Jacob added.

"What's the big deal? If you're meant to be here, fate will choose you again," Sloane told them.

Both ladies looked impressed.

"That's exactly right, Ms. Lolant. If you're meant to be part of the High Council, you have nothing to worry about," Lady Gray reassured her.

"And if you're not... you're gone." Lady Mauve cut her off. "By the end of this limbo, the two weakest ties will be out. Tomorrow, the new round of parabonding begins."

SIX

FOUR SPECIAL TALENTS

"ALL IN FAVOR of the non-bonds doing the right thing and stepping out of the competition?" Greg called for a vote the second the ladies left.

Marcy's hand shot in the air, followed by Anita and Tej. When Rick put his hand up, Hilde followed. After them came Jacob, who avoided all eye contact, and Vince, who looked me right in the eyes as he shrugged. He slowly raised his fingers. Finally, Nicolette's hand raised as well.

That left only one.

All eyes fell to Sloane.

She shrugged. "It's not up to us so this vote is moot, but I say let 'em shoot their shot."

Across the pool, I could feel Beck and Josie unclench. One person was on our side, or at least she wasn't actively against us. Those weren't great odds, but it was better than none.

For a moment we all sat in silence and mulled what

the ladies had said: Kate's intervention had spoiled the parabonding process not just for the four of us, but for everyone around this pool. And now we'd have to do it all again.

The others weren't happy.

But none of us non-bonds were dumb enough to try to plead our case. Not even Spade. Instead, Josie and Beck decided to duck and cover. They left the pool area and made their way back to the safety of her motel room. Both nodded at me on their way. I returned a strained smile. Spade went another way. During the meeting, he had covered up and shown some modesty. Now he stood and peeled off his shirt. Annoyed as I was, I couldn't help but sneak a peek at his chest.

I had felt it once. Just a solid wall of muscle.

Like Jacob, he had a swimmer's frame with muscular arms and a tight torso, but instead of wearing revealing little bottoms, his swim trunk shorts hung loose on his hips. You could see the tiniest cut of his leg bones. He looked delicious.

"How's the water, Marce?" he wondered.

"It's fine," she replied. Her tone was cool. She hadn't forgiven him for upsetting her parabond potential. Spade pretended not to notice. He retied the swimsuit cord on his hip bones. When he caught Nicolette watching him, he flashed her a wink. Then he launched himself into the pool in a fantastic flip, generating enough momentum to throw his body weight high in the air. The landing sent a tidal wave towards Tej, Hilde, and Rick.

Spade burst to the surface, pulling his wet hair behind his ears, his chest muscles shining. I could tell he expected accolades or the start of a contest or something. Instead, Rick just scowled and stood and left.

"Come on," he said to Hilde over his shoulder, and she quickly gathered her things.

Tej stood too and glanced at Sloane, but seeing her disinterest, he strolled to his own room alone.

Rick walked Hilde to her motel room, waited until she got inside, closed the door behind her, then headed to his own.

Spade swam towards Marcy and Greg, but she shuddered.

"I'm cold," she told her boyfriend, not looking at Spade. She climbed the steps out of the pool and wrapped herself in Nicolette's dry towel.

"Later, man." Greg, more conciliatory than his girlfriend, tapped fists with Spade in bro-solidarity, then followed Marcy straight out of the pool and into her motel room, picking up pieces of their discarded clothes as he went. Spade shrugged and settled for swimming laps by himself.

It wasn't a bad idea.

I would have loved to burn off some nervous energy as well, but I didn't move. Joining Spade in any way wasn't a message I wanted to send. After all, I still wasn't staying. He and I would not be partnering. Especially if the High Council needed to thin the herd.

"Well, this is lame," Anita murmured to Jacob. She

stood and stretched her long legs. He followed her lead. He dragged a pair of sweat shorts over his tiny Speedo and instantly looked ten times more attractive to me. He checked to see if Sloane and I were looking. We were, but Sloane made a big show of rolling her eyes. "Come on, Nicolette," Anita added, half-inviting, half-ordering.

Nicolette was surprised by the invitation, but quickly hopped up and fell into step with the perfect specimens. They even had exquisite posture as they strolled. The threesome walked across the concrete pavers together, but Anita really only wanted to exit with numbers. When she got to her motel room, she didn't invite either of the other two teens inside. Jacob saw that coming, but Nicolette, having just received her invite to join them, seemed surprised. She hesitated, probably wondering if she could gracefully make her way back to the pool, but we all knew she couldn't pull it off. Instead, head down, she went on to her own room.

I stayed poolside.

Being the new girl in so many situations had taught me the best thing to do in a tense scenario was often to stay. Running to hide in the privacy of your room, like Josie and Beck had done, was the easiest option, but if you steeled your nerves and stuck around, quieter people were almost always heard. Dissenting voices just took longer to speak. Sloane didn't disappoint.

"You can't take it personally," she said.

"What, that nobody likes me and if it were up to them, they'd immediately vote me out?" I asked.

"Exactly."

We both laughed.

"If they were meant to be here, they wouldn't be so worried." Sloane shrugged again. "Does *he* look worried?" She gestured at Vince, who hadn't budged from his chaise.

"He does not," I agreed. "Neither do you."

"Well, I doubt they'd pass me over three times only to kick me out when I arrived. My powers are too developed."

"You have powers?" This was the first really witchy thing I'd heard anyone say since we arrived.

"We all do. What are you, an empath? Can you energy-harness?"

"No. I..." I hadn't heard those words before, but something told me I could trust Sloane. I just hoped it wasn't her long blonde hair and symmetrical face. "I have vivid dreams. Sometimes..." How to put this so I wouldn't seem crazy, I wondered. "Sometimes they seem to guide my way."

"A caster." She nodded. "Honestly, that's a little common. I would have pegged you as an empath or even a lie-guard. But maybe you'll be two-fold. I'm a caster too." She clocked my uncertain expression. "Were your parents passed over?"

"My mom died when I was little. My dad... I don't know. But yeah. My aunt was passed over."

Sloane nodded. "It's like this: there are basically

four special talents. Casters see the future while they're sleeping. Your basic witch gets jumbled visions or murky riddles. When bad things are coming, they'll know. But a talented caster can see the future for multiple people, maybe even a whole town." She held up a second finger in her list. "Chemists understand the chemical, biological, and scientific makeup of potions and experiments. They're in tune with chemical reactions and propagate powerful herbal remedies and plants. My parabond, Tej, he's a chemist." A third finger went up. "Empaths are sometimes called Harnesses. They specialize in meteorological, mineral, or animal energies. Some witches can harness bad weather, others kind of talk to animals, I don't know how much, but they can at least make them come when they're called. It's tough to be a Harness or an Empath, as humans treat the rest of the earth so bad. Tapping into those energies is really exhausting. And lastly," her fourth finger rose into the air, "there are the lie-guards. Their power is built on illusions. Really solid illusions. The lie-guards make you see and feel things that aren't really there, but they make it so real you experience it as true. Their entire power rests in warping a perceiver's mind. The more that you doubt, the more power they have to exert. And that's basically it. Every witch falls somewhere in those camps. Some people have quirky party tricks, but those aren't that common. You can be two-fold, meaning instead of one, you're blessed with two powers, but it's rare to be a three or four."

"You shouldn't tell her all that," Vince said. He

swung his work boots off the chaise and kicked up the base of his scooter off the floor. "She might not get in."

Sloane stood, so I followed suit. "Please." She frowned. "They switched this whole thing up just for her."

"Or him." Vince nodded at Spade, who was smart enough to be listening. "Or Floppy Hat, or that other girl."

"His name is Beck," I pointed out.

Sloane shrugged. She didn't care. "I'm going to bed."

"Sounds like a plan." I nodded. Vince shrugged too. His warning gone unheard, he dropped his scooter and rolled away. Sloane and I started to depart.

"Mae, hold up a minute," Spade called me back. His voice cracked just a little, betraying his casual act. Sloane raised an eyebrow, but I waved her off on her way. She shrugged and left for her room.

"What?" I frowned and crossed my arms. What could he possibly have to say? There wasn't an apology on earth that would be big enough to keep me on board as his partner. He looked around to indicate someone might be listening, then beckoned me closer. We could both see there was no one left in at water, but I humored him and sat on the edge of the pool. "What... I'm listening."

"You still owe me for dinner," he said with a cheeky smile.

"I'm going to bed."

"I'm kidding." He lightly tossed himself in the

water and floated several feet away. "You know I'm kidding." He flashed another grin. It was the kind of smile that had gotten him out of many thorny things in the past, I was sure. I was embarrassed to say it was kind of working again. "No, actually..." He swam back near my legs, putting a hand on the concrete only inches from my thigh.

My skin buzzed in proximity. Defensively, I shifted out of easy reach.

His tone grew more sober. "I wanted to say sorry for how things turned out on our date. I'm serious. I pushed too far, too fast. I know that. I was wigging out over not parabonding. My mom was driving me nuts. I guess I was ready to try anything to help fate. But I ruined the good thing we had going. It was dumb. Super dumb... I didn't know what I was doing. Plus..." He sized me up, a grin twitching on his lips. "You've got to admit your breasts looked damn good in that little white top."

I flushed bright red.

Spade waited. He cocked an eyebrow, watching me carefully. Throwing such a bold compliment into the mix was a serious risk. But he could see that it was working. His eyes twinkled like he wanted to keep going, keep teasing, keep pushing, but instead, he stuck to his apology. "I wasn't my best self. And I'm sorry. Water under the bridge?"

His flattery had unnerved me, but I wasn't at a total loss for words. "Let's see... you tried to hump me and when I said no, you called me a prude."

"I didn't say that."

I gave him a look.

"I might have implied it," he conceded. "And that wasn't cool. I get it. But before I turned into a total douche-llama we were having a nice time. Don't you think? I had a nice time." He propped himself up on the pool ledge, his arms and shoulders showcased on the cement. There was that smile again. Water dripped from his hair. "A really nice time." He was careful and slow as he emphasized each word.

In spite of myself, I blushed. "Forgiven," I agreed.

Spade smiled. I smiled too. Maybe he was right. It was a stressful time for us all. Spade had behaved poorly, but that was all it was. A poor reaction to a stressful situation. This guy, the nice guy from the pool, from my class, from the first part of our date together, that was the *real* Spade. The guy who thought I looked cute in little white sweaters. The guy who looked pretty good in his swimmers as well.

He raked his hair back. "Just think, if it hadn't been for that nut job hiding your offering..."

"Don't call her that," I said. Just like that, the connection fizzled. "You don't get to charm away your own bad behavior and then act like she's some monster. You didn't know Kate."

"You didn't either! You barely liked her."

I frowned. "You don't know how I feel."

"I'd like to," he said quietly.

There it was again.

His voice stirred something deep inside me. I

thought I'd stayed by the pool to talk to Sloane, but had I really stayed for this? Did I want Spade to talk me into staying?

"It's getting late." I pulled my legs up.

"Is it? Let me see." He held out his arm with a wicked smile. A call back to our first date. We both knew he wasn't wearing a watch. He wanted me to touch his skin, trace a small circle, pretend to wind the hands of an imaginary clock. The first time we'd done it, that move had ignited a fire. It was the simplest form of intimacy.

The gentlest touch.

Only a graze.

But I didn't take the bait.

Seeing he'd gone too far, too fast, he gently reached out and peeled my arm off my own legs and draped my palm in his hands. I rolled my eyes but didn't flinch, so he kept a close watch to gauge how participatory I was feeling.

I didn't play along.

I also didn't pull away.

"Hmm." He examined my wrist, then looked into my eyes. "You're right, it's late. But it's not too late." I stayed perfectly still. "This time..." His index finger trailed over my skin, the delicate touch sending shivers down my spine. "There's no rush. We've got nothing but time." He smiled slowly, softly. We both hoped I'd move towards him, jump into the pool, maybe wrap my arms around his chest. I could smash our lips together, search his mouth with my tongue, and let his warm body push up against me on the blue mosaic tile. We could move things quickly, stripping off extraneous clothing. Skin next to skin, we'd be connected while keeping afloat in the deep end of the pool. That's what my body wanted. But in my head, I knew I had to stay dry.

He was trouble.

The ease with which he could manipulate my feelings tonight was simply more proof.

I wouldn't be baited so easily.

"Good night, Spade," I said, hoping my legs wouldn't betray me as I stood and walked to my room without looking back. I felt good about my decision to leave him in the cold. Especially as I realized, barely hidden behind their curtains, there were at least six other pairs of eyes at their windows watching.

I closed my door behind me and breathed a sigh of relief.

Day one of the High Council was over.

I had survived.

SEVEN

THE TASK OF SEVEN TRIALS

I AWOKE the next morning to the sound of cheerful piano music floating in from the pool. I looked around the shabby motel room and rubbed my eyes. The sun was filtering in through the blinds. It looked like a beautiful morning. My unpacked bags still sat beside the bed. I hadn't bothered to change clothes to sleep, just stripped down to only undies and a T-shirt, but now that I'd slept in the outfit, I'd have to switch up my clothes.

What to wear? It might be easier to choose if I knew what was on the agenda.

Fat chance.

I flopped the comforter aside and stumbled out from under the covers. My fingers fumbled with the suitcase zipper as I yawned, only half awake. The ladies hadn't mentioned a specific time for a wake-up call, but it seemed clear they were now ready to start the day. It took me a few rough tries to get going, but finally the bag unzipped in my hands.

I shoved aside my warmer sweaters and grabbed my new gray T-shirt from the suitcase. Next, I pulled back on yesterday's black pants from the chair by the desk. The weather seemed warm and inviting. Warmer than a fall day should be. Better roll on plenty of deodorant, I thought. Wouldn't want to stink up the whole High Council on my second day. I flipped to the front pockets of my suitcase and was surprised to discover, along with the sweat stick I was looking for, a large, bumpy white envelope. It was scrawled with my name in my aunt's messy writing. I grabbed it with a smile. Aunt Abeline had snuck this into my bag without me noticing. That was sweet. What was inside?

I ran my hands over it. Part of the envelope felt soft and smushy, the other part felt hard and square.

I ripped open the paper packaging and grinned.

Her package housed two things: a mouse deterrent buzzer, like the kind we had plugged in all over the lake house to prevent unwanted critters, and a brand-new pineapple T-shirt. The same fruity motif shirt I'd rejected at the store.

Aunt Abeline had also included a note:

For the day you're ready to stop blending...
Be true to yourself. Knock 'em dead.

. . .

P.S. Also... none of your new friends should be four-footed.

Aunt A

I looked down at the brightly colored shirt.

Had it really been only one night since I was back in the lake house with my aunt? It felt like a million years.

I loved the thought behind the purchase, and the extra treat of her slipping it in my bag, but I didn't change the clothes I had on. I was still in no mood for brightly colored T-shirts. And I never would be. The thought made me smile, but that was it. I wouldn't wear it. I tossed the shirt on the bed and plugged the buzzer into the wall. Immediately, I was greeted by the low-pitch hum of the small plastic box. Considering the state of this motel, the second part of her gift would indeed come in handy.

Maybe I should text her?

I was just about to, but then I started to wonder: did Aunt Abeline know that the High Council would be dumpy? Did she have some sort of insight into the place? Or was it possible this little buzzer was just a cute memory from home? Had my mother also stayed in limbo?

The décor in the place was certainly old enough.

Mom.

It was kind of messed up that she wasn't at the fore-front of my mind. I was here at the High Council. Her High Council. Here with her witches and all that entailed. I'd been so wrapped up in arriving and meeting all the other kids and learning all the social niceties, I hadn't given much thought to my mom in all of this.

But this was a big deal.

Stepping on these grounds, making these new friends, I already had a better sense of who she was. If Spade and I were to patch things up for good, if we could get along, I realized I could stay and learn so much more. It was what I really wanted. To gain more knowledge about my powers and discover more about my heritage. I was excited to hear more. If Spade smartened up, maybe he and I could really be partners. It was a big change from how I'd felt even one day before.

"Rise and shine, potential bonders." Lady Gray's sing-song voice at the door broke through my reverie. She rapped three times on the woodgrain, then moved on to do it all over again next door.

I guess the piano music hadn't enticed us out of our rooms fast enough. The ladies were ready to get things going. I threw my hair into a topknot and joined the rest of the teens as they were gathering by the pool.

"Mae, I saved you a seat." Spade waved me over.

The empty chair sat between him and Josie.

Most of the other teens already had plates of food on their lap.

I nodded and smiled, signaling okay, I'd come over, but I needed to get food for breakfast first. I wandered towards the long table set up by the pool with serving dishes and plates and cutlery. It was unclear who was running the buffet, but I didn't care. It was a welcome new addition. The spread had fruit and toast and eggs and bacon. Even English muffins. Everything smelled really great.

I fell in step in the line behind Beck.

"Hey. Sleep okay?" he asked.

"I did. How about you?"

"Josie was up half the night, but I can sleep anywhere." He shrugged. "Sorry we didn't warn you about Spade. That was dumb." We both glanced over to where they were sitting. Spade and Josie were each doing a great job pretending the other was a potted plant. For all her sales pitch to me about how Spade would make a fine partner, she really didn't like him.

"No biggie. You don't owe me anything." I gave him a reassuring smile. "I should have guessed this was how it would be."

Beck frowned.

I could see he had more to say, but Josie had noticed we were chatting together. Her neutral face had turned to a frown. The last thing I needed was anyone questioning my motives. I grabbed a couple pieces of toast. "See you over there." I hurried away from Beck and flashed Josie a big grin.

"Fancy meeting you here," Spade said, brightening as I took the seat beside him.

"Well, thank you very much," I greeted him back. But immediately I turned my attention to my other friend. "Beck's still loading his plate," I told Josie, playfully rolling my eyes.

"The boy can eat," she agreed, but didn't add on.

I wondered if I should keep the conversation rolling, keep teasing her man, or abandon that line of thought completely, but before I could decide, Josie picked up the slack.

"This is not exactly what I was expecting," she admitted.

We looked around the pool. Sloane and Tej were chatting with Greg and Marcy, but the other teens were quietly eating from the plates on their laps.

"What were you expecting?" I wondered.

Josie shrugged as Beck sat down on the far side of her. "I don't really know. Just... not this."

"Mae, check this out." Spade tried to interrupt us.

"In a second," I told him, then turned back to her. "I thought for a minute last night we might be tarred and feathered," I joked.

"Yeah. That wasn't great. But I can see how they felt. It sucks to hear our parabond connections haven't been finalized. Even after all this, we still might not get in."

"You and Beck will be fine."

She gave me a forced smile and shook her head. "Doesn't really ingratiate us with the others, does it?"

"It does not."

"Well, at least we've got each other." This time, her smile was sincere.

"We'll stick together," I agreed. This was the Josie I had hoped would be at the High Council.

Resolute.

Honest.

Decisive.

"You should try this English muffin, it's totally delicious," Spade cut in again. He tried to feed me, but I waved him off.

"I'll stick with my toast," I told him, then took a large bite to prove my point.

"I love breakfast," he said. He was just keen enough that I could tell that he meant it. The adoration in his voice over eggs and bacon was disarming. With a body like his, I seriously doubted that he often overindulged. Or maybe he did. Who knew how teenage guys filled their stomachs? "It's the most important meal of the day," he told me with a wink.

I just laughed. He wanted to add more, but the ladies were calling things to order.

It turned out the classical music I'd heard from my room wasn't a recording, it was being played live by Lady Mauve. She sat at a piano at the corner of the pool deck, which before now, I hadn't even noticed. With dramatic flourish, she brought her song to a close.

"Good morning," Lady Gray greeted us as Lady Mauve played her final notes. When the song was over, the shorter, stronger woman moved to stand beside our other host. "I hope you all had a good night's rest. I'm sure you're wondering how the fate selection process will begin, but you should know we're not going to concern ourselves with that today. Today is to allow your energy to rebuild and reconnect."

"So breathe," Lady Mauve clarified. "Because no one's getting cut today."

I exhaled the breath I didn't know I'd been holding. And I wasn't the only one. All around the pool, the color came back to our faces. We were all on edge.

"Did everyone get breakfast? Did everyone eat?" Lady Gray asked. We nodded. "Good."

"Well, what are you waiting for? Drop your dishes in the bin and let's go." Lady Mauve turned and marched away from the pool with Lady Gray by her side.

Quickly, we realized our assembly was on the move. We dropped our half-eaten breakfasts and plates in the bin with a clatter and hurried to follow. Vince took an apple as we went, noisily crunching into its skin. How he could still eat at a moment like this was beyond me. I was so tied up in knots I could barely breathe. The women took us around the front of the hotel to the parking area. Only, as we made the turn, we discovered all the vehicles had been removed.

"Where's my car?" Greg wondered.

"Temporary relocation," Lady Mauve assured him.

"Mine too?" Sloane asked.

The women simply nodded.

Where the cars had once been, there were now seven large black crates on the lot. Each one was about the size of a train car. As far as I could see, there were no doors or windows into the boxes. Each was a sealed container.

"What are all these?" Marcy voiced the question we were all thinking.

"This is what we're doing today." Lady Gray gestured grandly. "As we said, this morning is all about get-to-know-you exercises... on a fairly large scale. Anyone can have a conversation, but to really get to know each other, we think actions are stronger than words. Ladies, you'll each be locked in your own private box, and we'll create a scenario inside just for you."

"We're going in there?" Anita raised an eyebrow.

"Mm-hmm, and the boys will come room to room and help you out with your tasks and your little situations. Think of it like speed dating, with a task to complete."

"Except the tasks aren't easy," Lady Mauve warned.

"Yes. Well, they're geared to test your compatibility as a team under stress, as well as the limits of your individual capabilities," Lady Gray agreed.

That didn't sound good.

"Each one will help fate determine your destiny," Lady Gray went on. "You'll stay in the box together with your rotating partner until you either complete the task, or officially fail."

"You don't want to fail." Lady Mauve made that advice clear.

That didn't sound good either.

Lady Gray agreed. "Yes, of course. Try your best and work fast to solve the problems because you have six other compatibility tasks to get through."

"How will we know when to move to the next box? Will you hit a gong?" Greg joked.

"No gong, but don't worry. We'll move you forward. Don't you worry about that." Lady Gray shook her head. The two women snuck a small knowing look at each other. That subtle look was another bad sign. Something told me these tasks were going to be a lot more difficult than the women were letting on. "Any questions?"

I looked around at the group. I had a million follow-up questions: what was the task? How long would it take? How would we know it was complete? How would this help determine fate? If there were no doors or windows into the boxes, how would we even get in? I waited for someone to ask something, anything. But nobody offered any questions. I tried to formulate one of my own, but it was tough to come up with something coherent. I was feeling sort of woozy.

Weird.

I was thinking clearly a minute ago.

The grass under my feet grew fuzzy and I could barely make out the silhouettes of Lady Mauve and Lady Gray standing ten feet in front of me.

"When are we starting?" Marcy wondered. The words sloshed out of her mouth.

"Right now, Hot Lips," Lady Mauve replied. "We call it The Task of the Seven Trials."

But it was getting progressively harder to hear her.

"The seven what?" Greg slurred. He plopped down to the ground mid-question.

Suddenly, the yard started tilting. I put my hand to my head to try to stop the pavement from spinning. Lady Mauve and Lady Gray each crossed their arms. In front of me, I saw Vince crash to the ground, his half-eaten apple rolling out of his hand. Others around me started dropping.

My eyelids were so heavy.

I tried to wave the ladies over.

Something was wrong.

It didn't seem like I could keep standing. Instead of legs, my limbs became jelly. My body lurched to the left. Then right. I crashed into someone or something. We both tumbled to the gravel. Then everything went black.

EIGHT
THE KEYS OF FATE

"WAKE UP." Large, rough hands shook my shoulders. I peeled my eyes open and looked into the concerned face of Hilde's giant partner, Rick. "It's started," he told me.

I squinted and looked around, trying to get my bearings.

We were inside one of the black boxes. At least, from the activities the women described, I felt we had to be, although I couldn't see any of the walls, the floor, or the ceiling. But that's where the ladies had said we would start.

It didn't seem like a container.

Instead, it felt like Rick and I had been transported to a day at the beach. The nature around us was beautiful, but it wasn't peaceful. To my left, there was some sort of water flowing. A lot of it. Flooding in from the hill above, filling the sandy shore where we were standing with a rising tide.

The beach was soft and sandy underfoot. My sneakers were gone, I realized. In their place I could feel the earth beneath my toes. My feet were free, but my ankle had been shackled to a large stone.

Water continued to rush down the hillside.

Pretty soon it would soak into the hems of my pants.

"This is our scene? What do we do?" I asked, even though Rick wasn't privy to anything more than what I had heard. "Is this the task?" I raised my ankle. "To get myself free?"

"That seems reasonable to assume."

Rick had no impairment. I was the only one who was trapped. Already the rising shoreline was up to our ankles.

"The water just keeps coming," he observed.

"Right. If we don't undo this, I'm gonna drown. I guess that's what they meant when they said you don't want to fail," I groused. "Maybe you can turn it off at the source?"

"I'll check the hilltop," Rick said.

The dune of sand rose up behind us on a steep incline from where we stood on the beach. The hill went well above my head. He quickly scaled to the top, sand kicking up behind his heels.

"Hurry," I added, though it was completely unnecessary. I just felt like I should be doing or saying something.

The water continued to gush down the hill.

I knelt down to examine the padlock. I'd waited too

long to take a close look and now it was fully underwater. The rushing liquid was almost up to my calves. I could only see the details of the lock through the gentle undulation of waves, but it looked like an ordinary clasp. As far as I could tell, I was chained to a standard padlock. All we needed was the key.

"There's a chest full of keys," Rick told me, arms full as he came down the hill. "But I can't turn off the water. I can't even tell where it's coming from, not really." He dropped the heavy box on the sand with a thud. A huge pile of keys bounced inside. "How do we find the right one?"

"Process of elimination? The lock's gold, so the key should be too." I eliminated the silver and bronze options immediately.

Rick dragged the chest farther down the hill where we could both look inside. Already I could tell we weren't moving fast enough. The water was most of the way up my legs. When we knelt down to reach my ankle shackle, the level would be dangerously close to our faces. There was no time to lose. Without any real plan, we began grabbing keys and trying to shove them into the padlock.

"If a key doesn't work, fling it away. That way we won't get them confused," Rick suggested.

I nodded.

The first key he'd stuck in the lock didn't budge, so he pulled it out and hurled it away. But instead of it flinging out to sea, the tiny piece of metal twanged off what sounded like metal. A metal wall we couldn't see.

So it was true. We were inside one of the boxes.

Sloane's words from last night came rushing back. Some people were casters, some were chemists, some were empaths, and some were lie-guards. The lie-guards created elaborate illusions to fool our perceptions. They could create any vision they could think of; their power was in the details. So this beach scene seemed real, but we were inside one of the windowless metal boxes. This whole scene was something the ladies created.

It was a weird piece of knowledge.

In my brain, I knew the beach was fake. The rising tide, the gushing water, even the chain locked around my foot—none of it was real. But the reality of that knowledge went against everything I could see, hear, touch, or feel. Because it sure did feel like my life was in danger.

Sloane hadn't made it clear, and I didn't know the answer. Could a lie-guard's illusion really hurt the intended viewer? Could it kill you? I didn't want to find out.

The water had risen to my hips.

I was no longer able to look down and see what I was doing without my face submerging in the water. Luckily, Rick was a bit taller.

"I can't breathe and reach," I told him, shuffling my feet.

"It's okay. I'll keep going." He nodded.

I grabbed and prepped the keys for him to make the transition into the lock as seamless as possible. He strained his fingers into the padlock, testing each key, but soon his face was only barely above the edge of the rising tide as well.

"We've got to hurry," I said.

He strained his neck to keep his head above water.

"It's no use," I said worriedly.

Rick grimaced with effort. "I think I... I got it." He twisted the key in the padlock and the shackle released around my ankle.

"You did it!" Immediately, I pulled him up to his feet, and the rushing water stopped. The beach filled with silence but for our gasping breath. We both clawed our exhausted bodies up on the dune to rest. "Some get-to-know-you exercise," I muttered.

"I feel I know you better," Rick agreed. He smiled. It was the first time I'd seen him in anything but a scowl. It suited him.

"I guess. I'm Mae." I offered a handshake.

"Rick." We shook. His hand was huge and firm. "How long do you think we'll stay here?"

"I guess until all the other teams have completed their task," I suggested.

But Rick hadn't heard my answer. Eyes closed, he'd already collapsed on the sand.

"Rick?"

I reached out to revive him, but the blackness took over.

—

I woke up to the sound of rushing water. Immediately, I looked around for Rick, but he was gone. I was back in the beach box without him. The world had reset. The illusion was once again filling the beach up with water, but this time I wasn't shackled. All of my limbs were dry on the sand. It was Vince who was tied up below me. He lay flat on his back, his head propped on the sandy shore, not moving. The water was already at his ankles, rising in a steady flow.

"Hey, wake up." I splashed him.

Vince shot awake and sat up. Instinctively, his hand floated up to check his head, then moved down to the lock.

"The second task's started," I told him. I ran up the hill to find the treasure chest like Rick before me. Why hadn't I paid attention to which key opened the lock?

"I'm shackled," Vince called out to me, struggling against his tether.

"I know. The chest of keys is up here," I told him. But when I got to the chest that Rick had retrieved, it was far too heavy for me to carry alone.

"Hurry!" Vince shouted.

The water was past his knees.

"It's too heavy," I relayed back down the hill. Frustrated, I pulled my T-shirt away from my body and held onto the hemline to make it into sort of a fabric basket. Next, I shoved handfuls of keys inside the cradle I'd made. "Here." I scaled back down the hill with our precious cargo in tow. "Keys!"

"The lock is bronze," Vince noted. He made the same assumption as me that the color of the lock would match the color of the key.

"Last time it was gold... or silver... I don't remember, but the task is changing as we go," I noted. "Getting harder." The water was flowing quicker too, I'd noticed. Meaning he could drown that much earlier. But I didn't think it would be helpful to tell Vince that detail.

I sorted the silver and gold keys out of my T-shirt cargo and Vince quickly tested each bronze one. Any that didn't fit or match our color scheme, we dropped into the water.

But we weren't moving quickly enough.

The water level was already at his waist. Vince had to crane his head to keep his face above water while his fingers blindly stuck the keys into the lock. I wasn't as tall as Rick, so Vince was our best bet.

"There are more keys than this. Hold these." I gave him the last four bronze keys from the first group and climbed back up the hill. In the chest, I dug through the selection.

"Those didn't work. Hurry!"

In all, I grabbed twenty or so more bronze keys. "I'm coming." I made one last check of the chest to be sure I hadn't missed any and ran back down to him.

Vince had resorted to standing once more.

"You can't reach?" I said worriedly.

"Not while breathing," he admitted. The water had risen to mid-chest level. We would have to submerge underneath the water to test the rest of the keys. "You know what, forget this. I got it." Vince lowered one hand in a fist at his side and narrowed his eyes. He seemed to be concentrating deeply.

"Your powers?" I looked around. Nothing was happening. "Are you doing it?"

The water kept rushing.

"I don't..." He frowned. "It's not working. They must be blocking my harness." He tried again. He closed his eyes and dug deeper into his powers.

"Can they do that?" I wondered.

"It's not happening." He released the tension in his palm.

"Or they made you believe that," I realized.

We just looked at each other. I'd never seen a harness, so I didn't know what to expect, but magic powers or not, we had to keep going. I transferred the keys from my shirt into his.

"Why don't you try yours? Your powers," he asked.

"I'm a dreamcast," I admitted.

He snickered.

"What?"

"I just thought you were better than that." He shrugged.

"Give me those." I grabbed two keys from his hands and dove under water.

It was hard to keep under the current long enough

to put the keys in the padlock. I fumbled as I went, but I found I could test both keys in the lock in one breath. Maybe more.

Neither of them fit.

I pushed back to the surface and shook my head.

"Here you go, caster." Vince was ready. He handed me two new keys and I grabbed a couple more, then dove back to the bottom.

Great, so I was a witch, but not very powerful.

I shoved each piece of metal into the padlock opening, but none fit. Feeling disheartened, I resurfaced. The water had almost reached Vince's shoulders. The snarky look had washed off his face.

"We have to go faster," he told me.

I nodded. "Help hold me down," I told him, catching my breath. "That way, I can do more."

"Okay, I got it." Vince nodded.

I grabbed another handful of keys and dove.

Once I was down near the padlock, Vince put his knee on my back to keep me from floating. I shoved each key into the hole. When they didn't work, I dropped them onto the sand below. One after another, they didn't fit the device.

After the last key had failed, I swatted his leg to let me up.

Vince moved out of the way, and I shot up to the surface, huffing and puffing and filling my lungs.

When I could breathe again, I realized the water was up to his neck. He didn't say more; he was out of snide comments. He just offered new keys for me to try.

There weren't many left.

I grabbed another handful and dove. I injected the first one. And then tried the second.

It was more of the same.

None of them worked.

I moved to the third one, and on to the fourth one. Had we somehow missed the right one? Or cast it off on the ground? As I tested the fifth, my chest burned, and I could feel the cloud of carbon dioxide in my head. I shoved in the sixth, then the seventh. But to no avail.

When I breached the surface, I realized it was worse than I thought.

I could no longer stand. I had to tread water. The water level between us was now well above my head. Vince had his head tilted skyward to protect his nose and mouth. Water lapped at his cheeks.

"This is it," he told me. "All we got."

I nodded, grabbed the last remaining keys, and dove. As I descended, he took his last breath. The water flooded over his head.

It was all on me now.

I started again at the beginning. Key one, key two. None were a match. Key three... clicked.

That was strange. I almost pulled it out.

I tried it again.

I was so used to the little metal prong being rejected that for a moment I didn't know how to react.

But then I turned the key in the metal lock and the hook of the lock popped away from its shell.

That was it!

The padlock had opened.

I shoved Vince's ankle out of the trap, and he kicked off, up to the shore. I pushed off the bottom to the surface too, my lungs exploding with the need for air. As I breached the waterline, I gasped a huge gulp of oxygen, then swam over to the sand.

Vince clawed himself out of the water. Like soggy fish, we flopped on the shoreline. Again, and just as suddenly, the rushing water turned off.

For a moment, there was silence. It was so sweet. Our heavy breathing filled the air.

For a moment, it was peaceful.

Then the blackness took over.

NINE
BECK'S PADLOCK

THE THIRD AND fourth unlocking with Tej and Greg both went easier.

We had a bit of luck finding the true keys before the water dramatically rose, but even when everything went right, the onslaught of fear and adrenaline was an exhausting experience. It was almost too much to bear. There was no reprieve. No moment to catch one's breath. The only thing a completed task guaranteed was that in moments, the panic would begin all over again.

The blackness was our only solace.

It overtook me once more.

———

"Mae?"

The rushing water greeted me.

"Mae?" But so did a familiar voice. He called out to me.

I opened my eyes and Beck's concerned face came into view. "Hi." I smiled. I was lying flat on my back on the beach. He was kneeling above me. He grinned back, relieved, and for a moment I didn't feel panicky. Then the tickle of water began reaching my toes.

It was coming again. Just like before.

The water was gushing. There was no stopping the scene.

"No!" I kicked helplessly at my shackled foot, trying not to cry. I was locked to the giant stone once more.

"What do we do?" he asked.

"The keys are up there. The water will rise." Finally alone with someone I knew, all my bravado disappeared. I was exhausted. "Beck, I can't do this. Not again. I..."

I fizzled into pathetic sobs, knowing full well every moment I wasted would make our task harder on the other end.

"Whoa, hey. It's okay. I get it. This is hard." Beck wrapped his arms around me. He let me cry. I released another sob or two, then pulled myself together. What was I doing weeping into the chest of Josie's guy?

"Sorry. The chest's up the hill. It's heavy." I wiped the snot and tears off my face.

At least she hadn't seen me fall apart in his arms.

"I'm strong," he said, trying to cheer me up. "I can take it."

"Strong enough to lift the rock?" My tone despaired. I wasn't really asking. That thing was huge. Already, the flooding water was ankle-deep.

"Maybe..."

"I was kidding. The stone's a monster."

But Beck was willing to give it a go. He bent low and wrapped his arms around the awkward load. When he felt he was in a good position, he heaved with all his strength.

"Oh my god!" I couldn't help but cheer.

He did it!

He picked it up!

The stone moved, maybe an eighth of an inch or so, and then he dropped it with a grunt.

"It weighs too much." Beck shook his head. "But I bet I can drag it."

I narrowed my gaze, uncertain what he meant, but Beck jumped right in. He took hold of the chain right before my shackle and burrowed his heels in the sand. With that little bit of leverage, he tugged. The rock fortress slid forward a few inches up the hill.

I was shocked. "You did it."

"I didn't do much." He frowned.

"But it's something. I think it's enough. We can rise with the water level," I realized in awe.

Because of his leverage system, my foot was now back on dry land. It was a freakin' miracle. I could see the padlock clearly; it was made of gold metal.

"Go. Quick, get a bunch of gold keys," I told him with renewed vigor.

If Beck could shift the stone on pace with the rising water, we wouldn't have to worry about drowning while we were working. He could feel my energy return, and he scampered up the hill. I felt so relieved.

Around me, the water kept flowing.

In our original position where we'd awakened, by now it would have been up to my waist or higher, but now it only fell to mid-calf. For the first time in these get-to-know-you simulations, I felt in control.

I collapsed into a seated position on the sand.

Beck returned, and together, we put the first batch of potential keys into a small pile on the sand. Before even trying the first of the keys, we pulled on the rock and chain together and raised it higher on the hill once more, breaking the water surface level again. It was incredible. I could actually see the lock I was trying to open.

We took turns inserting and attempting to twist the keys. When the waters started to get too close for comfort, we simply dragged the rock and shackle higher.

"What are the other rooms like?" I wondered. We'd fallen into a comfortable rhythm.

Beck frowned. "Not great. They're all life or death but each different in task. With Sloane we had to squeeze through an hourglass with sands of time dumping on our heads. I got across a chasm with Anita.

Built a shield to stop the walls with spikes closing in with the little girl…"

"Hilde."

"Hilde, right. Nicolette was poisoned and we had to find the antidote. Her muscles seized and froze right in front of me. It was not a pretty sight. And I still haven't gotten to Josie."

"Saving the best for last," I mused with a wry smile. I hadn't seen Spade either.

Beck didn't see the humor. "The human body isn't built for this stress. Such prolonged fight or flight options will destroy our very nature and—oh, I got it." He interrupted his own thoughts when the key fit.

"Wait!"

Beck was about to turn the lock, but I grabbed his hand. He looked up, surprised.

"Sorry." I quickly released him. "What you're saying was right. The stress to our minds and our bodies… what if we don't finish? The task. You know, just for a little while. What if we give ourselves… give everyone… a little break?"

"The next task won't begin until this one is complete." He caught on.

"Exactly."

"Huh. Okay."

Together we adjusted the stone and shackle higher once more, but this time, we could both see the move had a different tenor. There wasn't a rush. Our next move wasn't urgent. We plopped back on the sand, side by side, and looked around at our surroundings. With the end to this task safely in our sights, the rushing water was no longer a deadly trap. Instead, it felt like a beautiful waterfall. For once, I could relax a bit. The whole scene felt calm and serene. While we knew in our heads that the beach wasn't real, merely an illusion, the details of the scenario looked impressively lifelike.

"Think of it like a little beach vacation," I told him. "With no sun and no skin…"

Beck grinned. "What, you're not going to strip?"

I slowly shook my head. I thought of Marcy's display of bare assets. She'd looked so great. That so wasn't me. "If anything, I'm gonna put on more clothes!" I laughed.

"I will too," he agreed. "Jacob and Marcy showed enough skin for everybody." Beck picked up a pebble from the beach and hurled it into the sea.

"Oh! Careful!" I warned.

The little stone bounced off a metal wall we couldn't see and ricocheted in another direction. We ducked, but our spot on the beach was well clear of the path.

"Right." His brow furrowed. "You know, for a second, I forgot where we were."

I realized I had too. Kind of.

For a moment, the contest, the High Council, the promise of parabonding—it had all slipped away. We were just two friends hanging out, chilling out on the beach. Never mind the giant weight around my ankle still holding me down.

"We could skip them, maybe?" I offered, referencing the stones. I stood and dusted the sand off my butt. The circumference within which I could search for the perfect pebble was small, limited by the chain, but I actually found one or two that looked pretty good. In a smooth motion, I chucked one across the water. It leapt once, twice, three times, then clanged on the hidden wall and tumbled into the water, sinking to the bottom.

Beck hopped up too. "Pretty cool. How'd you do that?"

"You've never skipped rocks?"

He shook his head.

"It's easy. Look for something flat, like that." I showed him an example. We searched around again and found a couple more pebbles that might work. Beck picked up a pink-and-gray beauty that was smooth and long. "Perfect. So you take it in your hands, and you just kind of skip it." I demonstrated again. My second stone flew out of my hand and flicked across the water, nimbly bouncing twice, then disappearing into the tide.

Beck mirrored my action a few times.

"It's kind of like... you throw it, but you sidearm it. It's a flick of the wrist and then you release, cuz you're trying to bounce it across the water, not toss it, so when you do, it just skips across the surface."

Together we tossed a couple more. Beck caught the hang of it pretty quickly.

"Pretty good," I told him. He grinned.

We each threw nine or ten, neither of us getting up

to more than three jumps. Either the motion wasn't right, or they'd hit the hidden wall. But Beck didn't fling the gray-and-pink one. Instead, he ran it over in his hand.

"You didn't toss it," I noted.

"I like the feel. It kinda makes me feel normal." He gave me a sheepish grin. "That sounded dumb."

But I thought I knew what he meant. "You're not normal," I admitted softly. "None of us are."

"Four of us are," he corrected. "Or we will be again."

We dragged my stone prison higher on the beach and sat down together, looking out over the fake ocean.

"Who do you think it will be?" I wondered.

"On the outs? Probably Josie and I."

"Don't say that," I chided. But when he didn't say more, I couldn't help but ask, "Why?"

"Just a feeling." He shrugged.

I could tell there was more to that story, but he didn't offer it, and I wasn't brave enough to push again.

"I know what you mean," I agreed. "I can't help but wonder if fate had it right, you know? The first time. Like maybe fate sent Kate into the mix to mess everything up. Maybe that was on purpose. We were done. You and Josie make a lot of sense, but Spade and I? It wasn't..." I trailed off. All the talk from the ladies of the energies mixing and the re-selections of fate was fine, but the truth was, everyone but me knew exactly who they were re-partnering with, and that only left me one option: Spade. A guy who knew how to apologize, and to flirt, and to press all my buttons. A guy who was fun, charming, and undeniably sexy. But he knew it. He knew exactly who he was. And he used it. Like a shield... or a weapon. To try and get what he wanted. Was that a person I could call my parabond?

It was a scary decision to make.

The challenges today had made it clear the Council wasn't playing. These get-to-know-you tasks were powerful, cruel, and deadly. Beck and I had managed to find a reprieve, side by side, but the message was clear: partnering with the wrong person would have serious repercussions.

Spade was sweet to me last night, and even more so this morning, because he had to be. He needed something from me, just like he'd needed something at the end of the full moon cycle. He needed a partner, and I was it. His only option. But what would happen on the day that I was no longer the only option? On the day that I needed something from him? How could I possibly trust him?

Beck was surprised. "I thought you liked him. Josie said you went on that date..."

"It didn't go great," I admitted.

He didn't ask for details and I didn't offer any. He chose his next words carefully. "Well, maybe this is fate's chance to match you with someone else." He gave me a hopeful look.

I couldn't help but smile.

"Tej seems nice..." he said. "Or Rick?"

I shook him off. "I couldn't do that to the other girls."

Together, without thinking, we took hold of the stone and shackle and dragged ourselves farther up the beach again.

What I really needed was a partner like Beck.

Someone strong and resourceful, thoughtful and caring, who wasn't just using me to further his own agenda. But I couldn't do that to Josie, and I knew in my heart he couldn't either.

"Well, don't quit," Beck said quietly, as if reading my mind. "If I'm in the High Council and you're not..." He didn't seem to know how to finish the thought. "I want to know you."

It was simple but loaded.

The sentence hung in the air.

I wanted to know him too.

But as Josie's partner and boyfriend, as jealous as she was, there wasn't much room for us to get any closer. Even friendly little moments between us, innocent as they were, made her uncomfortable. Outside this little round-robin, I knew we would both respect her feelings. Moments like this, one-on-one, hanging out together—they would soon be gone forever.

And she wasn't crazy to be on guard.

The truth was, I liked Beck.

I was pretty sure he liked me too.

If Josie hadn't been in the picture... I stopped that line of thinking. She was in the picture.

"Everyone should probably be rested." I changed

the subject. "We should maybe get moving again. What do you think?"

He nodded. "Maybe Spade will surprise you and you'll end up with a really great partner."

"Maybe." He handed me the key. I was about to twist it in the lock but stopped for one more moment. "Beck, do me a favor?"

He nodded.

"Don't tell Josie I cried."

Beck smiled. "It'll be our little secret."

We grinned at each other and for a moment, I wondered what would happen if we never completed the task. If we never opened the shackle and we never went back to reality. If Beck and I could stay smiling on this beach here forever. But the beach wasn't real...

I twisted the key in the lock.

The shackle fell from my ankle, and Beck immediately collapsed on the ground, unconscious.

"I want to know you too," I admitted to his sleeping body before the darkness took over, stripping the words right out from my mouth.

TEN

THE TERMS OF MY SELECTION

I AWOKE to droplets of water raining down from above.

"Hey. There you are. Sorry, I had to get your attention."

I sat up in the sand, wiping the wetness from my face to see Jacob tied to the familiar stone. Water had already crept up to his ankle. Taking in the scene, I sighed.

"The hits just keep coming," I muttered to myself, hopping up to my feet. "Can you drag it? The rock?"

Instead of refreshing me, the comfort of being with Beck had made me even more tired. Even though we'd both agreed to move on, it turned out I wasn't ready to be here with someone else. Especially not someone like Jacob. The wolfish way he'd leered at Marcy's body hadn't endeared him to anybody. He took hold of the shackle and tugged as hard as he could. It didn't budge.

"Is that what the others did?" He asked.

"They must have changed out the rock." I frowned. "The whole thing changes a little every time." I joined him and we tried to pull again, but he was right. We couldn't drag it. "Okay, I'll get the keys. Hold on." I ran up the hill. Had they actually changed out the stone? Or was Beck just really that strong? I shook my head. Focus on the task at hand. "What color is the lock?!" I yelled over my shoulder.

"Gold!"

"Okay."

My fingers scrambled through the collection of keys, and I gathered all the gold ones in the cargo hold of my shirt. I stirred through the chest several times, and satisfied by my thoroughness, I ran back down the hill. Jacob was already up to his knees in the water, but he was examining the ankle shackle closely. He looked up as I returned.

I slowed down so as not to kick sand in his face. "These are the gold ones."

"That's a lot of keys." He frowned.

My shirt was full of metal keys of all sizes and shapes.

"I'm pretty good at the details," he told me, starting to pick through the shapes.

"It's just trial and error," I warned. I dumped the keys on the sand so we both could help, but Jacob didn't start testing each one. He just continued to look. I shoved my first key in the lock. It didn't work, so I grabbed another one.

"Not that one," Jacob said, his eyes flicking over my choice.

I narrowed my eyes but tried the key anyway. He was right. It didn't turn. I grabbed another one. Another few. Stuck them in and turned, one after the other. Jacob just puttered. His super calm demeanor and lack of action was starting to freak me out.

"While we're here, I was hoping to have a delicate conversation," he told me. He held up a more antique style key to have a closer look, then, disappointed by something, dropped it in the water.

"Are you crazy?! You didn't even test that!" I frantically caught it before we lost it forever in the castoffs already resting on the sandy bottom.

"It doesn't fit." He shrugged.

"How do you know?" I shoved it in the lock. But he was right. It didn't fit. "How did you know?" I asked again.

"I told you, I have a pretty good eye for detail. For how things really are..." He smiled and went back to poking and prodding through the pile of keys without a care in the world. The water had risen to his waist. "Now about that conversation..."

He definitely had my attention.

"Is it fair to say you're not exactly thrilled with your choice of parabond?" He picked up another golden key and this time, his eyes shone. "Got it."

"Oh good." I breathed a sigh of relief, but Jacob didn't budge. "Then put it in the lock."

"I will. After you answer my question."

What a dumb thing to be playing with: his life. If he was wrong, the water would just keep coming.

"Put it in," I growled.

He sighed and did as I asked. He was right. The key fit. Out of a pile of more than thirty gold keys, he'd picked the right one on the first try. But he hadn't turned the latch.

"Your turn," he said. "Answer the question."

I shrugged. "It doesn't matter how I feel. It's all up to fate."

"But what if we could help? For instance, you and I could partner."

"What about Anita?"

"What about her?" He shrugged. "Let's just say I'm also not entirely thrilled with the terms of my selection."

I furrowed my brow. Someone was offering me a carrot. This should have been great news... so why did it feel like a trap?

"You don't even know me."

"No, but as I said, I have an eye for things, and I think you do as well." He waited.

Which is why I don't trust you, I thought, but held on to my tongue. Was the fact that he was aggressively handsome like Spade clouding my judgment? Was it possible that all beefcake jocks didn't have to be jerks? I shifted my weight onto my other hip and regarded him skeptically.

"How'd you know the right key?" I asked.

He smiled. "I'd tell you, but then we'd have to partner."

I rolled my eyes and waited.

His teeth broke through his lips in a grin. "I read the lock brand name."

My jaw fell open. It was so simple. The water rose so fast I'd never thought to look at the writing.

"Think about it," he said. "We'd be a good match."

"I'll think about it," I agreed.

We both knew that was all he could hope for. I wouldn't promise any more. Jacob nodded and turned the key in the lock. It unlocked his shackle, then everything around us faded to black.

ELEVEN
SPADE'S LOCK

THE GUSHING WATER WOKE ME.

"Last time," I muttered to myself. I was back in the shackle again. "Spade, wake up!" I shouted. I didn't see him, but it didn't matter. I knew he was here. He had to be. This was our last speed date. Once we'd succeeded and opened the lock, this ordeal would be over.

It couldn't come soon enough.

I turned my attention to the details of the lock before the water rose too high and it was too late to see them. This one was silver. But unlike Jacob's before me, there was no brand name.

"Damn," I muttered to myself.

"Saved the best for last," Spade said. He cheered coming over the sand dune, the giant chest of keys in his arms.

"You didn't wake me?" I asked.

"You looked so cute, lying on the sand. Like Sleeping Beauty."

"I won't look so cute when I'm dead," I complained.

"I dunno..." He grinned and wiggled his eyebrows.

"Gross."

Why was he in such a good mood?

I just rolled my eyes.

There was a comfort with Spade. I didn't have to put on a show or even hold my tongue. I didn't feel the need to be nicer or kinder. I was free to be my snarly, exhausted, bossy self. "Pull out all the silver. I'll test 'em in the lock."

"Sounds good. How did all the other tasks work out?"

"It's been a long day."

"Tell me about it. I almost died like six times. At least you haven't drowned."

"Yet." I frowned. He better not jinx it. I knocked on the wood chest between us. "Give me a couple keys to get started."

His lack of urgency in the selections was unnerving.

"I haven't found one," Spade said.

"What?"

"They're all different colors of gold. Like, that's bronze, right?" The key he held up was clearly in the auburn color family.

The water was up to my knees.

"What do you mean you haven't found one?" I had bent down into a lock-picking stance, ready to be handed a rapid-fire collection of keys, but now I straightened up to look in the chest.

He was right. Just a sea of gold options. There was nothing with even a hint of silver in the entire box.

"See?!"

"That's weird."

"Do you think they screwed up?" he asked.

"The padlock is definitely silver..."

Spade tilted the chest on its side and spilled out all the various types of gold keys onto the shore. It was a gaudy, gilded river, until finally, there was one glimpse of silver.

"There!" we both shouted.

Spade dug in and pulled out the solitary silver key. "Got it." He handed it over.

The water had reached my thighs. But that was fine. With the key in hand, we were going to make it out quickly.

"What a weird variation on the task," I muttered, kneeling down, holding my chin up to the sky to keep my head above water as I put the key in the lock.

"Did we do it right? That seemed too easy," Spade said.

My eyes flashed to his face. Talk about jinxing. I turned the key, but instead of feeling it click, I felt something snap.

"Oh my god." I yanked my hand out of the water in horror to see what I had felt was true. "It broke off. The key broke in the lock." I was still holding the round bow of the key, but the blade had splintered off in the device.

"No."

"I'm serious."

"You've got to be kidding."

"Why would I kid about that?" I didn't mean to shout at him, but this was really bad. "Can you lift it? Lift the stone? Or drag it?" I could feel myself panicking. Even if he could move it along, the task wouldn't complete until I was free of the rock. The lock here was broken. The key was stuck in its gears. We might never get out.

Spade tugged at the stone, but like Jacob, he couldn't move it.

I held back tears.

The water seemed to rush louder. I'd gotten so used to its never-ending pulse that it had faded into noise in the background, but now, with new momentum, it flooded my thoughts. The gush was so loud I could barely think. Would the High Council let Spade and I be trapped here forever? Would they let me drown?

But Spade wasn't giving up that easily. "Hold the chain tight," he told me.

"What?"

"Here, pull this." He grabbed hold of the chain and held it across the stone, taut from its origin on the rock, and gestured for me to do the same.

I snuffled and nodded, doing what I was told. I

held the links tight against the rock. "What are you gonna do?"

He dumped out the key chest and lifted the large wooden box into the air. "Tighter."

I yanked the chain as tight as I could.

He hoisted the crate above his head. "Arrghhhh!" With all of his might, he threw the box down on the chain links below. It smashed into the rock with a terrifying crash, gouging out a chunk of stone, but he'd missed the metal links. "Damn it." Spade retrieved the trunk. "Again."

"Okay." I steadied myself, pulling the chain taut.

Spade collected himself. Water gushed from the hinges as the chest emptied out. He picked it up in his arms. It was heavier now. Liquid seeped into its walls. "Ready?" His voice shook with effort. Higher he raised the box in his hands.

"Ready," I told him.

"Pull!"

As I yanked back, he thrust the chest towards the rock. This time, the crate made contact. It smashed into the metal chain, flinging me forward. I stumbled over the box, full of momentum, and tripped over the rock. I splattered into the water, my shackled ankle holding me back. I struggled to my feet and looked at the chain.

"It's working!"

The links had started to ease and dent. They were coming apart.

But so was the chest.

The impact was so strong, the hinges of the box

were starting to open. Small chunks of wood had already splintered off of the walls.

"This might be it. The last time," Spade warned me. He gathered the chest once more. Water gushed out of the box as he raised it up out of the water.

I nodded and readied myself. "Then we better make it count."

Even if the chest held together past the next throw, there were other things to worry about. The water level had risen so high, soon it would absorb all the impact.

One way or another, we were running out of time.

Spade grunted; the box was at least twice as heavy as it had been when he first raised it. Water spewed from its hinges, jetting out of all the angles, splashing in his eyes as he held it, pouring down his face and chest. Still, he lifted it over his head. "Ready?" He huffed and puffed, about to go under.

I grimaced and tightened my grip. "Ready."

"Pull!"

I yanked the chain as tight as I could with every ounce of strength that I had as Spade hurled the wood and metal box down upon the links.

Crack!

I flew forward on impact.

The chest split apart into a thousand sharp pieces, and I fell into the debris field, unable to catch my weight with my hands.

Spade collapsed on the sand, totally spent.

I had to swim to right myself, floundering in the waters to regain my footing, but that was great news.

Nothing was holding me back! The chain was broken. My leg was free. I wore a big clunky anklet, but I was no longer shackled to that big stupid rock.

"You did it!" I dug myself out of the water and raced up the beach towards Spade, who, still in an exhausted daze, had sat down on his butt. "Spade, I'm free!" Despite myself and our rocky relationship, I dove full on into his arms for a hug.

Adrenaline coursed through my body.

"You did it!" I shouted.

"I did it! We did it. Together!" Spade hugged me back and laughed.

"Yeah!" I let out a primal howl.

I was free. But even better than that, the trials were over. We survived. I felt out of my mind with excitement.

The sky seemed so blue.

The soft sand felt so fine.

I had never been so happy or so calm.

I beamed with deep pleasure and leaned on his arm.

Impulsively, Spade swung around and kissed me on the mouth.

I pulled back surprised. "Whoa, what are you—"

He pecked me again. Quicker now. Then stood still. To see my reaction.

I stared back in shock. What had he done?

If only he knew how I'd manipulated my stay two rounds ago to spend every moment I could alone on the sand here with Beck. Or how I'd discussed his betrayal with Jacob. If only he knew how little trust I put in anything he said. Or how I doubted every single thing that he did, wondering if he was only doing it because it directly benefitted him. If only he knew that just one day ago, I had sworn I would rather leave the High Council forever than be stuck partnered with him. Or how my suitcase still remained unpacked on the chair by the bed... would he want to kiss me then?

He raised an eyebrow and gave me an enticing smile. The coaxing started with his lips, but it sparkled in his eyes. My heart beat right through me. I couldn't hold back. Or think long term. Or do the right thing any longer.

"Spade," I murmured his name.

"I'm right here," he whispered back.

The tenor of his voice lit a fire in me.

I just couldn't hold it.

I leaned into him.

His head tilted towards me.

We came together, lips to lips.

I shut my eyes.

I felt his energy move in. Sweet and slowly, we embraced. It was soft and gentle for a moment. Then, all at once, the floodgates opened. His lips pushed for more and I received him. Full of passion. Full of purpose. Intensity shot between us, curling my toes, singeing all my nerve endings.

He tasted sweet as green grapes on midsummer's eve, handpicked by farmers.

Plump and juicy on my palette.

I remembered this kiss. His kiss. From days before. And I recalled the ways he'd hurt me. It was all still there, inches below the surface. But for once, I didn't care. I just wanted more.

More.

Deeper.

His five o'clock stubble scratched at my chin.

I wrapped my arms around his neck, digging my hands into sandy hair.

"Mm-hmm," I moaned with satisfaction.

His lips parted and his tongue searched my mouth. I welcomed his breath and cataloged the vibrant sensations. I loved how he kissed me so quickly and sweetly, then so long, deeply, and hard. It fulfilled me completely. Called me back to his beckoning. Over and over. When our tongues rolled together, the massage warmed through my skin. He pulled me closer, our bodies colliding. We got down into the sand. We were soggy from the sea and a little sticky, but damp hair wouldn't stop this, nor the cumbersome folds of wet clothing.

We were dripping together. Every inch of us soaked.

His chest felt so warm and strong and good.

I melted into his embrace.

He lifted me half on top of him, lying back on the sand, and I let myself climb over him. I wanted to disappear. Let my flesh become his flesh. Let our energies get messy.

Spade wasn't right for me. He wasn't even good for me, but I didn't care.

His fingers were exciting.

Their touch so enticing.

Their caress made me forget the last few hours.

All the insanity.

All the ugliness.

There were only his exploring palms, cupped on my bottom. Applying just a hint of pressure, pulling me in.

"Come here," he told me.

And I did.

All we had was this moment.

His kiss.

In his arms.

On his chest.

There was nowhere else I'd rather be.

Our chemistry was thrilling.

I wanted even more. To squish every inch between our bodies.

He wanted more of me too. I could sense it.

He was panting for it.

He shifted my weight, bringing me higher around him, and I was happy to meet him, but when I swung my leg across his body, the heavy cuff around my ankle clanked against his tender shin.

"Ow!" He squirmed and grabbed his leg.

"Oh gosh, the shackle," I said, looking down. "Are you okay?"

"I'm alright."

"Sorry."

We both burst into giggles. It was a strange interruption.

The passion faltered. And for me, the moment was over. I climbed off his chest. He rubbed his leg. Back to being perched side by side, we both looked down at my foot.

"It's still locked," I noted. I picked up the big iron casing and dropped it back on the sand. "Does that count?" I wondered. "Did we complete the task?"

"I don't know," he admitted. "Does it matter?"

Spade tried to lean in and reignite our chemistry, but I no longer felt so desperate. Or happy. Or sloppy.

"Of course it matters," I told him, closing the door to intimacy between us.

He frowned for a moment.

Then the world faded to black.

TWELVE
CUTE PARTY TRICKS

I AWOKE for the eighth time to the sounds of rushing water.

"No!" I sat straight up, eyes wide in terror. The tasks should have been over. Why was I still at the beach?

But I wasn't.

As the sleep shook out of my head, I realized it wasn't the sounds of the beach that awoke me, simply a plumbing tap flowing in the ceiling overhead. Somewhere in the hotel, someone was running a shower. I was back in the safety of my room. Wrapped up in my bed. It was true. The Trials of the Seven Tasks were officially over.

Under the covers, I discovered I was still clothed in my gray T-shirt and dark pants. However, neither showed or felt any signs of the day's drastic wear and tear. Had we really completed all seven unlocking experiences in one day?

It felt like forever.

It felt unreal.

My location had changed so drastically, but my wardrobe remained untouched. It was like we'd never started. Someone had, however, let my hair out of its messy ponytail and tucked me into bed.

Similar to this morning, there was cheerful music wafting in from the quad, but unlike this morning, it wasn't classical or live. Someone had turned on a radio or found a playlist or something. It was a nice reminder of the world beyond the High Council. Every now and then I could hear an excited exclamation. My peers were already gathering by the pool.

Suddenly, I felt very hungry.

I wasn't sure how long the trials had taken, but I was ready to fill my belly. I grabbed my hair elastic off the table and stacked my long brown hair back on the top of my head. Once that was finished, I checked my wardrobe. A bit wrinkled, maybe, but still fine to be seen in. I headed out into the dusk to greet the others.

The atmosphere by the pool was light and airy.

Lady Gray and Lady Mauve were nowhere to be found.

Just as well. I wasn't ready for another round of whatever they had in store.

"Mae!" Nicolette and Hilde cheered.

I happily waved over at them.

Although we'd all been kept separate, it felt like we'd all survived something bigger together. Now that we'd escaped the trials forever, the people at the pool were reveling in their newfound freedom. Plus... most of the kids already had a beer in their hands.

"Mae-mae, Greg snuck 'em in," Marcy told me. She not-so-secretly waved to a case of beer they'd stuffed under a chaise. "Help yourself." She took a swig from a can of her own, winked, then jumped back in the pool, today properly suited in spandex. The bathing attire still didn't leave much to the imagination, but it was better than bra and panties.

I ignored the beverages and followed my nose. "Smells amazing," I said, looking over Vince's shoulder. The grill was chock-a-block with burgers. "Where did they come from?" I wondered.

"Here waiting." He shrugged.

"Beef, with cheese, or veggie." Tej pointed out each one, his mouth already full. "So good."

"Thanks." I helped myself to a burger, then stacked my plate with veggies and snacks. I was so hungry I couldn't even wait to find a place to sit. Standing by the grill, I sunk my teeth into the delicious melee of bread, meat, and condiments. I happily chewed beside Tej. We silently, pleasantly munched together. Seeing how we filled our hungry bellies, the others made their way over for dinner as well.

"I'm surprised you would eat that." Anita frowned, not moving from her chaise, a can of Greg's beer in her hand. "You know they drugged us."

"Mm-hmm. They've been doing it all day," I agreed.

"What are the chances they'd do it again?" Tej asked, mouth still full.

"Pretty high." Vince laughed. As if to prove his point, he took another huge bite of his meal.

We all did.

Everyone found this hilarious.

After everything we'd been through this afternoon, we were all too hungry to care. If the ladies were about to toss us into another life-or-death situation, at least we'd attack the new thing with full stomachs. But then again, maybe we didn't have to worry. Our two fearless leaders were nowhere to be seen.

After the initial need to feed had subsided, people floated back to the comfort of the plastic deck chairs around the pool. Unlike the first night, today the girls clumped together while the guys hung out near the beer.

"Remind me never to try speed dating," Sloane moaned, brushing her long blonde hair back from her face.

"As if you'd ever have trouble dating," I complained.

Hilde shook her head in disbelief. Her eyes were wide and wild.

"More like speed torture," Nicolette agreed, rolling her eyes.

Hilde laughed especially loudly, then took another swig of a beer.

I eyed her. "How many of those have you had?"

"Two," she said, then recounted. "This is my three-d."

I frowned.

"I think you've had enough," Sloane told her gently.

Hilde instinctively pulled the can away from us as if she could hide it by keeping it on the other side of her shorts. "I call my own boss."

Sloane and I both rolled our eyes. However many she'd consumed, the girl had already had too many. Behind her back, when she wasn't looking, Josie slipped something into the can. She shot Sloane and I a wink.

"Let the kid do what she wants." Anita shrugged.

Hilde smiled at her ally and tried to prove us all wrong by taking a giant swig. "Ugh!" She spit it out. "It tastes like soap! You did that!" she accused Josie, who shrugged.

"That's just how beer tastes. It's not good."

The rest of us nodded.

Hilde frowned but didn't take another sip.

"So Josie's a chemist," Marcy concluded, grinning.

"I prefer the term Master of Foreign Medicine." Josie had loosened up as well.

"What's everyone else's secret sauce?" Marcy leaned in close to let us all know that if we considered our powers a secret, they would be in good hands. No one answered. "Buncha chickens. I'll go first. Animal Empath." She closed her eyes and dropped her hands to concentrate. By her hip, her fingers curled into a ball. Suddenly, a great bird swooped in from the sky and soared dangerously close to the guys. They scrambled to duck as the giant wings went past. Greg spun around and shot his girlfriend a look. She gave him a sweet smile, then mimed cracking a beer. He pulled one out of the case and tossed it over to her. "Thanks, baby." She winked at her man. Marcy passed Hilde the fresh can of suds. The young girl smiled wide, but Sloane took it right out of her hands. She passed it off to me.

"Cute party trick." Anita scowled.

Marcy shrugged and took a swig of the beer she was drinking herself.

"I can harness too," Hilde said. She dropped her hands the way that Marcy had done and balled her fingers into her palm. Half the water in the pool shot up in the air, whirling on the wind, but Hilde couldn't hold it. Without warning, she gasped and released it. The wind disappeared as quickly as it had come, and the pool contents sloshed back into the giant mosaic tub in a huge rush. The water rocked and roiled against its concrete sides.

The display caught the guys' attention. From the other side of the patio, they hooted and cheered. Hilde blushed.

"Take a bow, girl," Marcy encouraged.

Hilde stood and gave a little curtsy. The others clapped, but Rick and Vince frowned.

"Two empaths and a chemist walked into a bar..." Marcy joked. "Any lie-guards?" She said the word with reverence, staring each of us down. It was clearly the talent at the top of her hierarchy of skills.

"Dream-caster," I admitted.

"Same," Sloane agreed.

We all looked at Anita. She rolled her eyes.

"I'm not giving you ammunition. You're my direct competition. Or did you forget, tomorrow this little gathering gets culled from fourteen to ten."

No one had forgotten, but the reminder was a little sobering.

I looked down at the beer that was still in my hands. To ease my own tension, I cracked it open and took a big swig. The liquid that filled my mouth was wheaty and warm. It didn't make me feel any better.

"I'm also a chemist," Nicolette admitted. We looked up, surprised. Somehow, in the round of confessions, we had missed her completely. Happy to have some attention, she grinned. "I know how to make truth serum."

"Ooh," Josie and Sloane both said, grinning.

That sounded like fun.

"Well, what are you waitin' for? Get to it," Marcy commanded.

Nicolette bit her bottom lip for a moment, uncertain, then burst into a smile, her doe eyes flashing with mysterious charm. She left us to poke around at the buffet ingredients and pick some flowers from the field, presumably to make some kind of potion.

"You know how to make that?" I asked Josie.

She shook no.

"It's not gonna work." Anita rolled her eyes.

"You don't know," Marcy corrected. "I bet she can do it."

"You're a party pooper," Hilde told Anita, then laughed, her shrill giggle still sloppy and overly pronounced. The older girl's dark eyes stormed.

"She's just a kid," Sloane reminded Anita.

Across the pool, Rick could also sense the danger and stood. He walked over to us. Vince followed. Beck glanced over too. Greg was walking the guys through an especially dramatic story that Jacob and Spade were clearly enjoying, but Beck seemed like he was looking for a chance to escape. Still, he didn't move.

"You should say sorry," Sloane told Hilde. "That was rude."

"I don't wanna." The younger girl pouted.

"Come on, Hilde. It's time for bed." Rick eyed us warily.

We could all tell from her body language that Hilde didn't want to go. But she wasn't drunk enough to talk back to Rick.

"What's *your* secret power?" Marcy asked, eyeing him salaciously. But Rick ignored her.

"He's another chemist," Hilde whispered over her shoulder, speaking at full volume. She got to her feet and put a finger up to her lips in a shushing motion to instruct us to keep the secret, but her finger missed her lips.

"You should be ashamed." He glared at the group of us.

"We're not her keepers," Anita snarled.

"Just because someone couldn't hold half a brewskie. Seriously, she drank half." Marcy giggled, but Rick didn't crack a smile.

"Say goodnight, Hilde," he instructed.

"Goodnight, Hilde!" Hilde giggled but followed her partner away. Rick walked her back to her room, and we all watched her go inside. After the door had closed, he sprinkled something in the doorway. Some special spell, I supposed, to keep her locked in until morning. After that, he went straight to his room.

"Who would want to bond with a ten-year-old?" Vince muttered.

The rest of us nodded.

So I had proof. I wasn't the only one with an imperfect partner. I glanced over at Spade. He was chuckling with Greg, kicking back in a chair, super cool and relaxed. Although... lately with him, I'd seen more good than bad.

"Oh good, you're here." Nicolette came back to our huddle, happy to see Vince. "You can be my truth serum guinea pig."

"Truth? You? Not happening." He hopped on his scooter and slid out of her reach. Still close to our group, he did a few funky tricks, but you could tell they were for his own benefit, not ours. He couldn't care less if we watched.

"Nice wheels," Marcy catcalled after him. But Vince didn't bother to respond. Still, we watched him. Nicolette could see the group's attention had floated to her parabond. And he didn't even want it. She frowned, disappointed her serum was brushed so easily aside. But Nicolette didn't have to worry for long. After a couple failed spin moves and a few sloppy landings, we grew bored of watching Vince's little scooter. Nicolette tried to intercede and bring the group back to her elixir, but instead, Marcy dramatically flopped back on her chaise.

"Why the heck did the High Council choose this place for their Judicial Studies? The pool isn't even ten feet wide," she complained.

Nicolette bided her time.

Beck, who'd sensed an opening in one of Greg's stories, had made his way over to our little cluster.

"Will the pool size interfere with your studies?" Sloane teased.

"No..." Marcy frowned. "Well, maybe." She winked, not one to take a real slight.

"This isn't judicial anything. This here is just limbo," Josie corrected.

"And you dumb dumbs are revealing all your secrets before they've made their final selections," Anita reminded us.

"If they revealed the true Council and then didn't pick you, they might have to kill you," Vince added over his shoulder, a little ways off. We all looked at him in shock. "After today's trials, is that really so surprising? You need to check your situation." He tucked his wheels under his arm and headed to his room. But we all knew he was right.

It made sense.

Weeks ago, Spade had warned me that there were strange deaths associated with various aspects of the High Council. Those rumors now seemed true. But it was still hard to imagine an organization would be on board with such drastic measures.

"My trials were pretty dangerous," I admitted.

Others around the group nodded.

"Mine too," Sloane agreed.

"Maybe they really would kill us," Josie said worriedly.

We all grew quiet.

"Come on." Marcy groaned. "What a buncha drama queens. I wanna see another party trick. Where's Nicolette?"

At her name, she brightened. "Here."

"Show us the magic. Truth serum victim?" Marcy polled us.

We all shook our heads.

"Whoever it is, you have to swallow this. But be warned, it doesn't taste good," Nicolette apologized.

"Beck volunteers." Anita smiled.

So far, he'd just hovered in the background and hadn't said a thing. But now was his chance. "Fat chance, Anita."

"Josie, aren't there truths you'd like to hear?" Anita goaded.

"Maybe Jacob should take it," I deflected, knowing full well how surprised the girl would be to hear how her partner truly felt.

But Josie was intrigued. "Does it hurt?"

Nicolette shook her head. "It only lasts a few minutes. Tastes bad though."

Josie grinned at Beck, wiggling an eyebrow, but she left it up to him to decide.

"Why don't you try?" he asked me.

"Hey, I tried to help you. You're on your own." I grinned.

Beck sighed. "Fine. It probably won't work anyway."

"Actually, it works about ninety percent of the time," Nicolette said, handing it over.

"That's not how you get him to drink," Anita scolded.

But Beck didn't care. He chugged the potion down.

"Yay!" Marcy clapped.

"Ugh. Super bad!" His tongue shot out of his mouth in disgust.

"I tried to warn you." Nicolette shrugged.

"Guess it's not the kind of thing you can slip in someone's drink." Sloane frowned.

"That's good. One day of people secretly drugging me was more than enough," I said.

"How long 'til it's working?" Josie wondered, eyeing her boyfriend.

"Almost immediately," Nicolette said.

"Well, how will we know?" Josie wondered.

"I feel totally normal," Beck told us, but we could see his pupils had expanded into black, shiny globes.

That was how.

"Ask a question," Nicolette instructed.

Marcy's eyes sparkled with mischief. "Beck, describe your... package."

"Fairly average. Circumcised. It does curve a little to the left."

My eyes bugged out of my head. All the girls started laughing.

"Josie, is that accurate?" Anita wondered.

But his girlfriend just grinned. "Keep it above the belt, ladies," she told them.

"Beck... have you ever committed a crime?" Nicolette asked.

He looked up and to the right, accessing some long-ago memory. "I stole a Kingfisher comic book from the Reader's Market in seventh grade. Mr. Reader caught me and when I wouldn't confess, he washed my mouth out with soap."

We shrugged. That wasn't nearly as interesting an anecdote as a verbal description of his manhood.

"What about at school? Ever cheat on a test?" Sloane asked.

"No. I just do badly." He shrugged. "I'm failing science."

"Even with a chemist for a girlfriend?" Marcy laughed.

"Beck," Anita said, leaning forward. "How do you feel about Josie?"

"Uh, I think he's coming out of it." Nicolette watched his vitals.

"She's really pretty and super smart. Way smarter than I am."

We smiled at Josie. She blushed.

"She has this fire in her belly, it's kinda hot, actually. When we fight, the making up is just exceptional. But she gets mad at me a lot. I know it's hard for her to trust me. Spade really screwed her up."

Josie's pleasure fell off her face.

"Beck, that's enough." I tried to stop him.

"But she can trust me. You know?" He shrugged. A faraway look came onto his face. "I'll never leave her. I'll never hurt her."

"Okay, Beck. Thanks for sharing. That's good and plenty." I tried to end things on a high note.

"But..." Anita prompted him again. As much as I had tried to help him wrap things up safely, Anita was out for blood.

Beck sighed. "I really, really love her. God, the girl's the absolute best. But... I wish we didn't parabond."

THE PARTY WASN'T OVER, but Josie left immediately. Beck followed quickly.

Of course he did.

Did he even know what he'd told us? Or did Nicolette's potion work like some kind of hypnosis? I didn't know. We just watched from a distance. At first Josie refused him entry, but eventually he worked his way back into her room.

"You know what he said, making up can be exceptional." Nicolette tried to grin and keep the camaraderie going. It received a lukewarm reception.

"I love making up," Marcy agreed.

I couldn't help but nod. Making up with Spade had been pretty incredible.

"Who have you made up with?" Anita frowned.

"Duh. Greg. We fight, like, every day," Marcy told us. That actually didn't sound as romantic as she was hoping. The rest of us grew quiet. The party was mostly over anyway.

Spade and I had made up.

Sort of.

Seeing the lumpy bits of the other kids' parabonding partnerships made me feel a bit better about our rocky relationship. Also... the thought of his tongue pushing into my mouth helped. I blushed just thinking about it. So what if he'd tried to rush things the first time? Josie was right. It was a bad first date. They happened.

I was definitely attracted to him then.

I was even more attracted to him now.

There were a lot of things about Spade I really liked. Did it matter that I couldn't trust him? Did it matter that I wasn't one hundred percent sold that he was actually a good guy?

I was glad when I said goodnight to everyone at the pool that he didn't try to flirt with me or put on the Spade charms. I was a little worried that I'd have to fend off some midnight advances and tell him to cool it, as I wasn't ready for another make out session, and I certainly didn't want him to spend the night in my bed. But I was also a little insulted that he didn't try.

When I said I was off to bed, he'd just looked up, given me a nice smile, and said goodnight. In seconds, he'd gone back to his chatting with Tej.

Didn't he *want* to sleep with me?

Wouldn't that act solidify our bond in the eyes of fate? That's what he'd thought before. Yet now... not even a glimmer. Barely even a glance. Hadn't he liked kissing on the beach? And all that flirty flirt he'd given by the pool... *he* was the one who always kept this party going, opened those gates, pushed his way in. And now, he was giving me nothing? That didn't sit right with me.

"Can I speak to you for a second?" I frowned, crossing my arms in front of me.

Spade looked up, surprised. "Uh, sure." He nodded at Tej, then followed me a few steps away. "What's up?"

"That's it?" I frowned.

"What's it?"

"See you later?" I left the platitude hanging in the air.

Spade seemed confused.

"That's all I get? After we *kissed*?" I whispered, dropping my voice. "After *rolling around*?"

"Did you want something more?" He stepped a little towards me, his voice growing thicker.

"No." I immediately stepped back.

"Then see you later," he said each word clearly, now emphasizing a frown.

"Fine. See you later." I stalked away.

But Spade caught up. "What's the matter?" he asked.

"I just thought..." I trailed right off. "What's your deal?"

"My deal? What's yours?! First I move too fast, now I move too slow. What do you want, Mae? In that little heart of yours. What do you want from me?" His voice grew tight.

"I want you to be real," I snapped. "The real you." My voice grew louder.

"This is me!"

That was too loud. We both looked over at the others. A couple teens raised their eyebrows. But we ignored them.

He dropped his voice once more. "All I've ever tried to do is give you what you wanted. You want a relationship, I can give you that. You want your space, I'll give you room on your own. It makes no difference what I'm giving. I cannot win. I'm always doing something you don't approve of. I like you, Mae. I think you like me... but I sure as shit can't tell."

I glowered at him. How dare he act so grand? Claiming I was the sole reason our relationship was doomed to fail. "I'm going to bed," I told him.

"Fine... see you later." Spade made a point of saying those same words again. He stalked back to the pool while I marched to my room.

I couldn't believe him. Acting like all the turbulence in our relationship was my fault. How about his hot and cold behavior? Trying to hump on the first date, then blowing me off by the pool.

That wasn't *me*. That was *him*.

I'd made my interest abundantly clear. It wasn't my fault he only moved at one speed. Full throttle. That wasn't my fault... was it? Maybe he and I were just better off as friends... or enemies... I lay awake on the top of the sheets for hours, trying to figure it all out.

Sleep was impossible.

At around two a.m., I completely gave up. I peered out the window. The concrete pad and pool area were deserted. If I was quiet, I could head out and swim laps and nobody would know. It might be good to let out some pent-up energy.

I pulled on my black one-piece bathing suit. Unlike Anita's cut out masterpiece or Marcy's bra tops and bikinis, my swimsuit was all business. I slipped out of my room and tiptoed across the cement panels with a towel wrapped around my hips. The patio lighting was low, the water mostly lit by moonlight, its reflection rippling in the mechanical pattern created by the circulation pump. I knelt by the edge and dipped my fingers into the pool. Without the warmth of the sun, the water was a bit chilly, but that was exactly what I'd been hoping for. It was the perfect temperature to pump my legs and arms through a few lengths to relieve some stress and get my endorphins flowing. Once I'd done that, I'd hop out, curl up in my warm bed, and sleep like a baby 'til morning.

I dropped the towel on the closest chaise and dove in.

My body shot across the water, curving down with my entry, then gently moving back up to the surface. The cool, crisp liquid tingled every part of my skin, and I broke the surface feeling energized and primal, but I swallowed the gasp of exuberance and instead flattened my hair back out of my eyes while treading water. The pool was even cooler than I had expected, but if I kept moving, I felt confident my body would adjust. I picked up one stroke, then another, and soon I fell into the rhythm of swimming back and forth, hitting one wall, striding forward, turning around, and doing it all again.

What was I doing here at the High Council?

Growing up, Aunt Abeline had always made all our living arrangements, and while I wasn't always happy about her selections or the frequency of their changes, she was the adult in charge of my life, and I went along without a care in the world. Who was the adult in charge now? The two ladies? They basically drugged us and pitted us against each other, then left us alone to figure it out. Me? Was I now in charge of my choices? I had jumped on the first boy who had tried to kiss me. A boy who had a history of treating me poorly. A boy Beck had just told the group had a history of wreckage with Josie. Kissing him? That was how I chose to deal with this stress?

He didn't even try to sleep with me!

Which, I mean, it was true, I didn't want him to... so, I guess that was a good thing. Why didn't that feel like a good thing?

This was all so dumb.

Could my decisions really be trusted? I was so lost in my own thoughts I didn't see the person who had come to join me until I swam up to their legs dangling in the water. But it wasn't Spade.

It was Josie.

"Couldn't sleep either?" she asked.

I knocked my head back and dipped my hair in the pool to sweep stray hairs out of my face. "Just burning off some energy." I shrugged. "Are you okay? That truth serum stuff was pretty awful."

"Yeah, fine. Great." She scoffed at the thought but didn't add any details.

I tried to think of something comforting to tell her but came up a bit empty.

Beck had always been a touchy subject between us.

"He was just worried that if we parabond, I might get hurt," she told me.

"Right. Of course." I nodded. I could see she wanted to move away from the topic, and I was happy to oblige her. "What do you think we'll be doing tomorrow?"

"Whatever it is, it'll be intense... cutthroat."

"My get-to-know-you task was to stop me or my partner from drowning," I agreed.

"And you're swimming now?" She raised an eyebrow.

"It's a lot easier when you aren't tied to a shackle," I told her.

"Mine, we were on top of a car, surrounded by junkyard dogs. Like, six of them, and we had to get through this chain link fence to safety." She shook her head, remembering.

Now that the ordeals were over, we could sort of

laugh about it. It wasn't funny exactly, but it was definitely absurd.

"Do you think they would have let us die?" I wondered.

"Yes." Josie's answer shot a shiver through me. "Mae, this is all very real."

"It *felt* real, but Sloane said the lie-guards can make you think things that aren't actually... it's like a magician's illusion."

Josie was quiet for a moment. "No. It's not like that. You misunderstood. The lie-guards play with your perceptions, but when they're successful, they literally trick your brain into being," she explained. "Which means it is true. All of it. All the pain and the stress and the hormones your brain releases to combat the imagined scenario, that's all real. The illusion won't kill you, but your brain can."

"If my mom could take it, then I can too," I said. I could tell bringing up my dead mother made Josie uncomfortable, so it was time to switch topics again. "So you and Spade, huh?" I raised an eyebrow. "Is that bad to say? I mean, is it fair game? Because I know Beck was kind of out of his head when he said it. It's just... when I first got here you were defending him, and..."

"He never told you about us? Me and him?"

I shook my head. Spade had never said a thing.

She laughed bitterly. "Why am I surprised?"

I pulled myself out of the pool to sit beside her and

wrapped a towel around my shoulders. I hugged my knees into my chest and I waited for her to begin.

Josie sighed. "We used to be an item. A thing. We were—I *was*—totally in love. Spade was my first kiss, my first dance... a lot of firsts." She raised an eyebrow. I knew exactly what she meant. "We were sure we'd parabond. I had our whole futures set. Then I met this girl, Clara VonProd."

I could already see where this was going.

"She wasn't a lifer. You know? A townie. I'd been there my whole life, and she was new to the party. You grow up in a small town and sometimes people's vision for your life can be... well... small. She had these dreams and ambitions. It was cool. She could do these crazy tricks on roller skates, and she wore them, like, all the time. I really liked her. Clara VonProd. Even her name was, like, boss. We clicked right away. Spade and I would just hang out in the park and watch her practice. She loved an audience. One of those. You know the type? Then my parents got me that stupid car." She shook her head. I knew the car she was meaning. I'd seen it break down several times. "It was a dump when I got it. Still is, really. But they thought it would be good for me to learn basic automotive maintenance. To never get trapped with a flat tire, that sort of stuff. No offense."

Josie had once fixed and subsequently totally destroyed my bike's tires. I still couldn't fix that wheel. I waved her off. Again, I knew what she meant.

"And when we got it, we couldn't wait to drive

around town. Drive to school, no more bus... just my boyfriend and me. But it turned out to be a lot of work. A lot. And when I'd roll under the car... she'd roll into his lap."

She paused, still embarrassed for the past version of herself.

"Clara VonProd," she went on. "I should have known. You know? I should have. That's the thing. I'd come out from under the carriage and they'd both be all red-faced and jittery... but I just didn't put two and two together until we went to junior prom. We all took a limo together. Clara didn't have her own date. I guess she didn't bother cuz she planned to make use of mine. I lost track of them for a little while, but when I got bored, I went looking for my guy. Spade was my boyfriend, so I thought we could dance a little or take some cheesy photos. But instead, he had Clara undressed and naked, pinned against some bathroom stall. And lucky me, I found them. Like, mid-thrall. I still remember." She shook her head. "I couldn't find him, so I stopped in to use the washroom. I had hiked my dress up—it was cute, short with black sequins— and dropped down my undies. There I was, my thong around my ankles, when I saw her red strappy sandals and a pair of men's Oxford black shoes. They were his daddy's dress shoes. Earlier in the night, he worried that if he scuffed them he might never hear the end of it." She chuckled. "But it was definitely both of them. They were in the next stall. Playing around."

"What'd you do?" I asked. I was shivering and

ready to get out of my wet swimsuit, but there was no way I was missing the end of this story.

"I peed, knowing full well they were kissing or grinding or humping beside me. I don't know... probably with his hand down her bra. How disgusting. Thankfully, I never heard a peep outta the stall. I always thought how unsanitary. You know? Of all the darkened halls in that stupid prom location, why hump in the stalls? How many other girls had they heard pissing or farting or who knows what else, cuz, you know, that's what you do in the toilets. But Spade didn't care. He went to town. I washed my hands, then went back and tapped on the bathroom door. I said, 'I know you're in there and I know you're with Clara.' Inside, I heard them adjusting, then I stepped back, and he opened the door. Spade said something like, 'oh, good. I've been looking for a way to tell you.' Then walked right by. Clara VonProd was so disheveled. She ran right after. They didn't wash their hands, and for us, that was the end."

"What a dick." I shook my head.

"I held it together, but I left. I went to the parking lot to cry. I should have taken the limo home, right then. I should have gotten out of there, you know? But I was still being dumb and considerate because that oversized car was supposed to be all of our rides. Can you believe it? You hump my man in the women's bathroom and I'm still going to worry that I don't take your ride." She shook her head at the naiveté of younger Josie. "Finally, Spade came out. Clara VonProd followed. I thought they wanted to talk to me. To apologize or explain the situation, but they walked right by, got in our limo, and drove off. They left me crying in the parking. I had to find my own way home."

"Dude."

"Yeah." She nodded. Her face grew a smile. "She couldn't keep him. Once all their sneaking around was over, the thrill was gone, and he didn't bother to keep her. He just went a little nuts. Like, a new girl every Tuesday. He started lifting. Bulking up, you know? He developed that cocky persona. He dumped me on prom night and immediately became someone I would never, ever want. The next day, I saw Clara VonProd crying. Served her right. I already did my crying. But now, yeah, I guess you're right. He leaves a broken trail wherever he goes." She shrugged.

"Lucky me," I said.

"I didn't mean you. Oh geez. You know what I mean."

"It's fine. I asked for it," I agreed. I meant that I had asked for her story, but I realized I could have just as easily also been describing my interactions with Spade. I knew he was trouble, but I still let him get in my head. I still let him get in my pants. Metaphorically. Why did I have so little willpower? I should have left the High Council when I first had the chance.

Josie shrugged, the faraway smile returning. "The funny thing is, that's also the night I met Beck."

"Now *that's* a story worth telling," I encouraged. "He was your knight in shining armor?"

"He's my best friend," she agreed, a little sadly. "Sorry if I get a little defensive sometimes. About you and him. Now that you know the story, I'm sure..."

"Even I can see the parallels." I nodded. "But you have nothing to worry about. Because I'm not Clara VonProd. And Beck is not Spade."

"No, he's not." We both nodded in agreement.

"Besides, you guys are the closest things to friends in Plumpkin that I've got." I stood.

"Heh. Same." She followed. "Isn't that sad?"

"It is what it is." I hugged the towel around my skin, ready to swap it out for a warm blanket and bed. We strolled back across the patio stones together. "There is one thing. If Spade treated you so badly, why are you pushing me to partner with him?"

Josie scrunched up her face. "Well, he might have changed," she started. But then sighed. "And you don't have another viable option. So maybe it's better to accept the hand you've been dealt?" It was a reality I didn't want to her to say. Neither did she. At least not out loud. The truth felt so uncomfortable she jumped in again. "Well, I guess it's time to work," she told me.

"How's that?"

"Your dreams. You're a dream caster. Your dream may help in tomorrow's activities."

"I never thought of it like that," I told her. "And with that sort of pressure, I might never sleep again."

"No, don't think of it like pressure. It's a pleasure."

"It'll be something. But who knows," I countered.

"I might not even dream. I don't think I had any last night."

"Well, I'll see you in the morning."

We parted ways.

"Night." I closed the door in my motel room. After the late hour, my swim, and Josie's conversation, I should have been asleep on arrival, but that last thought she gave me had stayed in my brain. Could my dreams really help in my experience tomorrow? Only one way to find out.

I stripped out of my wet suit and hung it to dry in the bathroom, primed myself in a T-shirt as a nightshirt, and readied for bed. I felt super exhausted. But when I lay down, all I could hear was that damn mouse deterrent buzzer. Its hum filled up the space.

Aunt Abeline. I silently cursed her gift.

I should have remembered to take it out of the wall before I got into bed. I would never sail off to a helpful dreamland with that high-pitched buzz in my ear.

I dragged myself to the far wall where the device was plugged in and tugged the prongs from out of the wall. There. I expected a delightful silence to fall over the room, but instead, faint voices drifted in through the wall of the adjoining room.

"Guys, they're gone," Marcy told someone. "I don't see anyone by the pool."

"That was close."

My ears perked up, but I couldn't really make out the identity of anyone's voice other than that of my neighbor. I leaned closer to the drywall, trying to hear.

"Do you think they were plotting? Making their own alliance?"

"Doesn't matter what they were doing. The numbers are on our side."

The voices chuckled.

"Well, the coast is clear. We wanna get to bed," Marcy told her guests.

"We wanna get to something..."

"Greg!"

"Alright, alright."

"Keep it in your pants."

"See you tomorrow."

All the voices were muddled. I couldn't make out who was who.

Marcy opened and closed her door. My eyes flitted to the window to put a face to the other conspirators, but no one walked past. What had I just overheard?

But Greg and Marcy weren't finished.

"It's too bad, you know. I kinda like Mae-mae."

"I like her too..." Greg teased his girlfriend.

"Oh yeah? What do you like about her?"

"Maybe a little of this..."

Marcy squealed in pleasure.

I winced. Ew. That wasn't strategy talk I was overhearing.

"How about..."

"Ah! That tickles. Stop... stop!" Marcy squealed.

"Oh," Greg moaned.

Their bodies thumped against the shared wall of our room. I jumped back in surprise. Through the plaster, both Greg and Marcy gave off excited giggles. Their scheming or planning was done. All I could hear was a festive bit of banter between a happy, romantic pair. They moved farther into the room, seeming to crash into everything around them, until the sounds grew more and more muffled. But every so often, I could hear a guttural grunt, or a squeal, or a laugh.

I should have left them to their private encounter, but instead, I sunk down on the floor by the outlet and leaned my head against the wall. It was gross of me to listen to their lovemaking or their make out or whatever it was they were doing in the privacy of their own bedroom. But I just couldn't leave it. I couldn't stop myself from listening. Icky as it was, I just couldn't will myself away. The sounds of two partners who loved and cared about each other was so alluring. That undeniable trust...

I wanted a parabond like that more than anything in the world.

FOURTEEN
DREAMS OF TOMORROW

THAT NIGHT IN MY DREAMS, I entered a beautiful castle. Through the double doorway entrance was a great arching entry with cathedral ceilings and a decadent pendant light shining on all four of the walls. Large tapestries hung on the surfaces, their intricate designs slightly yellowed with age. The space felt solemn and deliberate, like an antechamber big enough to sweep the world's problems away. It was grand.

I walked forward, knowing the route to take immediately, but as I moved farther into the building, the walls started to give way. The structure became unsound. First, little crevices split the columns, spitting dust and bits of drywall. Then the cracks grew into fissures. I watched them rupture the walls.

I moved down the antechamber faster. With each step over the threshold, the majestic world came tumbling to the ground. Walls and ceilings crumbled around me. The beautiful tapestries ripped from their homes and floated to the floor. As they landed on the rugs below, both deteriorated into ash.

I couldn't save them. I could barely save myself.

I hurried on, fearful my momentum was both dismantling the castle and destroying my ability to save it. Our only hope, it seemed, was if I moved quickly enough, I could stop the collapse in my mind.

I burst through a second double doorway, this one glass and mahogany. I shoved both doors open when really, one would have done. In my haste to escape, I stumbled out into the courtyard. At its center, a water fountain gushed. Around the liquid display, symmetrical green hedges created a waist-high maze, but it was clear, all routes led back to the fountain. The second the French doors closed behind me, all the fear and the noise of wreckage inside disappeared.

And I was no longer alone.

The two ladies sat at a marble table, a deck of playing cards between them. They were playing a game of war. And around them, in a haphazard circle, all the other parabond inductees watched the game.

There was an excited hush over the crowd.

Lady Mauve played a six.

Lady Gray played a four.

The teens gasped, and Lady Mauve collected her win. Then the women flipped again.

I moved a bit closer.

Lady Gray now flipped first. She pulled a four. The teens let out a groan. But Lady Mauve, sure as she was, turned up a two. Lady Gray was victorious. They each had one win apiece.

The teens nodded to each other.

A gust of wind whirled up from the table, and the ladies slammed their hands down on the cards to protect their next turns. But it didn't matter. The wind got there first. It kicked one card up off the pile before Lady Mauve's hand could secure it. It flew right into my hands. I looked down at the card. Some artist had drawn the king of hearts face card character with a knife thrust in his head. The suicide king.

I shuddered.

I slipped the card back on the table with the game, but neither Lady Mauve nor Lady Gray bothered to pick it back up. Instead, it blew to the ground and out into the garden. No one seemed to care that the deck was no longer a full set.

Once the wind died down, the women faced off once more, and the game began its rhythm again. Both women drew. Lady Mauve's five beat Gray's four. Then each woman slammed down a king. The crowd gasped.

A tie.

The ladies glared at one another. The tension thickened the air. All eyes moved to their fingers. In tandem, they flipped again.

Bam!

Two queens to follow the kings!

In the cheap seats all around the ladies, the teens began to sputter in shock. No one had ever seen such a pattern.With the cards they played next, one lady would earn a huge win. But Lady Mauve had other plans. She reached across the table to Lady Gray's pile, picked up the queen of clubs, and ripped it in half. Then, suddenly, before anyone could respond, before Lady Gray could even react to what had been done to her card, a huge duck fluttered onto the table, beating its wings, squawking.

I sat straight up on the floor, eyes opened wide.

Ooh.

I grasped my neck in pain. Hunched in the corner of the room, I had fallen asleep with my ear still pressed up against Greg and Marcy's adjoining room. My entire body groaned with discomfort. Humans were not meant to sleep slumped against a wall.

I pulled myself up from the hard-backed position and rolled my neck and my shoulders to release some of the stress. Next door, there was nothing but silence. Greg and Marcy, it seemed, were both peace-fully asleep in her bed.

I stumbled away from the outlet and the mouse buzzer and sat down at the small desk underneath the window. The chair groaned under my weight. It was still very, very early. The sun was only barely starting to break through the horizon, but before I collapsed back on the bed to keep sleeping, I tried to write down everything I could remember from my dream. If I was a dream-caster, I didn't want to leave anything to chance. I made notes while the dream was still fresh.

But it wasn't as useful as I'd hoped.

Even as I transcribed it, the details started to fuzz. When I'd chicken-scratched out everything I could remember, I looked out the window at the early morning glow. Everything felt still. In the midst of the sea of concrete and patio furniture, a mama duck and three small ducklings were using our swimming pool's water as a pond.

FIFTEEN
THE BATTLE BEGINS

"MORNING," I murmured to Sloane as I came up behind her. She was pouring her coffee. Patiently, I waited for her to finish with the pot. The same classical music and breakfast spread awaited us this morning, but today we were wary of eating the food. Only Vince had made up a plate.

"If they drugged the coffee, they got me," Sloane said. She gave a little laugh.

"You and everyone else," I noted.

There were mugs in almost everyone's hands. A little caffeine pick-me-up after last night's liquid courage. She nodded and moved on.

"A new day begins," Jacob said brightly. "Top me off, partner?"

I was still pouring my own cup, but he held out his mug, so I obliged.

"Have you thought any more about my offer?" he asked, his conversation volume dropping. We moved on to milk and sugar.

"Not really," I admitted.

"Well, you should."

"What do you have against Anita?"

"It's not about punishing her. It's about thriving. With you."

"Does she know what you've been planning?"

"Of course not," he whispered. "Does Spade?" He raised an eyebrow.

Busted.

After all, I was now whispering too. But I wasn't the one who instigated this conversation.

"Coffee, yes!" Marcy bounded towards us. "I am famished! Why is nobody eating? Oh, because of the drugs?" Her questions weren't really directed at us, so I turned back to reply to Jacob, but he had already melted away into the group. He sat himself back beside Anita. When he saw me looking, he gave me a little eyebrow raise and a nod. I moved around the pool and sat beside Hilde. She looked green.

"Wanna know how to beat a hangover?" I offered.

She nodded in misery.

"Feed it lots of grease." I tucked my legs under me. "Course, on a day like today, you have to weigh the odds. If I eat the bacon, will I be drugged by a powerful witches' coven? If the odds are yes, and they are," I admitted, "then maybe the hangover doesn't seem so bad." I grinned at the young girl. The least I could do was try to make her laugh. Hilde suffered a smile, then went back to holding still for fear her insides might projectile vomit out of her mouth. It was good for her to suffer, I thought to myself. Help her learn a little moderation. I knew Rick's watchful eye was upon me, but I felt mostly that he would approve of my candor.

Suddenly, the piano music that had been the backdrop of everything this morning came to an end. Lady Mauve looked up from her place at the keys.

"Why is only Mod Squad eating? You all need your strength."

Vince grinned wide between giant bites of pancake.

"We don't want to be drugged and manipulated," Anita said.

I was surprised—her straightforward, nasty charm wasn't only reserved for fellow teenagers.

Lady Mauve laughed. "Oh, please, we're not going to drug you twice without you knowing. Not in one week. How lazy and predictable." She seemed insulted that we thought so little of her. "If we were gonna drug something today, it would have been in the coffee."

"Told you," Sloane murmured to the group, undeterred, taking another sip.

Everyone looked down at the cups in their hands.

Tej actually spit out the swallow he'd just consumed.

"Oh, relax, Short Stop. The drugs are here." Lady Mauve shook a bottle and put it out on the piano. "And if you want your shot at the High Council coven, you're each gonna swallow a pill. So don't be dumb.

Eat the breakfast. For the battle this morning, you'll need all the strength you can get."

Lecture over, she sat back at the piano and whipped up a jaunty melody.

We looked at each other.

"Get it while it's hot," Vince snarked.

Rick motioned to Hilde, and the two of them went up to the buffet. If there was anyone who would benefit from a full stomach, it was her.

"You're sure it's fine?" Nicolette asked worriedly.

Vince dragged a piece of toast around his plate, sopping up any last drippings of eggs and syrup, and shoved it in his mouth in reply. He gave her a gross grin full of half-eaten pancakes. "It's delicious!" he said through a mushy mouthful.

"Real nice." But she joined the line.

After that, the rest of us followed. There was safety in numbers.

I noted Hilde took my advice and piled the greasy bacon high on her plate.

After getting my usual toast with butter, I relocated poolside to be closer to Josie and Beck.

"I overheard something," I whispered. They started to lean forward, but I shook my head and casually looked around the pool. I didn't want the others to know we were talking. I kept my voice low, but didn't lean in. "I think the others are planning to team up. Greg and Marcy for sure. But there were others, I over-head them. I'm not sure how many."

Josie nodded, like she half expected it. We glanced

around to see who might be watching, but it was still safe to talk if we kept our volume low.

"There's more. Jacob wants me to partner. Leave Anita and Spade in the cold."

"Well that's great, isn't it? You were looking for another partner," Beck said. But Josie and I shared a look.

"Spade is the devil you know," she said in a worried tone.

I nodded. Spade wasn't that great, but for all we knew, Jacob might be far, far worse.

"What do you want to do?" Beck asked.

We all clocked Spade coming towards us.

"I don't really know." I answered honestly, then sat back to greet my potential partner. "Hey."

"Geez, I slept terribly," he said, plopping down in the next chair.

It wasn't much of a greeting, but who was I to demand more from him? Although Spade was usually the captain of the charm police, it was unreasonable to expect that he would win me over with every word that he said.

"Well," I admitted, "this won't make you feel better." I filled him in on the first piece of information I'd already shared with the others: there was an alliance building against the two of us, Beck, and Josie. And there was nothing we could do about it.

"Well, that's just dumb. It should be survival of the fittest," he objected.

"If that were the case, they think we've already failed," Josie reminded him.

"Hey," Spade called across the pool to Greg. "What's this? You guys have some sort of secret alliance? You trying to knock us out of the coven?"

"What?! No." Greg laughed. A bit too hard.

"Every man for himself," Tej agreed.

"Or woman," Sloane corrected.

Spade shrugged, satisfied. "See, there's no alliance. You're reading too much into things."

"And you're not reading enough. I know what I heard."

He bit the head off his muffin without unwrapping the paper dress. "I just asked. They denied it."

"What else are they gonna say?"

Spade looked down at his empty plate. He squished up the wrapper. "I'm gonna get another sausage."

"You do that." I sat back in my chair, frustrated.

Of course they'd deny a secret alliance. By its very nature it was meant to be secretive. That didn't change what I'd heard. If Spade couldn't see that, then he really was a fool.

A fool who would leave me hanging.

I sunk back in my chair and watched as he picked out some new breakfast meat. In the background, the tenor of Lady Mauve's piano playing changed. First slowly, then more suddenly. All this time, her music had been softly building in the background, relaxing and sweet, not overpowering, but now her playing became louder, more insistent. The music garnered our attention.

Lady Mauve was a talented musician. Her melody slowly expanded, doubling back on itself to grow in complexity and thematic resonance, again and again. As it bloomed in strength and volume, it silenced not just me, but the whole group of us, meeting our ears, invading our hearts, and striking at chords deep inside.

Her fingers danced in nimble dexterity. She reached high and low on the ivory keys.

My skin goose-pimpled in anticipation as her notes built and bubbled. Somehow their sounds encompassed my hopes and fears into the spinal cord of her tune.

It was like we were hypnotized.

No one spoke.

No one gestured.

We were mesmerized by the undulation of song.

Expertly, she created her base, then swooped us up into soaring refrains. Her piano skills were displayed so deliberately, audibly hammering themes home, holding them close, then tossing them out when no longer useful. Her song reverberated through our very essences, sometimes in multiple octaves at once.

My breathing calmed.

My body relaxed.

There would be a fight ahead.

The music spoke to me.

Today required battle.

But I would take it on.

Whatever was coming for me. I would fight for what was mine, the melody told me.

I could hold off all the others.

Lady Mauve's fingers soared on the keyboard. Sharper, more visceral now.

We were warriors, the lullaby warned me.

We would fight for our rightful spots.

We would be ready, her song informed me.

It called us out.

It raised us high.

If our entry into the coven was a birthright, the music instructed, *then we must rise and be victorious.*

There was no one to stop us.

We were just.

We were strong.

Like a dragon, the song breathed fire into us. The flames flickered and burned in our souls. Higher and higher the melody dragged us.

Until the sound dropped down to a whisper.

The fight begins.

The same melodic theme played the directive over and over.

The fight begins.

I closed my eyes, breathing in this message.

The fight begins.

My spirit calmed from strength deep within.

I would be ready.

The music whimpered and wound quieter, continually replaying its message until it was gone in the silence, like a whisper on the wind.

Peace washed over me.

The alliance didn't matter.

I knew I would win.

Silence hung for a moment, then slowly, I opened my eyes.

All around me, I could see the other parabonders do the same. The music had taken us all on the same salient journey to find our deepest spirits and fortify our strengths from within.

The battle loomed ahead.

Lady Mauve stood from the keys and joined Lady Gray, who was watching us from the head of the pool.

"Right." Lady Gray nodded to her partner. "Let's get started."

SIXTEEN
ARE YOU OUT? OR ARE YOU IN?

"TODAY, fate will begin its culling. Fourteen of you arrived, but four will leave before the sunset tomorrow. The first two today, the other pair tomorrow. You may have noticed for now, we speak of you as individuals and not as parabonds. In our eyes, the bonds have not yet been made. You should consider the same. It is our belief that fate will renegotiate at least some of your partnerships."

I looked around.

Only Greg, Marcy, Tej, and Sloane seemed self-assured. The other teens didn't know where to look. At their previous partner? At the others in the group?

No one said anything.

"Today, no parabonds will form. It's every man and woman for themselves. Is that clear?"

We nodded, though the task was clear as mud.

"The job is simple. Find your way back with a partner, any partner, and be the first four pairs to jump in the pool."

"Wait, so we can finish with anyone?" Greg seemed to have only just tuned in.

"Anyone," Lady Mauve agreed.

"Even dudes?"

"You catch on quickly," Vince said.

"If it's four partnerships... that's eight. What happens to the bottom six people?" Tej asked the more pertinent question.

"We're so nice they get a second chance." Lady Mauve rolled her eyes.

Lady Gray nodded. "The bottom six will run the course again. The final pair to the pool in that second round, I'm sorry to say, will be rejected by the High Council coven, removed from this limbo, and sent on their way home."

Home.

Said here like a threat.

"So, it's a race," Sloane said.

"Of sorts." Lady Gray nodded. "Yes."

"Can we use magic?" Little Hilde's voice surprised us all. The full meal had done wonders for her green complexion, but she still looked worn out and worried and small.

Lady Mauve grinned. "You're a witch, aren't 'cha?"

"Well, what are the rules?" Josie wondered.

"You need rules?" Lady Mauve frowned.

"Yes, of course they do," Lady Gray agreed.

"Fine. Don't kill or maim another human. And if you see somebody dying, even through no cause of your own, help them. We don't want to have to fill out a bunch of paperwork."

"Let's keep it clean," Lady Gray agreed.

If someone's dying, then help them? What sort of macabre elements did this footrace entail?

Lady Gray picked up the bottle of pills that had been resting on the piano and opened the lid. She made her way around the pool and sprinkled one yellow capsule into each of our hands. Obediently, I held out my palm. She shook a pill into my hand and moved on. I looked down at the capsule. The drug was encased in some kind of vibrantly colored coating. It was impossible to tell what was inside of the pill.

"More questions at this point is basically stalling." Lady Mauve's look dared us to ask for more clarification. No one in the group was so dumb.

"Fate requires action," Lady Gray reminded us, returning to her rightful place at the head of the pool once all the little yellow pills were delivered. "When you awake from the drug-induced slumber, the task will begin."

"Bottoms up." Lady Mauve smiled.

I looked around the pool. Were we actually doing this?

Greg and Marcy, Tej and Sloane, and Jacob and Anita all took their pills immediately. As he swallowed, Jacob even shot me a grin. Rick waited until Hilde had swallowed hers. It took her almost a full bottle of water to force it down, but eventually, she did. Then he followed. Vince shrugged and popped his pill into his mouth. Nicolette trailed only moments behind. Josie and Beck locked eyes and swallowed together.

That left only me and Spade.

He was waiting for me.

"See you on the other side?" he asked.

I nodded.

As an act of faith, he went first and popped his pill.

All eyes turned to me.

"What of it, Ms. Kinglsey? We're all waiting. Are you out?" Lady Gray asked.

Lady Mauve smiled. "Or are you in?"

I swallowed it down.

SEVENTEEN
WAKING UP IN THE FOREST

CRACK!

"Whoa!" Marcy's squeal and the crunching of tree boughs awoke me.

Shhh!

Several voices hushed her at once.

"I know. I almost fell," Marcy whispered back.

"You're gonna wake them," said another harsh whisper. Maybe Tej.

"Quiet." Sloane's voice cut out all further discussion, and a silence overtook the forest once more.

No, not silence.

All around me, I could hear gentle grunts and rustling. Moving leaves, creaking branches, heavy breathing. There were tiny movements happening all around and a thousand little sounds. In every direction, nature was bending to human will.

I blinked my eyes and looked down to get my bearings. I was tied to a tree branch, or a couple branches.

A bough, maybe. Whatever it was, I was at least twenty or thirty feet up in the air, with nothing but a mix of grass and weeds and dirt below to break my fall. My fingers fumbled with the rope that held me, but it disintegrated in my hands.

The creaking and cracking, I realized, was the other teens disembarking from the forest. All around me, the sounds they were making were growing farther away. They were getting lower to the ground.

I sat straight up.

The race had already started. There was no time to waste.

"Spade?" I whispered out into the foliage.

I looked down below me. To the left I thought I saw him, but instead, it was Greg. I looked him right in the eyes. For a moment, we both froze. Then, two trees over, Josie started to stir.

"They're up!" Tej warned the others.

"Go!"

"*Go, go, go!*"

Any pretense of moving quietly dropped from the alliance, and the other teens started racing down their trees. One after another, they descended through the forest until their feet found solid ground.

For Josie and Beck, the sudden motion was a rude and rapid awakening.

"Mae! I'm here," Spade shouted. He was twice as far from my perch as the others had been. "Start climbing down," he instructed, as if I needed to be told.

"I knew they were teaming up on us." I was seething.

We were already behind. The other group had hit the ground running.

"Beck, come on!" Josie called, already finding her footholds.

"Where are we going?" I wondered.

"We follow them," Spade shouted, watching their departure.

"I'm gonna climb up to see where we're going," Beck told us, already ascending.

"There isn't time!" Spade shouted, but Beck didn't listen.

"No, he's right," Josie said. "It's more important to know where we're going."

"We?" Spade sneered. "Come on, Mae." He and Josie had already reached the soil. I was the third to land on the floor of pine needles.

"We're on the same team," I said.

"No, we're not," Josie and Spade said in tandem.

"Did you get an invite to the other alliance?" I asked them. "No? You? Then take the help you can get." They refused to acknowledge this was their situation, so I ignored them both and turned to Beck. "What do you see?!"

He had already started to come down. With his long arms and legs, he was able to move fast. "Through the forest there's a quarry, then the motel's in a big field on the left. But there's a lie-guard mirage on the right. My perception of the illusion was broken cuz I went up the tree and not down. It's a fake reflection."

"They didn't expect someone to check." I was impressed.

"See, his climbing already paid off," Josie told Spade.

"Only if the others choose wrong, which they might not." He wouldn't concede the point so quickly.

"We'll catch them," I told them both.

"If there's a quarry, there's gonna be scree. Grab the sturdiest stick that you can," Spade told me.

"What the heck is scree?" I asked.

But Spade was already running. "You'll see when you get there."

I didn't want to see when I got there, I thought to myself. That was why I asked. But I didn't say it. Everyone's stress levels were already right through the roof. No point in snapping at him. Instead, I just ran forward, looking for nature's pole.

With Beck back on the ground, we raced after the others through the trees too, picking up suitable branches as we went. "It's like tiny pebbles that land-slide together," he told me, holding up the brush as I snapped the perfect stick in my hands. "Scree."

"Thanks." I nodded.

"I was gonna tell her," Spade bickered.

"Well, you still can," Beck snapped back.

"Hurry!" Josie instructed.

The other group had a large head start, but we could definitely catch up. It was always harder setting the pace in a race than following. They started strong, but if Beck was correct about the geographical land the race would take us over, the distance wouldn't be easy. They would tire. Being in the underdog position, adrenaline surged through me. I felt confident we could catch at least some of their group. And if we could catch them, we could pass them.

We raced through the brush, sometimes seeing broken shrubs and branches where the others had passed. Other times, we forged ahead totally on our own. But we were quick on our feet, and I felt confident we were closing the gap.

Suddenly, we broke through the edge of the trees, just like Beck had said we would. The four of us gasped for air, taking only a moment to survey the new surroundings. It was a quarry. The giant hole carved in the rock by a mining company years ago was dramatically wide, with jagged angles spanning out in all directions. East and west were the farthest distances to go. It would take forever to make your way around the man-made pool. Straight down and through the depths was a much shorter journey, but also far more physically demanding, with a steep slope full of tiny rocks and gravel: the scree.

And that was only the beginning.

After that first hill was a deepwater source, then a tall climb on the other side of the quarry.

"There they are!" Josie pointed.

Jacob, Greg, and Vince led their pack, sliding down the hill, kicking up plumes of gray dust as they skidded down the slope. Tej and the girls were more carefully picking their way down the steep hillside. Rick stayed dutifully by Hilde's side.

"See, scree." Spade pointed.

"Gee, thanks." As if I hadn't already put that together.

"This is gonna be fun. You done this before?" Spade asked me. I shook my head while he checked all our sticks.

Who the heck would have done this before? Apparently Spade.

"It's like surfing. But instead of water, it's sharp rocks and a forty-foot fall." He grinned, trying to lighten the mood.

I just nodded dumbly.

Josie and Beck also listened. While Beck talked a good talk, it was clear only Spade had traversed something like these tiny rocks before.

"Put your stick behind you, lean your weight back towards the hill, feet parallel to the slope. Look for the tiny rocks and make use of the slide. The rate they're moving, we can beat them. Easy. You go first, and I'll catch up."

I nodded, looking braver and more secure than I felt. As per his bidding, I dropped into the rocky terrain, every step sending a cascade of pebbles down the steep hill. I propped the tree branch behind me like he'd shown, and it did make me feel sturdier and more connected, but when everything around me dribbled down the mountain with each move I made, I couldn't really gather any speed.

"Embrace it. Embrace the slide!" Spade shouted.

"I'm trying!"

"You go," Josie told Spade. "We'll follow."

"Watch and learn." He nodded. "Try to keep up," he told Beck over her head and jumped onto the hill.

"Try to keep up," Josie mimicked after him.

"Let's do this," Beck said.

I heard Spade coming, zipping and ripping into the gravel, using the stick like a rudder behind him, careening in beside me from a much faster speed. He made it look easy.

"Just trust your body. You got it. Keep three points of contact, but let the slide do all the work. When it's going, that's a good thing. You want everything to be rolling. You simply move with it. Come on." He jumped out in front and scurried his feet on the ground. He ran much faster than common sense told me he should, but he gave a little hop and caught the rocks sliding around him. In seconds, he fell into rhythm with the stones. He was right, the tiny rocks of the hillside did catch him. After that, they continued carrying him. They were doing all the work.

"I can't believe I'm doing this." I ran out behind him, leaning back on my makeshift pole. "Woo-hoo!"

Spade was right. If you worked with the hillside, not against it, you could ride a thousand tiny rolling rocks. The wind whipped through my hair. Behind me, I heard Josie and Beck also start steamrolling down the hill. With our pole points for balance, we moved much quicker than the other alliance, and we reached the quarry water at almost the same time as the other ten.

So much for their head start.

"We did it!" I cheered, coming to a stop in a plume of gray smoke.

Josie and Beck pulled up as well. At the last moment, a larger rock caught on Beck's stick, stopping his momentum. He pitched forward, smashing into the stony ground between me and Josie.

"Way to make an entrance." I giggled when I could see only his pride was hurt.

"Little help." He shot up a hand and I pulled him to his feet.

"We gotta keep moving," Spade complained. "Come on, we swim for it." He pulled off his shirt.

"Are you alright?" Josie checked on her man.

"I'm good."

"Look." I grabbed Spade's shoulder and I pointed at Vince.

The surly boy held his hands down by the sides of his body and stood very still. His fingers curled into a ball. Around him, the quarry water bubbled and stirred until suddenly, the liquid broke into two different bodies, arcing ends elevated, exposing the wet ground underneath.

"What the..." Spade's mouth fell open.

"Whoa." Beck raked his hand thru his hair.

The other teens ran in between the parted water.

"How the hell is he doing that?" Spade wondered.

There was no way to describe what I saw with science. The water simply divided itself and held up its walls like a shelf. The teens on the other team ran across the quarry's mushy bottom.

"He tried to do something like that in the seven trials," I told the others. "The black box stopped him."

"Yeah, but today they said we could use magic on this course," Josie noted. "He's an empath. Harnessing the water."

"He can't hold it. There's no way to hold that." Beck shook his head.

I was surprised. From his tone, it was clear Beck knew what he was talking about.

He was an empath too.

"Should we follow?" I asked.

"Too dangerous." Beck shook his head. "It'll close."

He was correct. Only inches behind them, the path was already starting to falter. Vince couldn't hold it forever, and any moment, all that water he had pushed to the sides would come rushing back in.

"They can run faster than we can swim, even in sludge," Josie said worriedly.

"So we don't swim. We boat. Take off your shirts. We'll use 'em like ropes," I suggested. "Tie the four poles together." I stripped off my shirt and tied it with Spade's, then I tied our fabric rope through the four little branches. Beck and Josie could see what I was getting at. They quickly did the same.

I couldn't help but peek at Beck's physique.

He was just as pristine a specimen as Jacob or Greg

or Spade. He just never flaunted it. What was with these guys and their superhero physiques? To be a man-witch, did you have to have six pack abs? Not that I was complaining. But it was a little intimidating.

Under our T-shirts, Josie and I had both opted for modest, functional swimwear. We weren't interested in giving a free show to anyone today.

"I'm the strongest swimmer, so I'll rudder," Beck offered, and we launched our primitive raft into the water.

"Not sure you're the strongest swimmer, bro," Spade disagreed, but I just shoved him onto the front of the boat.

"We need strength in front too," I said, assuaging his ego. "Lead us to safety."

We piled on, Spade in the lead, then me, then Josie, and finally, Beck. The little structure held our weight. All four of us paddled with our hands.

It was clear the alliance was back in the lead. We could see their progress ahead of us as a gaping hole of pushed, harnessed water led their way. The cavity moved with them as they crossed in the middle of the man-made lake. Although we couldn't see any of their bodies, we knew they'd all gone in together. The whirlpool created by Vince's balled fist looked like a moving partition. And Beck was wrong; Vince was much stronger than he'd initially assumed. They'd been crossing for almost two minutes and still, his barrier held.

They were twenty feet ahead of us and several

more feet to the right. But once more, we were gaining. Working as a collective was definitely smarter than individually swimming. We were cutting through the water much faster as a team than we would one on one.

"They've got a huge advantage," Josie noted.

"Well, what's our advantage?" I thought on my feet. "The race isn't survival of the fittest; they expect us to use our talents. Our powers. To prove that we belong in the High Council."

"Keep paddling!" Beck instructed.

"I'm a chemist. I can't just whip up some potion in the field," Josie complained.

"Well, I'm a dream-cast, and there isn't time for a nap," I agreed.

"Did you dream about this?" she wondered.

I shook my head. I didn't bother to admit to the others that my only dream since we'd arrived here in limbo had been as exciting as watching other people play a card game.

"Well, I can harness bad weather," Beck admitted.

We looked up into the sunny, cloudless sky. That was three of us useless, one to go.

"I'll think of something," Spade growled.

"What are you?" Beck asked.

"A lie-guard," Josie told me.

"You're a lie-guard?" I asked, surprised.

Spade nodded. "Don't sound so shocked while I'm saving your butt."

"No, it's just... you never told me."

"You never asked."

That was true.

"Okay." He grinned. "I got something." Spade sat up, kept his arms low like Vince had done, closed his eyes, and focused.

Suddenly, we heard screams from the mud.

"Oh my god!"

"Look out!"

"There's another one."

"What is that?"

"Get me out of here!"

"It's not real!"

"How can you tell?"

"Quarries don't have alligators."

"They're an illusion."

"Are you sure?"

"It almost got me."

"How can you tell?"

"Oh my god. Oh my god!"

Spade released his concentration and went back to paddling with the rest of us. He seemed to be huffing and puffing from the act.

"What did you create?" I questioned over his shoulder.

"A couple gators. Down in the mud."

I could see why the others were screaming.

"And they're hungry." He gnashed his teeth like a gator might have.

Our little boat was almost on top of their water

hole. We could actually see the others down in the cavity floor as they ran.

"How is Vince still holding the walls?" Beck couldn't believe in his competitor's stamina.

In answer, we paddled as hard as we could.

From inside their water crater, some of the alliance began noticing us.

"They're gaining on us," Tej shouted.

"Let's bring in some reinforcements." Marcy stopped and let her arms fall to her sides.

"Leave us alone," Josie shouted, but that didn't deter the other girl.

Marcy closed her eyes and breathed deeply, harnessing her inner powers. She connected with something deep inside, smiled, then started to run again.

We looked to the sky, but nothing happened.

"I don't get it, what did she call?" Spade wondered.

Caw, caw.

A seagull circled overhead.

"Oh..." he realized.

Caw, caw.

More birds flew in.

"Oh no," Beck added.

Caw, caw.

"This isn't good, guys," Josie murmured.

"Animal empath," Beck agreed from the end of the boat.

"It's just a couple of birds. What's the big deal?" Spade shrugged.

Suddenly, a dark cloud floated over the quarry, housing us all in its shadow.

Caw, caw.

Only, it wasn't a cloud blocking out the sun. It was birds. Hundreds of birds, swarming the sky above us.

"This is gonna be bad," Josie warned.

They wafted for a moment more, circling above us, floating aloft, and then the first few started to dive.

"Incoming!" I shouted.

"Get down," Josie instructed.

We were able to duck the first few feathered creatures, but as more and more birds dove down into the water, it was clear on our makeshift vessel that we were about to get mauled.

"Jump ship!" Beck ordered, but we were already abandoning the boat.

All around us, sharp beaks and flapping wings dive-bombed into the water as if we were their fishy dinner.

"The logs! Get under!" Josie screamed before diving back underwater herself to avoid being attacked by the swarm.

We ducked under the log raft. The branches did a good job of hiding our eyes and faces, but the bird wings beat down on the wood sticks as the fowl lunged and dove from above. We were attacked from every direction. The pelting was swift and sudden. The makeshift boat we'd built couldn't take the drubbing and broke apart at the seams.

Luckily, as quickly as it had come, the feathered onslaught abated.

Marcy's call for reinforcements lasted only twenty seconds or so.

"Everyone okay?" I checked.

The others nodded.

"It's slowing," Spade noted.

"I told you. Anything so potent just isn't sustainable," Beck agreed.

The chaos above us dissipated back to thin air. Marcy's birds did her bidding, then disappeared back out of the canyon. We held onto various pieces of our man-made sea craft, but it was clear the structure was too broken to reclaim. It would no longer take our weight.

"Swim for it!" Spade instructed, and the four of us were forced to leave the safety of the raft poles for good.

But we weren't the only swimmers.

Beck was right. At some point during the onslaught, Vince had finally lost control of the waters, so the other alliance was now also forging ahead, bobbing through the waves, dragging their exhausted bodies up on the shore. All fourteen of us were much closer together than any one of us could have hoped.

"Call it off!" Marcy shouted towards us.

"Concede to the real parabonds!" Greg bellowed.

"See who fate gets to the pool first," Spade called back.

Suddenly, Greg got really still, arms at his side.

"Something's coming," I warned. Above us, we heard a rumbling.

"Holy crap," Beck said, pointing. A giant boulder shook loose from the top of the quarry and tumbled towards us, picking up momentum as it headed down the hill.

"It's an illusion. He's a lie-guard," Spade told us.

"You willing to bet your life on that?" I asked him.

"I'm not!" Josie shouted. She and her boyfriend dove left.

Spade watched the stone barrel down. "It's an illusion, I'm telling you." He didn't flinch, just stared straight ahead, trying to break apart the perception of the rock with his doubt. The giant boulder picked up speed. I looked between Spade and the path of the rock. It was coming right for him.

"Spade," I said, worried.

"It's not real," he told me.

"Spade," I tried again.

"It's not..."

"Come on!" I grabbed his hand and we jumped to the right, landing in a heap together. The giant rock whizzed past us, inches from where we'd been standing, its wind in our faces. It landed on our beach location, the place where we'd just been standing moments ago, with a deafening crack. The ground beneath us shuddered.

Tej and Greg high fived.

"Maybe it was real," Spade said, a shocked look on his face. "Are there rock empaths?"

"I don't know, dude. Let's not get ourselves killed," I told him.

"My ankle," Josie shouted, doubling over. Spade and I looked at each other and ran to her side.

"Did you hurt it?" he asked.

"Did you land funny?" I added.

"Someone get a boo-boo?" Anita catcalled from farther up the slope.

"Ohhh," Josie cried in pain. "I'm fine," she whispered so that only we could hear her. "Just giving them some distance so they stop trying to kill us... and maybe the lie-guard finish line will take its effect?"

"Smart." I nodded. "Here, we'll help you," I said much louder. I took her arm over one shoulder, and Beck took the other. We pretended to hobble up the hillside, creating our own non-magic illusion. Spade scouted ahead.

Sensing our weakness, the other group seemed to forget all about us.

As they got closer and closer to the finish line, it had probably occurred to them that even in their alliance, because of the numbers of winners and losers the ladies had set, two people in their gang of ten still wouldn't be safe through round one. At some point, it would have to be everyone for themselves. I hoped that time would come soon.

"It's working. Look." Spade pointed ahead. On the

right, far back in the field, we could see the motel and the pool. The alliance ran straight for it, Anita and Nicolette bringing up the rear.

"Are you sure it's an illusion?" Josie said worriedly.

It looked so real.

"I know what I saw," Beck said, but Josie and Spade still didn't seem sure.

"Change your perspective," I suggested to the others.

If Beck had seen the truth by climbing up the trees, not down, maybe we could see the cracks in the lie-guard mirage through a perspective change too. I dropped down in the grass and the others did the same, an angle the ladies were doubtful to have thought of. From our unexpected low vantage point, the truth was abundantly clear.

It really was an illusion. The motel on the right was a mirage.

"Told you," Beck said, pouting.

"I guess part of a witch's skill set is being able to decipher the deceptions of others as well. That was smart thinking, Mae," Josie said. "Let's go."

We ran in the opposite direction, dropping the ruse of Josie's injured foot. I thought we were home free, but unfortunately, Nicolette noticed.

"Hey!" she called for attention.

Because they'd run so far in the wrong direction, I couldn't hear the follow-up to whatever she said next. But when I peeked back over my shoulder, I could see she had caught up to Vince, gestured in our direction, and clearly convinced him. They knew they were headed on the wrong course, and now they had started to come this way. It was only a matter of time until the others would too.

"Whoa!" Josie screamed as something sent her and Beck tumbling to the ground.

"Run!" Spade told me. "Go!"

I didn't turn to identify the cause of the other couple's collapse, just kept running. The tide had turned. All the teens were now coming. It was all I could do to stay ahead of the pack. On the brink of exhaustion, we ran forward as fast as our wilted legs could carry us.

"They're closing in!" I warned. Any advantage the lie-guard had given us would be eaten up in a moment's notice. Our little group of four was being caught by the alliance's five couples...

Five beats four.

My dream!

Maybe it really was part of a vision. Was this the war game that the cards were playing? The ladies played head-to-head against each other. And those were the first cards they played. I tried to remember more of the details.

Five beat four... but then four would beat two.

Four plus two was six.

Six of us would end up running this whole race for a second time. And Josie, Beck, Spade, and I were the four. Somehow, I was sure.

There wasn't time to mull it over.

I ran as fast as I could, but the tall, lanky bodies of Jacob and Sloane were just built to be faster. They caught up with me, then blew past. Even Tej, the tiny powerhouse, could run like the wind.

"Four beats two," Sloane said just loud enough for me to hear.

Her blonde hair flowed like a river behind her. She wasn't even huffing.

"I know," I gasped. "What does it mean?"

But she just shook her head. "Watch out for the suicide king," she called over her shoulder. She didn't stop or break stride.

Great, so I wasn't the only one with dreams of cryptic card game messages.

Having had the dream was easy. Interpreting the vision correctly while running for my life was a bit more of a challenge.

Jacob, Tej, and Sloane were first to come to the end of the field. The path tapered into a wall of dirt almost eight feet high. Like a natural retaining wall built out of the ground, the dirt wall elevated the pool beside the motel almost a full story higher than the grass of the field. Tej dropped a knee and in a smooth motion, he boosted his partner up into the air. Sloane vaulted her body over the ledge then draped back down the dirt wall to help him follow her up. They both made it look easy.

On the grass, Vince passed me too. He caught up to Jacob. The two boys raced at the wall at full speed and, like impossible rock climbers, scrambled themselves up, catching their body weight on mere fingertip grips and using their upward trajectory and momentum to haul their bodies to safety.

"Holy crap," I muttered. It was like they defied gravity.

Spade, who'd been watching the others climbing the dirt wall and not watching his footing, stumbled to the ground. His shoe was caught in a terrible bramble. He struggled to get it out. I raced towards him.

"It's stuck!" he told me.

"It's just an illusion," I said, practically falling over him. "One of the others is a lie-guard, and they're holding you back."

"I know, but it still feels mighty real." Spade looked around at the field ahead and behind us. Our lead on the pack was disintegrating. Everyone was catching up. Nicolette, who'd turned sooner than the others, was only moments from hitting the wall. Vince was already waiting to pull her up.

"Go," Spade told me. "I'll change my perspective. Go!" Surprised at his vehemence, I picked myself up and ran to the wall. Vince struggled to pull Nicolette up to his level, but they managed. How was I supposed to climb this wall alone?

I dug my fingers and toes into the sides of the soil, but there were very few footholds. It was slick mud and crumbly dirt. There was no way I could get up the wall without Spade's help.

"Mae, over here!" Jacob appeared over the ledge. "Give me your hand." He reached down.

The sun glinted around his head, giving him a haloed effect.

I glanced behind me.

Spade's leg was still caught in the bramble, but he was trying to see the branch from an unusual vantage point to release his perspective. A glance farther back told me Anita was still coming, but she was far back on the course. It looked like she was hobbling.

But she wasn't the only one coming.

Rick had thrown poor Hilde on his back, and he was moving them both across the field, racing for two, making up ground on Greg and Marcy and Josie and Beck.

For a moment, I hesitated.

Sloane and my own dream vision had warned me to watch out for the suicide king. But who was that? And look out for what? Was it Spade?

I hadn't seen who created the bramble his foot was trapped in, but I knew he was a lie-guard. Was it possible he'd created the trap himself? Why would he do that?

Or was it Jacob? I still didn't know his witch-y power, but from his constant arrogance, I guessed it was a doozy.

"Come on!" Jacob insisted.

"Okay," I agreed.

"Take my hand," he told me. I reached out my arm and we clasped hands together. "Gotcha." He pulled me up the eight-foot wall. I used my legs to propel myself. We were able to do it together. I dragged my weight over the ledge. At the top of the course, we collapsed together, mere feet from the motel pool that marked the finish. Two couples were already across. "Let's do this!" Jacob grabbed for my hand, ready to jump in the pool together, but it didn't feel right to just abandon my friends.

"Hold on," I told him. I looked back at the field below me.

"It's okay," Jacob tried to reassure me. "The ladies said for this round, we could partner with anyone."

But I still didn't budge.

Spade was lying on the ground with his leg bent at a wild angle, trying to give himself a new perspective to break his foot free of the thorns. There was no way he had cast that illusion on himself. He hadn't given up on trying to break it, and in my heart I knew he wasn't the suicide king.

"Mae, come on! We've gotta do this." In frustration, Jacob raked a hand through his hair and rested his palm on the back of his head. For a moment, his bicep pointed right into his head, like the placement of the knife in the king of hearts card.

Of course. That was it.

My dream was referencing Jacob. He was the one of whom I had to beware.

"I can't," I said.

"Sure you can."

"I mean I won't. I'm not going," I told him. "Spade, come on!" I shouted encouragement. I wouldn't betray my partner. Jacob was probably the one who put his foot in the trap. "Just take off your shoe!" I shouted. "You don't need it. We're at the finish!"

Spade listened. He untied the sneaker, and that was enough to break the spell. His foot fell free. He scrambled to his feet and raced to the dirt wall just as Hilde and Rick arrived at the base.

Greg and Marcy and Josie and Beck came crashing through the final stretch of the field, only twenty or thirty yards to go. We had to move fast. Rick put Hilde up on his shoulders.

"Climb, girl," he told her.

Obedient, she did as she was told. He was already so tall; she had a good angle to reach the upper level. All she had to do was swing up her legs.

"Take my hand," I told Spade, reaching down for him.

"You're being stupid," Jacob told me. His voice had gone shrill as he threw his arms up in disgust. We could both see the others were coming. They were closing the gap. His plan to get me to forsake my old partner hadn't worked as he hoped. "You'll never lift him."

"Then help me!" I told him.

But Jacob wanted no part of our team. Instead, he turned and leapt for the pool without a partner. There was a bright flash of light and some sort of force field shunted him back. It tossed him aside, and he collapsed on the concrete paver.

"You need a partner to cross the finish," Nicolette chirped, behind the finish line, as if she was the only one who had put that fact together. Jacob lay motionless, temporarily stunned.

"Come on!" I told Spade. "We gotta move."

The others were coming.

Spade took three footholds up the wall, then leapt to clasp my hand. Our fingers connected. For a moment, I could hold him. But Jacob was right, I wasn't strong enough to make the link last. Within seconds, our grip disintegrated, and he tumbled down, back on the grass.

Hilde scrambled up over the ledge.

Like me, she turned and held her arm out for her partner. But if I couldn't lift Spade, there was no way she could handle Rick's heavier bulk. The boys saw this too. They tried to run up the wall like we'd seen Vince and Jacob do before them, but neither Spade nor Rick could get enough momentum. Rock scrambling looked easy but was a dedicated skill.

Jacob sat up, still dazed. He shook it off. "Mae, they're coming," he pleaded with me. Getting back on his feet.

"Try your foot here," I directed Spade, ignoring Jacob's looming presence.

There was no way in hell he and I would be crossing that line.

"It's cuz of me you're even up here," Jacob said, his tone changing. For a moment, I thought he might kick me back over the edge. But instead, he tried to drag my elbow. "You and I are partners."

I yanked my sleeve away. "No, we're not."

"Ignore Jacob, focus on me," Spade ordered. But I couldn't.

Jacob reached for my arm. "Come on, Mae."

"No." I couldn't be coaxed, so he moved in behind me, into my blind spot. I didn't like it. "What are you doing? Just give me some room." I glanced down at Spade, but he was helpless to assist me, trapped eight feet below.

"She's not your partner," Hilde snapped beside me.

I was grateful for a second voice. Jacob swayed to and fro. Hovering just behind me.

"Just go." I tried to shoo him again. I had hoped he'd give up and just wait for Anita's arrival, but something told me he wouldn't be put off so easily.

Suddenly, he grabbed me around the waist.

"I'm the reason you're up here. Like it or not, you're my new partner." He yanked me up in the air.

"What are you doing?! No! Oh my god. Let me go!" I fought against him, but his grip was really strong. "Spade! *No*. Help. Spade!"

Jacob dragged me poolside, a sick smile plastered on his face. "Right this way, little lady," he told me.

"We're not partners," I shouted. "We're not anything! Let me go." Much as I struggled, he was too strong. He had picked up and dragged me. I couldn't fight him off on my own.

But suddenly, I didn't have to.

Hilde raced to my rescue. She swung all her weight at him, pounding Jacob's arms and peeling back his hands where they had twisted my skin bright red in his grip.

"Let her go!" she screamed. "She's not your partner!"

"Leave her alone," the others from behind the finish line also started to chime in. The force field that stopped Jacob from exiting solo also limited them from reentering the field. But they stood as close as they could to its boundary and shouted their disapproval from the pool.

"Shut up. Just... shut it. We're doing this!" Jacob lurched me forward.

"No, we're not." I punched and kicked.

The ladies did nothing. A sick smile of interest danced on Lady Mauve's face.

Hilde and I kept up our battle. We punched and kicked and dragged and smacked. For the moment, it was working. Jacob couldn't move me forward and fight both of us off at the same time. I bit at his skin and kicked at his groin. He was losing his hold.

"Let her go!" Hilde screamed. "You can't have her!"

"Fine." Jacob dropped me like a brick.

Hilde tried to catch me or give me comfort, but Jacob wasn't finished. His arms reached out and grabbed her. He yanked around the waist of the smaller girl instead.

"You'll be my partner." He scooped her smaller frame under one arm.

"No!" she screamed.

"What? *No.* Stop it. Stop it," I cried. She and I had fought him off like a rabid dog when he was dragging me, but little Hilde was an easier choice. His size over the younger girl gave him a big advantage. Since he could hold her with one arm, the other was free to fight me. We weren't going to win the second battle. "Let go of her!" I charged at him, but Jacob smacked me to the ground. "Spade! Rick!" I screamed. I couldn't stop him. Hilde was trapped in his grasp. I could see the fear in the younger girl's eyes. "Hilde," I whimpered, unable to save her.

Suddenly, like a lion, Rick roared over the wall.

"Get your hands off her!" he shouted. He was on them in an instant, stripping the girl from Jacob's hands. Rearing back in red-faced fury, he punched Jacob in the gut. The handsy boy barreled over and fell to the ground only feet from where I was still curled. "You don't get to handle a woman!" Rick shouted. "She said no. She doesn't want to go with you."

For a second, I thought Jacob might get up and charge. I ducked for cover. But instead, he sniveled and slithered in the opposite direction. Keeping his eyes on Rick's fuming, hulking body, Jacob inched backward. Rick kept coming forward, raging hot and staring him down. His bravado fully dispersed, Jacob wiggled farther and farther back out of range until, to duck him completely, he took himself right over the ledge and landed on the field below.

I peeked up from my hiding.

Even this departure didn't slow Rick's anger.

He leaned over the ledge too, and for a moment, I thought he was going to follow Jacob down onto the grass to beat the guy into a pulp. But Rick stopped at the wall's edge. His chest was still heaving. I was wrong. He had no intention of going over. Instead, he held his arm out for Spade.

"Thanks, man," Spade said.

Rick pulled my partner up to the top of the ledge in one smooth motion, lifting him up with ease in a way I never could. The boys clasped hands and nodded to one another. They released their grasp, and Rick turned and held out his hand for a sniffling, shell-shocked Hilde. "Come on," he said.

I watched from my crumpled position as she slid her tiny palm in his, and together they jumped into the pool.

Another partnership final.

Spade looked in my direction. Below us, the final two couples had arrived at the base of the wall. On our level, he offered me a hand to pull me back up to my feet. I gratefully took it.

"You helped Rick," I noted. "And Hilde."

"Well, you were making such a racket." Spade grinned.

I smiled in spite of myself.

"You ready? Come on." He held out a hand, prepared to jump into the pool like we'd seen the others do. Beneath us at the base of the wall, we could hear a commotion as Jacob seemed to be fighting with the other teens. He was still trying to get the upper hand or find someone of whom to take advantage. Anita had finally made it to the end of the field. She was definitely limping. Spade gave me an encouraging smile. Was I ready to do this? I was about to put my hand in his and jump across the finish together, but something stopped me.

The ladies... the war game... I just couldn't shake off my dream.

This wasn't how it was meant to finish.

"Five beats four, but four will beat two..." I murmured. I looked up at Spade wide-eyed, the picture becoming clear. But the random numbers didn't make sense to him. They didn't make sense to anyone but me.

Suddenly, I knew what they meant. I dug in my heels and pulled back.

"Spade, we shouldn't cross," I told him.

"What? No," he objected.

Both Greg and Beck appeared over the ledge. They dragged their bodies up to our level, being pushed by their girls from below. They heaved their bellies and clawed at the grass on the upper level to get their centers of gravity over the wall. They'd both learned the better technique from watching Rick and Spade. Greg managed to roll his body over the ledge first. But Beck was only moments behind.

"If we jump, we're safe." Spade gestured wildly. But I wasn't budging.

The boys, now both firmly on the upper level,

immediately turned around and anchored their lower halves to lift up their partners. We had only moments to decide our fates. On his own accord, Jacob's fingers clawed over the ledge again.

"I know. I know we'd be safe, but that's not the end goal. There would still be another round. Then it's four against two," I told Spade.

"Or every man for himself," he countered.

"That's not true, and you know it. We only beat Jacob with Rick and Hilde's help. If it's those three in the final battle," I said, pointing at Jacob, Greg, and Marcy, "they'll team up on Josie and Beck for sure."

"Well, that's too bad for Beck and Josie," Spade cried.

With Greg pulling her waist, Marcy was about to reach our level. If we were going to beat them, we'd have to cross now. But I was too sure. I shook my head. Spade saw our victory deteriorating in front of him.

"Mae, this is it. No second chances."

"I know, but I can't. Five beats four. Four beats two."

"There could be a million ways to interpret those particular mathematics." Spade was desperate. "Come with me. We'll figure it out together."

I dug in my heels and shook my head. "You'll have to drag me." I looked him right in the eyes. He glared back, but the stare was twinged with sadness.

"Then I'd be no better than Jacob," he told me.

Marcy kicked up her leg. Greg helped her roll free of the ledge. Helplessly, Spade looked at his options.

"Spade, you can trust me. This is right. We can save them."

"Who? Josie? Or *Beck*?"

Beck had almost managed to drag up his partner. Jacob had already rolled himself onto the higher level. I didn't justify Spade with an answer.

"I chose you over Jacob," I reminded him. He nodded.

We both knew my decision had already been made.

Greg pulled Marcy up to her feet. They saw us waiting but didn't falter. The lovebirds grabbed each other's hands, and they jumped into the pool.

Lightning scorched across the sky, followed by a clap of thunder.

"Round one is complete." Lady Gray's voice echoed across the field, booming and decisive. We all spun to look at her. She raised both arms and flexed her hands. When we looked back at the field, the terrible ledge and other features of the race were gone. It was all an elaborate illusion. For a moment, we just stared, shocked at the disparate change to our senses. It had all seemed so lifelike only seconds before. Then Spade went over to the now empty field and scooped up his shoe. He tied it back on his foot.

"Well, wasn't that cute. Now you have a sense of how it's played. Round two will be shorter. And for two of you..." Lady Mauve looked at me, Spade, Beck, Josie, Jacob, and Anita. She dragged a thin, bony finger across her neck. The universal sign for death.

"Time for a rest," Lady Gray added. It wasn't clear if the rest was for her or for us. "We begin at dusk."

The women turned to depart, but Lady Mauve stopped for a moment and looked me right in the eyes. "Spade and Mae." She frowned. "Interesting choices. Hopefully not ones you will live to regret."

EIGHTEEN
REST

"BOLD MOVE, WAITING FOR YOUR BOYFRIEND," Greg said, laughing at Spade, taking a playful shot at his chest.

"I figured you could use all the help you could get." Spade jabbed him right back, then cuffed at his head. Greg dodged easily.

Josie grabbed my arm and pulled me away from the boys. "You waited for us? Why?" She frowned. This was news to her.

I shrugged. "If we didn't, Greg and Jacob would have teamed up."

"Got that right." Greg held up a hand to high five Jacob, but the loser from the last round was in no mood to play. He ignored the outstretched hand and stomped right by, stalking straight to his room and slamming the door. Greg shrugged and gave himself a high five. He and Marcy and some of the others strolled away.

"You shouldn't have done that," Josie snapped.

"What Josie meant to say was 'thank you.'" Beck enveloped me in a big hug, which I accepted but pulled apart from almost immediately. I could feel the dagger eyes of both Josie and Spade.

"You're welcome," I said awkwardly. "Wasn't just me though, Spade was on board."

Beck looked up to him, as did Josie. He set a hard smile and nodded.

"Well, you shouldn't have done it either," Josie said. "But thanks."

"It was nothing," Spade agreed.

"Mae!" Hilde rushed over. I dropped down lower so she could wrap her arms around me. We smashed together in a warm embrace.

"You put up one hell of a fight," I told her, gripping her little body.

"I can't believe you have to do it again," she murmured as Spade joined us.

"We've gotta make sure Jacob doesn't come back at the end of round two," he said with a wink. Hilde giggled but held on to me. Rick approached.

"Thanks for your help," he said. He offered Spade a handshake, which he took.

"Thanks for not making it something I'd regret," Spade agreed.

Rick turned and shook my hand next. He nodded. The words and actions were formal, but I could tell something between us had changed. For the biggest and youngest in the competition, Spade and I were no longer strangers. With Rick and Hilde, we were friends.

"Let's go," he told the younger girl. "They need time to prepare." Rick nodded at both of us then departed. I gave Hilde's shoulder one last squeeze, then off she ran to follow him.

"How do we prepare?" I wondered, taking note of Rick's wording.

"We rest." Spade shrugged. The sweet charm he'd put on for Hilde had disappeared.

"Spade," I beseeched him. But I deserved what I got. I had forced him to do things my way and put his spot at the High Council in serious jeopardy, and for what? For Josie and Beck. He was right to be annoyed.

"Four will beat two," I assured him, repeating the vision's mantra.

"You better get dreaming," he told me. "I'm gonna go rest."

"Do you... want company?" I asked, trying to regain that old spark between us. The spark that he always ignited. Anything to smooth out the decisions I'd made. I raised an eyebrow suggestively.

Spade just looked at me blankly and shook his head. "No." He headed to his room.

I deserved what I got.

"He needs it," Tej informed me, walking by and overhearing. "The rest."

"Like we both do? Like I might dream again?" I wondered. I was way too hopped up on adrenaline to see that happening.

"Nah, I don't know about dream-casts. But for lie-guards... it's like a limit on your credit card. After an expensive round of shopping, you need to wait until you spend again." Tej shrugged. "The balance resets."

"I've never had a credit card," I told him.

"Well maybe it's time to talk to your bank." He chuckled. "He's reached his spending limit." Tej shrugged and strolled away. I watched Spade close the door to his motel room, alone and annoyed. He'd reached his limit on something.

"Good job out there," Sloane cut in as she walked back to her room.

"Thanks," I said. "And thanks for your warning about the suicide king."

"You wouldn't have gone with him anyway." She shrugged.

How did she know? I wanted to ask her more. But she threw the comment over her shoulder without slowing her stride, so instead I rejoined Beck and Josie. The girl was busy laying out a game plan. I looked around, surprised to see them strategizing out in the open. But after I stopped my partner from finishing the contest in order to stay and try and help them, I supposed our mini alliance was officially out of the bag.

"I was just saying I'm gonna see if I can whip some things together that we can bring to the course for round two. Some sort of chemical reactions," Josie whispered. "So make sure you and Spade have pockets."

"Will do," I agreed, although Spade was no longer likely to take orders.

"There's not much I can do if it's nice out," Beck complained, looking up at the weather.

"You can help me," Josie offered.

"Maybe there is," I countered. "You said you've harnessed bad weather? Like snow or rain?"Beck nodded. Josie frowned, uncertain. "Well, you can probably use those same tools in the sunlight, you've just never tried it. Maybe you can harness it into heat or fire or... I don't know... something?" I looked at their faces, worried I sounded a bit dumb. I had no idea how the harnessing really worked, but the logic seemed sound.

Beck dropped his arms like I'd seen the others do. For a moment, the sunlight seemed to spark a bit brighter. "Huh. Alright. I'll work on it." He didn't seem convinced. "Unless... you need me?" Beck looked to Josie uncertain.

"It's fine. I can build the potions on my own."

"And I guess *I* will take a nap." I wanted to laugh. What a dumb superpower. Sleepytime.

But they nodded and didn't see the humor.

What silly magic to have. The others were casting magical spells, creating chemical reactions, manipulating physical parts of the universe with their mind-bending science, or even creating elaborate illusions out of thin air, and I had to try and have a nap. It was incredibly frustrating.

Our plan decided, we parted. I went right to my room. With all this going on, how the heck was I supposed to drift off to sleep? I couldn't activate my brain. Or was it deactivate? How did my brain need to act in order to drift off?

I didn't even know that. How could I help the others?

Was there a way to start the dream-cast process?

The others dropped their arms and got really still. I looked doubtfully at my bed. It seemed pretty dumb to lay down and try to force a slumber. How would I ever sleep with three thousand things running around in my head? But it couldn't hurt to try. I lay down on my back, opened my arms, lowered them at my sides, and grew very still. I tried to concentrate.

Sleep, I told myself.

Dream-cast, I internally whispered.

Begin dreaming, my inner voice instructed.

Nothing happened.

It wasn't working.

But I was saved from further worry when someone knocked on my motel door. I hopped off the bed and went to open it, thinking it might be Spade. Or Josie. Or Beck. But it wasn't any of them. Nicolette stood in the doorway.

"Can I come in?" She looked uncomfortably to the left and right, worried that someone might see her, so I stepped aside to let her enter my room.

Inside, her discomfort only grew.

She looked around the room, at once intensely curious and nervous. I waved to the end of my bed, then sat in the chair beside the desk. I was surprised at how the mattress sagged under her body, but then she adjusted herself and things seemed normal again. I raised an eyebrow, waiting. Everything about my space seemed to distract her, but I was in no mood to be an exhibit at the zoo. I sighed. I could feel myself growing more agitated. After all the excitement of the morning, I guess I was tired. Maybe I really could make use of a nap. Since this was her visit, I had waited for Nicolette to start the conversation, but she was taking too long.

"What's up?" I tried to sound friendly, but I couldn't help the tiny edge of annoyance from creeping into my voice. If Nicolette noticed, she didn't show it.

"What Jacob tried to do with Hilde wasn't cool. And you. That dude has got to go."

I nodded.

"It was smart how you saw right through him. Vince thought for sure you would fall for his charms," she told me.

"I've got enough trouble with the charmer I've got," I said, then stood. So this was just a chat? "I don't mean to be rude, but I've got a big night ahead of me." I started to usher her out.

"Anita sprained her ankle," Nicolette blurted.

"What?" I stopped with my hand on the door.

Nicolette stood but didn't walk towards me. "That's why she was so far behind the rest of the group. She can barely use it."

"Unless it's an illusion," I said.

"It's not." Nicolette shook her head. "To maintain a

ruse like that for hours... a lie-guard would have to be incredibly powerful."

"I'll take your word for it."

"And the ladies," Nicolette barreled on, "they said, 'finish with a partner.' It doesn't have to be your parabond. Any partnership will work. Voluntary partnership," she added. "Just remember that."

"Okay..." I agreed. "Thanks."

Nicolette seemed to relax a bit, having said what she came to say.

"Why are you helping me?" I wondered.

She shrugged. "You didn't put yourself above your friends. I could use a friend like that."

I opened the door for her departure, but she stopped.

"I think you're meant to be here," she said sweetly, exiting my room. "But if I'm right, and you take my spot... I'll hate you for the rest of my life."

I looked at her closely. She wasn't trying to intimidate me, just stating the facts. I sighed. "Sounds fair," I told her. Then I quickly closed the door.

NINETEEN
ROUND TWO

EVEN AFTER A HOT BATH, I wasn't successful at napping. I was totally exhausted, but when I lay on the bed, all I could do was stare at the walls. My mind reeled. The first round of the parabonding tasks were very physical. That was a surprise. I'm not sure what exactly I'd expected it to be. A school dance? An elaborate game of hide-and-seek? On some level, it made sense to get our bodies moving. By having us overcome so many obstacles, fate was given plenty of opportunity to intervene on our behalf. Even my dreams were a product of fate.

If I hadn't been told I was a dream-cast, would I have ever noticed an errant vision about a card game? Would I have stopped Spade from finishing? Would I have thwarted our passing? That was all fate.

So how could I learn and prepare and do it better next time?

I should have talked more with Spade. Ahead of

time. Told him the plan to save Beck and Josie... But of course, until we were in it, I didn't really know that was the plan in my mind. There was no guarantee that was what my dream even meant. There was a chance that I was wrong. I wasn't very sure of my interpretations. Yet.

I thought about my mother. I wondered which of the four fields of witchcraft was her superpower. Was she always able to use her abilities at top speed, or did they grow and mature over time? Would I even get more time to develop?

I stared at the frayed walls.

Since sleep eluded me, I decided to reread the notes I'd taken on the last dream instead. I picked up the small notepad. It had all seemed much clearer when I'd taken the pen to paper. But the details I'd remembered on the course were correct. There I was in a beautiful, crumbling castle, and the two ladies were playing their game of war on the courtyard steps. They each dropped their cards with dramatic flair.

Five beat four, then four beat two.

The suicide king blew away. Just like how Jacob fell back over the ledge.

After that round came two kings and two queens.

Was that Beck and Spade and Josie and me?

The queen would fold... and then a duck barged in. That was it. The whole thing. I tapped my pen on the desk.

Their five pairs did beat us four, that part came true. So tonight, our four would beat Anita and Jacob's two. At least, that was what I hoped. So why didn't I feel good?

It was an unanswerable question. Just a feeling. A nervous energy, not a statement of fact.

Over time, my mind drifted back to my mom.

Sierra as a teenager.

I tried to imagine what she was like, toughing it out in a training field like this, learning her witch powers. I bet she was a lie-guard. Their powers seem most impressive, and my mom impressed everyone that she met.

What about Aunt Abeline? Did she also have powers? Not enough power to be accepted to the High Council, but at least a little witchy power? I had never seen her act in any way that didn't feel normal, or human. I gave a small shudder. Were we no longer human?

Out in the courtyard, Lady Mauve started playing the piano again. I was surprised. How was it possibly time already? I glanced at the clock. I'd been daydreaming for hours. But with no new dream-cast fortune-telling to help with our futures, I'd have to hope that my earlier sleep interpretation still applied to the plan.

Five beat four. Four would beat two.

I splashed water on my face, retied my sneakers, and went out to the pool.

"You were right." Beck startled me out of a daze I didn't know I was in. "I got something." His eyes shone.

"That's great," I said. I was happy for him, but I couldn't bring that tone to my voice.

"What's wrong?" He noticed immediately.

"She picked the wrong horse to ride," Jacob said. He came by with Anita, who was propping her bad leg on Vince's scooter. "Should have changed lanes while you had the chance."

"You snooze, you lose," Anita added, which would be a pretty proficient insult to make against any dreamcaster, except in this case, the thing I had missed out on was stealing her partnership from under her nose. She hadn't thought that through.

Protectively, Beck put his arm around me to shelter me from the snide pair. While I was fully prepared to fight my own battle, I had to admit his embrace felt safe and warm.

"We'll get 'em both on the course," Beck and I both said quietly at the exact same time. We both looked at the other and laughed.

"Whoa, synchronization," Spade noted.

I jumped a little at his approach. Without thinking, I extricated myself from Beck.

"I know, funny, right?" I tried to chuckle. But neither guy said anything more.

"Okay." Josie joined us, keeping her voice nice and low, drawing us near her. "I've prepared a few chemical reactions." She tilted open her T-shirt, and we could see she had prepared several socks that were crammed with ingredients and powders and talc. "You each take one, stuff it in a pocket, pull it out if we need it. You all have pockets, right?"

We did.

"Some of them need activators," she added. "Which I will hold on to. So make sure you tell me and don't try to use them on your own."

Spade looked doubtfully at his sock.

"They're clean," Josie told him, as if a bit of dirty laundry was all that could go wrong with this plan.

Lady Mauve finished her keyboard melody.

"Competitors, please." Lady Gray waved us over.

We hid our chemical pods and joined the others by the pool. The teens who were safe this round had gathered in the chaise loungers, waiting for the spectacle to begin. They wouldn't miss the show for the world. At my arrival, Hilde gave a small wave, which I returned with a wink.

As we approached, I couldn't help but train my eyes on the bottle of yellow pills.

"It has come to our attention that Anita has suffered a leg injury in round one of the competition. She has tended to the wound as best she can. However, for round two, she would like to have the added use of a scooter to walk. This is outside the realm of the rules we have set, but still adheres to the purpose and spirit. The Council has therefore approved her request, barring any objections from the other competitors. Are there any objections?" Lady Gray asked.

"You gave her your scooter?" My question wasn't for Lady Gray, but for Vince. Until now, I'd really thought of him as above the fray, but maybe he was as manipulative and backstabbing as the rest of them.

He simply nodded.

"Why?" I wondered.

"Because she asked." Vince shrugged. "If you wanna beat up an injured kid for your spot in the council, fine by me. Whatever floats your boat."

"But it's not fair," Hilde complained.

"Life's not fair," Tej chimed in.

"Fine, we're good. Whatever." I frowned.

"No, it's not fine. Are you nuts?" Spade jumped in.

"Think about the terrain. Is a scooter really such an advantage?" Josie wondered.

This was true.

"They must have thought so," Spade argued.

"They could just be desperate," Beck countered.

Suddenly, overhead, a thundercloud clapped.

"It's time to begin." Lady Gray frowned. "What's your decision?"

We looked to Spade. I'd taken so much from him already. I figured he could make this call.

"Fine," he said. "She can use it."

Jacob, Anita, Greg, Marcy, and Tej gave off small celebratory fist pumps in the air. I looked over at Vince. He caught my eye and shrugged. Beside him, Nicolette looked miserable and wouldn't meet my gaze.

"Alright. With that decided, ladies and gentlemen..." Lady Mauve moved between us, shaking a little yellow pill into each of our hands.

I looked at my teammates. Spade nodded with a tight smile, and Josie patted her full pocket. I acknowledged each of them and gave Beck a rueful smile. He cocked his head and shrugged. Together, we raised the pills to our mouths and swallowed them down.

Lady Gray raised her arms. "Let round two of the reaping commence."

TWENTY

THE SECOND BATTLE

I AWOKE to the splatter of large raindrops hitting my cheeks and forehead. Another droplet burst on the bridge of my nose. It sloshed onto my eyebrow and ran into my eye socket as I flickered my lashes open to stare straight into the sky. My head was tilted heavenward. There were dark clouds above where I was lying, and more rain was starting to fall. The water pooled in my eyes, and I squinted and tried to wipe it away, only to discover I couldn't move my arms.

Or my head.

Or my body.

I could barely move my face.

The drugs had some bad reaction, I immediately feared. But no… that wasn't it. My body was able… I just couldn't move it. Something was impeding my limbs. A lot of something.

It was dirt. I was buried up to my chin in the soil.

I shifted my head to the left, then the right. It was

hard to see with the heavy fall of rain pelting steadily now, but I felt I made progress. With each rotation of my head, I wiggled a bit freer, and I was starting to get my bearings in the field. As I maneuvered my position, the ground around my face gave way, and soon I could see blades of grass and other features of the ground. My body was buried, it would seem, under the sod of the field, somewhere between the retaining wall of soil and the quarry.

"Spade?" I called into the night sky.

"I'm here," he said. "Work your fingers."

"I'm trying," I replied.

"I'll be out soon," he told me. I wasn't sure if that was true or if he was keeping up appearances. Neither of us said much more since we had no way of knowing if Jacob and Anita were buried nearby or far from us. But his technique was correct. Through repetition of tiny movements, things in the dirt did start to give way. The ground hadn't had time to pack down on top of us, so inch by inch, I was able to wiggle my hands towards the open air.

I kept my eyes closed against the rain, but the wet dribbles on my cheeks actually felt good. They reminded me that I wasn't dreaming, that this was all happening, and that this was a real-life scenario from which we had to escape.

My right hand burst through first.

I wanted to shoot it out into the air, but my progress was labored. After my hands were free, I still had to wiggle out my arms as well. I'd been buried the way one might choose to sit in a hot tub, with my head lying back at the surface, arms and shoulders floating nearby, and my legs and waist buried deep below the surface. With the tiny progress inching forward, my upper body was almost free. I had pretty much established full mobility when I felt someone move in above me, blocking the falling rain. I opened my eyes.

"Hey," Josie whispered.

She was covered in her own mud, head to toe, but she was up and out of the ground. Around my back, she sprinkled something from what was once a white sock. It was now a muddy mess.

"I'm turning the ground around you into quicksand. Don't struggle or you'll go deeper. Let it loosen for a minute, then Beck will pull you out," she whispered.

"I'm right here," Beck added.

I could hear him behind me, though I couldn't turn around. "Okay. Thanks." I nodded.

"There. You're good." She hopped up and ran in what I could now see was Spade's direction. He was doing better than me at digging himself out of the ground. But with Josie's help, I would be out soon as well. Whatever she mixed into the soil started to work almost immediately. I could feel the dirt around me changing, growing looser and messier.

"I'm gonna pull you backwards," Beck told me. He leaned into view, and I could see he was covered in mud as well. "Hi."

"Hey."

We smiled at each other. I held out my hands, which he took. His grip was warm and firm.

"Ready?"

"Ready."

Beck tugged. It hurt a little as the dirt tried to suction me back into its clutches, but the strength of his arms worked on the quicksand. Bit by bit, my body came out of the ground.

"Should I kick?" I wondered. How did quicksand work?

"Just hold on," he told me. I could hear the strain in his voice, but Beck didn't give in. I let myself fall loose like a rag doll and using energy reserves deep inside, Beck dragged me out of the pit. Success. We fell back on the grass, breathing heavily.

I got up first, free of my burial.

The rain made the dirt on our faces dribble in chocolate-colored streaks.

"That's what I'm talking about." I grinned. I offered Beck a hand to pull him up to his feet. He grinned and took it. I wiped my eyes. Josie had also managed to retrieve Spade, and they also struggled to stand, out of the quicksand. I was relieved to see they were free, but even without the chemical concoction, Jacob and Anita really weren't far behind.

"Which way?" I asked as we joined the other two.

The rain made everything tough to see, but I was pretty sure the quarry was at our rear. The ladies had said this course would be shorter, and it seemed to me that we were at the back of the large field. If the quarry was behind us, that meant both the motel pool and the finish line were up ahead, on the left. But in this downpour, it was tough to be certain of anything. I looked at the others. We all embodied muddy, drowned rats. But there wasn't time to even point that out. We spun on the spot, looking for a better vantage point to figure out our specific location, but it didn't seem to make a difference. The lead we had on Jacob and Anita was evaporating. It was time to go.

"We run forward," Spade said, not waiting for approval. "At the clearing, we'll see what direction."

It was as good a plan as any.

The terrain wasn't a flat field like it had been in round one. Whatever machines they'd used to dig the holes we were buried in had also dug up the grass all around. But Spade was right with his general intention. Without good information, the best course of action was to keep moving forward and reassess as we went.

Our foursome ran headlong into the storm. It was hard to see even two feet in front of our faces. The pelting rain and the dark clouds above sucked up all the light on the field. Time and again, I tripped and lost my footing. My body slammed into the ground wrists-first, but I picked myself back up and just kept running. There wasn't time to fret about bruises.

"Quicksand was smart thinking," I called to Josie.

"Yeah, but I thought we could use it at the wall." She shrugged.

"What's in our other potions?"

"Chemical reactions," she said almost automatically, as if it was necessary for her to deflect any hint of her magical abilities. I suppose in her past, it was. "I've got a superglue and a knockout potion, and also the antidotes for each of those potions... just in case something I created doesn't work like I hoped."

We ran blindly forward, trying to keep pace with the boys.

"Smart," I agreed.

"Beck's idea." She played it off, but she had impressed me. Not only had she thought of three different chemical reactions that might be useful in a magical footrace, but she'd parceled them out and brought along the antidotes, just in case they didn't go off exactly as planned. There was no way I could prepare like that. To contribute my part to the battle, I had literally been told to go and take a nap. And I didn't even do that right.

"Crap." Spade let out a low whistle. Ahead, he and Beck slowed to a stop.

"What now?" Josie wondered.

We pulled up beside them and saw what they saw: to the left, through the sheets of rain, we could see the eight-foot wall in front of the motel and pool, just like we expected.

But there was also an eight-foot wall and a ledge to the right... and directly in front of us... and even behind our backs, in the direction we just came from.

"Lie-guards," I whispered.

In total, there were six identical eight-foot walls,

motel buildings, and pools to choose from, but only one that held the true finish line.

"Which one is it?" Josie asked.

We spun in circles, trying to make heads or tails of the choices ahead.

"The rain's too thick to really tell," I said.

"I can thin it out," Beck offered, looking up to the skies. "But then my power will be spent."

We looked at each other. Was this a good use of his talent?

"They're getting ahead!" Josie shouted.

To our left, Jacob and Anita had escaped their burial slots and had run straight at the motel room mirage on our farthest left. Anita was hobbling along on Vince's scooter as best she could. They hadn't bothered to analyze the many directions and try to pick the best one. The other teens had simply picked a spot on the horizon and started to run.

"We gotta catch 'em!" Spade worried.

"Only if they picked the right direction," I said. "Beck, do it. The thin-the-rain thing."

Beck put his hands to his sides and closed his eyes. For a moment, nothing happened. Josie, Spade, and I spread out, looking in every direction, ready to spot some small detail. Anything that would show us the right way to go.

"It's not working," Spade complained. "They're getting farther."

"Wait for it." I believed in my friend.

Between us, Beck concentrated.

"This isn't working!" Spade spat out again.

"Just hold on!" I smeared matted hair off my face.

"You've got this," Josie told him.

Beck's fingers clenched. The rain stuttered.

"You're doing it." Josie nodded.

"That's it," I added.

The storm thinned above us, then dribbled, then stopped. Without the torrential downfall, the air grew strangely still. We looked at one another, no one speaking. The air felt cold against our wet skin.

"Okay, which one is the right path?" Josie asked.

Even without the rain pelting down, all the motel illusions looked the same.

Spade dropped to the ground to peer from a different perspective, but this time, the ladies, or whoever had built this illusion had thought of that response.

"I can't... hold... it..." Beck warned.

The thunder cracked, reverberating over the field.

"I got it." I put my hands down in the grass and kicked my legs up in the air. "Grab my feet," I shouted. Josie grabbed my ankles. Upside down and low to the ground, it worked. I was able to break my perception. "Not it... no... no..." I checked each potential direction, including the one Jacob and Anita had run in. "Not there..." I told them. We all breathed a sigh of relief. The others had picked the wrong destination.

"Hurry," Beck cried. His whole body was shaking.

"There!" I pointed. The real motel was two ledges to our left.

"Let's go!" Spade shouted, leading the charge.

Suddenly, a lightning bolt scorched the earth in the spot where Spade had just stood. Beck fell back in a heap. The rain pummeled back down on our heads.

"What the hell, Beck!" Spade yelled.

"It wasn't me," Beck said, standing back up. "I didn't do that."

"Like hell you didn't!" Spade was incensed. He marched straight at him.

"It didn't." Beck held up both hands, but he didn't give ground. Spade stalked right in his face, his hands balled into fists. But just then, another bolt of lightning cracked down from the sky. We all jumped. Again the ground was singed in a spot where moments ago we had stood.

"The ladies!" I shouted. "They're changing things! Making it harder."

"Can they do that?" Josie wondered.

"They just did!" I had to shout to be heard above the storm. More lightning and thunder. "Don't you remember? There are no rules! Just, 'don't die.'"

Chunks of hail had started to fall.

"Run!" Josie shouted, but none of us had to be told.

We ran as fast as we could, forks of lightning striking at our heels.

"Oh my god!" I stumbled, reeling forward, my body getting ahead of my feet. But Beck reached out and grabbed my hand, keeping me upright.

"I got you!" he shouted.

We ran full speed towards the hotel. Jacob and Anita caught on quickly to our determined path and changed their course to converge with the rest of us as soon as they could. I was pretty sure they were still a good ten or twenty feet behind us, but in the storm, with all the thunder and the lightning, with the hailstones the size of gumballs, it was hard to tell who was leading the charge. I could barely see two feet in front of me. The uneven ground constantly tripped me, but thankfully Beck hadn't dropped my palm. His strong grip kept me upright and encouraged me forward. I held tightly to his hand. Nearby, I could hear Josie and Spade huffing and puffing, and although I couldn't always see them, I knew they were running close as well. Suddenly, out of nowhere, we smashed into the eight-foot dirt wall at the front of the pool. The storm was so bad I hadn't even seen it coming.

"Look out!" Beck and I hit it first.

Quickly, we tucked into the wall's protection and tried to wipe the rain and mud from our eyes. The barricade of dirt offered only the tiniest bit of shelter. But its presence meant we were almost at the end of the task. The ordeal was almost over. We were home free and out of the storm.

"Come on." I pulled the others into the shelter, happy to see them arrive. Spade first, then Josie. We all huddled together. Quickly, I let go of Beck's hand. But neither of the others seemed to notice. Beck and I offered each other flattened smiles. Our handhold had achieved its purpose. Now it was on to the next hurdle.

"It's gonna be harder, even slippier, to climb in this storm," I noted, squinting at the ledge above us and the rivers of water now sliding down through the dirt.

"You got this." Beck offered his hands in a cradle format for me to go first. I looked at Spade and Josie, but neither flinched. There was no time to talk things over. Jacob and Anita would arrive any second. I stuck my foot inside in his hold.

"Ready? Up!" He scooped up my leg like a cheerleader, and I shot straight up the wall with momentum. When my frame was on par with the threshold above, I scrambled up over the ledge and swung my leg in from the side. Spade did the same boost for Josie. The rain pelted down, but she easily climbed. We flew up the wall. I dragged the final appendage of my body over the ledge just as a crack of lightning sizzled the spot where I'd rolled aground.

From behind the pool forcefield, the onlookers gasped.

"There!" They pointed.

"Beck, lift Spade up next," Josie instructed. "He can pull you up from above. Mae and I will cross through the finish line. Come on." Josie smiled, offering her arm to me. "We did it!" She was ready to jump into the pool.

"What? No. We should help lift the guys up," I told her. True, we couldn't do much, but we could still them breach the corner. Spade was already putting his foot in Beck's hands.

"Ready? Up," Beck told him.

"Alright, fine. But let's start first with Spade," Josie told me.

"Okay…" I agreed, but this seemed a little off. "Why?"

"Oh, cuz Beck's so much stronger. You know. He's my hero."

The hairs on the back of my neck stood on end.

I looked out over the horizon in the distance for Jacob and Anita. Way back in the field, they were still making their way. I thought they might be closer. Had they chosen the wrong illusion again?

That didn't make sense. Had Anita re-injured her ankle?

Something was off.

Something was wrong here too, I realized. I sensed it. I couldn't put my finger on what, but I felt it in my bones.

"Beck, wait!" I shouted.

He had been helping Spade to climb higher. But immediately, he responded to my voice. Suddenly, I knew what was strange. It was Josie's demeanor. She was being too nice. Too verbose. Too helpful. I had just held her boyfriend's hand running through the grassland. She had seen it. She always saw everything. The real Josie should have been livid or jealous. She would have treated me coldly. That's just how she was. But this Josie was the perfect teammate, cheering us on for the win. Urging us forward. It stopped me cold.

"I kissed Beck," I blurted out.

"What?" She raised an eyebrow.

At my confession, both Josie and Beck were surprised.

"I'm sorry. I have to admit, I kissed him. Between rounds. On the break. I'm so sorry. It just happened," I admitted again, watching for weakness. Josie barely flinched. In Beck's hands, Spade was almost high enough to put his hands on the top of the ledge. I purposefully stood in his path.

In my pocket, I began to finger my sock full of chemicals.

"Beck, tell them the truth," I told him.

"Mae." From below, Beck was confused. "What are you doing?"

"I'm sorry, honey," I told him. "But I think they should know." I turned to Josie. "I'm in love with your man. I put my tongue in his mouth. We made out til Christmas. I'm sorry, Spade. Sorry, Josie."

"'Til Christmas?" Beck sputtered.

"Can we talk about this after the finish line?" Spade asked through gritted teeth.

"It's fine." Josie smiled again and offered her hand. "Everyone makes mistakes."

"Beck!" I shouted.

"It's not them!" He also knew it.

In one motion, I threw my sock full of chemicals on the supposed Josie, who screeched at the blinding whirl of powders and instinctively shoved me right back. She dragged the white talc out of her eyes and in the powdery mess, it became clear: I was right. It wasn't really my friend.

It wasn't Josie. It was Anita, in lie-guard disguise.

I had no time to cheer though. Her shove careened me onto my knees, the momentum from her push carrying me backwards right off the cliff. I couldn't stop it. I twisted over the ledge and fell back to the grassy landing a story below, landing with a heavy thud.

"Oh," I moaned.

Everything hurt. But still, I had to stand. The phony Spade tried to sucker punch Beck and brush past him, but I recognized his muscular back. At him, I hurled the rest of the powder bomb I was still clutching, and he transformed back into Jacob as well.

"Get off of me!" The unmasked boy yelled. But Beck had his claws on his back. He yanked him back down to our level. I looked up at the ledge far above us. Anita prowled at the top, waiting for her man, but without her partner she was still stuck in limbo. Alone, she couldn't cross the finish.

"Keep him down," I ordered. "I'll get the others."

Beck nodded, taking jabs and punishment from Jacob's feet and hands. The other boy tried to kick his way out of grasp, but Beck held fast. It was a tough fight between them, their strengths being evenly matched, but luckily, since the ledge was so high above him, it was almost impossible for Jacob to climb up to the next threshold without Beck having the opportunity to pull him back down. For the moment, we could hold them off.

I ran blindly back into the storm. "Spade! Josie!"

"Over here!" they shouted.

I raced my way back to the scooter I had seen all the way from the top of the pool. Josie and Spade were trapped in some kind of larger knot of bushes that had magically grown out of the ground.

"They trapped us," Spade told me.

"And assumed your identities," I added, snapping branches from the outside.

"They can do that?" Spade was surprised.

"Well, they did," I said.

"How'd you figure it out?" Josie asked.

I laughed bitterly. "You both were being too nice."

"Glad my trust issues were used for something positive!" She grinned.

"I'm a nice guy," Spade complained.

I ignored their feedback and worked on the bramble instead.

"Come on," Josie encouraged. "Beck can't hold them off for much longer." She was watching her man take Jacob on. He was making a valiant effort, but also taking a violent beating from his hands. We all knew Jacob was open to playing dirty. Beck couldn't hold him off on his own for too long.

"I got this," I told them. I leaned my chest far out, over the bramble.

"What are you doing?" Spade asked.

"Just stand back. Wait for it..." I stared up in the sky; the thunder rumbled. At the last second, I dodged to the side as a lightning bolt singed my old position. It burnt a hole in the brambles right through to the grass. "Go, go!" The hole was large enough for the teens to squirm thru, their bodies wiggling free in single file.

"Come on! We can do this," I yelled.

Lightning cracked again, this time almost getting my side.

The three of us raced across the field back to the dirt wall.

"Hurry! Help!" Beck yelled from the pool ledge, but it was too late. "Argh!"

Jacob kicked himself free on the wall. Beck couldn't hold him. He climbed up the ground. Anita pulled from above. They were both at the top of the threshold. They would finish any moment.

"Oh my god!" Josie yelled.

I turned to my friend. "What's in my sock?"

For a moment, she stuttered. "Super glue!" she said, remembering.

"Anita's covered in it. Jacob too. If you activate it, maybe it'll slow her down," I told her.

Josie pulled out the sock with the activation ingredient. "She's too far. There's no way I can hit that."

"I can. Give it here." Spade put out his palm.

Josie hesitated for a moment, then handed over the ball. Spade took the sock, cupped it like a football, and threw it up onto the field. Even in the rain, his aim was dead on. It exploded into a ball of powder on Anita's back. She screamed. A direct hit.

"You did it!" we cheered.

The sock burst into a cloud of dust.

Anita choked and coughed, but she still dragged

Jacob's lower half over the ledge and out of sight. They were gone.

Nothing happened. They were the first pair to cross. Disappeared from view.

"Damn it." Spade sighed.

"Too much glue had worn off," I realized, downcast. "The rain washed her."

It was over.

We had lost.

Their team finished the challenge first. Now what? Who would be the final team to cross?

Four beats two.

I had been so sure we could survive as a group, I didn't even consider what we'd do if or when there was only one spot left between us. I looked in the eyes of the others. Just a moment earlier we'd been working as a well-oiled machine. Could we now turn on each other so quickly?

Everyone was thinking about it. But no one made the first action. Instead, we stared at each other.

I looked helplessly at Beck. "What do we do?"

"They're stuck!" Hilde's voice carried down from the pool.

"What?" I turned and looked up to the ledge raised above us.

"She's right. Oh my god. They can't move!" Marcy laughed.

"You did it," Tej confirmed.

Greg hooted and hollered.

More voices started to float down.

"You did it. You guys did it!" Nicolette shouted.

"Jacob and Anita are glued to the ground!" Sloane confirmed.

It was the voices of all the teens who were waiting for us by the pool. They could see what was happening up on top of the ledge. Jacob and Anita hadn't crossed the finish line after all! They were glued, stuck together, and they were also adhered to the ground. Josie's chemical elixir had worked as intended!

We raced to the ledge where Beck was waiting.

Together, the guys boosted up me and then Josie, and when we climbed up over the upper ledge, we could see Hilde and the others were correct: Jacob and Anita had twisted and glued themselves together in a tangled heap that had fastened them to the ground in a human pretzel.

They were trapped.

Josie and I grinned at each other and made our way up over the ledge. We swung ourselves up onto the pool level.

"You cheaters!" Anita wailed.

"Says the girl who built a boobytrap." Josie laughed. "And tried to fake an injury..."

"And passed herself off as someone else," I added. "That's the pot calling the kettle black."

"Let us go!" Jacob snarled.

"We don't have the antidote. Spade does," I said sweetly.

Just then, Beck gave Spade a boost up to our level. My partner swung his legs over the threshold and used his upper body strength to roll himself up onto higher ground.

"And I wouldn't help you defeat my worst enemy." Spade laughed. We all did, because in some ways, the hyperbole was true. "Come on," he said to me, holding out his hand.

I narrowed my eyes, surprised. "You forgot Beck." The last boy was still on the ground. He'd lifted up Spade to pool level, but now we had to go back together to drag him up.

Spade didn't budge. "I didn't forget. We're not a group of four, Mae. You can't save us all. You can only parabond with one. Me," he said.

"Damn it, Spade!" Josie rolled her eyes and went back to help her partner.

I was torn whether to continue reasoning with Spade or just go back without him and help Josie try to lift Beck. There was no way he could climb up the wall without us. "It hasn't come to that," I told Spade.

"For me it has," he said. His face darkened. He stepped closer and spoke quieter. "I saw you take his hand."

Busted.

I glanced at Josie. Thankfully, she hadn't heard us. She was busy, bent over the ledge, trying to lift up her man. "I was falling." I crossed my arms. "And it was nothing. It didn't mean anything."

"Well, this hand does. It means everything. Are you with me? Or not?" He stretched out his palm with raised eyebrows. His body language asked, *what will it*

Plenty of the antidote had landed on the other team.

"Good choice, Spade," Jacob commended him.

"Haha, so there." Anita laughed.

They started rustling, preparing to break free of their glue bonds.

"What did you do?" I stared at Spade, shocked.

But he simply stared back, stood still, and waited, apparently fine with unleashing the opposing team just inches from the end of the course. He raised an eyebrow again and watched me. *What will it be?* his blank face seemed to ask. *Go back to the others? Or finish with me?*

I shook my head. If he thought I was coming with him, he was kidding himself. I broke eye contact and dove beside Josie to help her yank up Beck, both of us leveraging our weight and each lifting an arm to help him gain traction up the eight-foot stretch. It was working, but surely, unglued, Jacob and Anita would cross the finish line first.

"Come on, you can do it!" I strained, lifting with every ounce of courage and strength I had left.

Beck swung his leg over the ledge, and both Josie and I fell back. He scrambled his torso onto the top level. He was up! Anita and Jacob still hadn't managed to escape. They had yet to cross the threshold. There were still a few seconds to cross. I looked around for Spade's hand, ready to grab him. Ready to jump. To run for our lives. Every second would count.

"Go!" I shouted.

Beck was up on our level. He grabbed Josie's hand.

I scurried to my feet, ready to grab Spade...

Only...

Jacob and Anita hadn't gone anywhere. They hadn't gotten free. The glue hadn't disintegrated. They were still trapped, stuck together. Had Josie made the antidote wrong?

I stood, dumbly taking this in. "What happened?" I looked to Spade, then at Josie and Beck, who ran past me and jumped in the pool. Their tandem bodies' impact made a huge splash.

"Why didn't it unglue them?" I looked closer at Jacob and Anita.

Josie resurfaced, having achieved her liquid finish.

"I didn't give a real potion to Spade," Josie told me. "He didn't have the antidote. He didn't have a thing. Just baby powder."

My mouth fell open.

"I didn't trust him." She shrugged.

"Well, good decision, I guess," Spade agreed. "Come on." He offered me his hand, but I just glared. How could I possibly parabond with someone who just turned on his friends?

A gross betrayal.

"Come on, Mae. Finish it," Hilde encouraged me.

"Come on, Mae," Sloane agreed.

"Finish it," Greg said.

"Finish them off," Marcy cheered.

"Finish the round," Lady Mauve said quietly. "We're all waiting."

"Or let us out," Jacob sneered.

There were only two choices. I could pair with a horrible person, or I could give up and let Jacob and Anita take my spot.

Every eye was on me.

Time to decide.

I gave Spade a small shake of the head. I would never, ever trust him again. I slapped my hand in his palm. His grip felt scaly and rough, like the snake he'd proven he was. Together we jumped into the pool.

TWENTY-ONE
THE ALLIANCES ARE OVER

AS SPADE and I resurfaced in the pool, a bolt of lightning cracked through the sky, followed by a deafening crash of thunder. In surprise, I shuddered and looked over my shoulder. The field and the wall and the other features of the last round were gone, and while I'd landed only a foot or two away from Josie and Beck, it felt like I was completely alone, isolated on an island. There was no one to comfort me. I didn't look at any of my fellow survivors. I couldn't face them.

"Round two is complete," Lady Gray announced. "The fates have chosen."

Anita and Jacob were also released from their fray. No longer glued or stuck together, they silently untangled.

"Anita and Jacob," Lady Gray instructed, "please say your goodbyes."

"You all deserve each other," Jacob said and he spit in the pool. He turned on his heels and marched out.

"Better luck next time," Marcy catcalled after him. "Oops, won't be a next time." She and Greg laughed. But Jacob didn't look back.

Anita didn't say a word. She walked away, her head held high.

The ladies gathered themselves to follow the losers out but paused for one final message.

"Tomorrow brings round three," Lady Mauve warned. "No rest for the wicked. By the end of round four, two more mice will be out."

"Sleep well," Lady Gray added. Having said their goodbyes, they left us on our own for the night.

Spade swam to one side of the pool, so I purposely exited on the other. Beck and Josie avoided us both.

"Guess that alliance is over." Tej grinned as if I weren't right there to listen.

"Alliances are dumb. We have no control in fate's selections," Sloane said.

"So what? Stop trying?" Greg frowned.

"Fate will weed out the ones who aren't supposed to be here. My message hasn't changed." She shrugged.

"Anita didn't have any powers," Nicolette blurted.

"What?" Several teens asked at once.

"It was all Jacob." Nicolette shook her head.

"Not even dream-casting?" Marcy wondered.

Nicolette looked down at the ground, miserable. "Not even that. She told me."

The group nodded. No one had seen Anita do anything otherworldly, so that made sense. Of course, it didn't look like dream-casts could conjure any fancy maneuvers, so who could tell with a witch.

"And Jacob? Why was he cut?" Greg asked.

"Because he was an awful person," Hilde said.

The others nodded.

"Too pretty," Greg agreed, scoffing at his one-time friend.

"He got saddled with the wrong chick." Vince shrugged. Beside him, Nicolette grew smaller in her chair.

"I know what that's like." Spade scowled, shooting me a look.

"Right back at 'cha." I rolled my eyes.

Spade had the nerve to chuckle. Suddenly, I just couldn't help myself.

"I can't believe I trusted you. Again! Josie was right. You think only of yourself."

"*I* think…" Spade was shocked. "*Me!*" He rolled his eyes so hard that he shook his whole head. "*Please!* If there's anyone who couldn't trust their person, it's Spade!" He referenced himself in third person. "You and Beck have been making goo-goo eyes at each other since the day we all arrived."

"That's not true." I glanced around the pool. We had everyone's full attention. Some were slightly curious, some were keenly interested, but everyone was staring. A few had knowing smirks on their lips. Beck shook his head with adamance, a cross look on his face. Josie just watched, disgusted.

The accusation hung in the air.

I shook it off, but Spade wasn't finished yet.

"Since day one, you've been shopping for a new partner. What happened, Mae? Beck wouldn't drop my sloppy seconds? His precious Jo was too hard for him to quit? I saw what you did. Walking around, kicking all the guy's tires. Who's better than Spade? Who's next on the list? I guess Jacob said no?"

"Jacob came to me! I turned *him* down."

"You did? Oh, I'm grateful. So, so grateful. Thank you, Mae. Thank you so much for keeping me here. Swinging. *Dangling*." His voice was sickly sweet, but he snapped back to attention. "I'm not dumb. I see what you're thinking. You never thought I was your equal. You never thought about how I felt for a minute. You thought you could boss me around, say whatever you wanted. Put out your tits hot and cold."

I blushed, acutely aware of the others.

"But I'm done, Mae. So done. I get it. I know who you are. I've always known." He laughed bitterly. "*I couldn't be trusted?!* Who's the real fake and the fraud?" He stared right at me, eyes blazing, until I had no choice but to blink first. He stalked back to his bedroom and slammed his motel door.

Vince let out a low whistle. "And I thought we were a rough fit," he said to Nicolette.

She nodded.

He scooped up his scooter from the lawn where Anita had left it and waved a vague goodbye. That was enough melodrama for one night. He was headed to bed.

"Come on," Rick told Hilde. Obediently, she got up and followed. Spade's dressing down had made her less certain of our friendship, I could see, but I offered a small, forced smile, which she returned. We gave each other a little wave goodnight.

"See you in the morning. Get some sleep," Sloane told me pointedly.

Tej followed.

"Come on, babe." Greg offered his girl a hand up. But instead of standing, she leapt into his arms. He scooped her legs around his waist.

"Home, Watson!" She giggled. "No, wait, who's the famous chauffeur?"

"Miss Daisy," Greg suggested, strolling away from the party.

"No, the guy who was driving Miss Daisy. It's called *Driving Miss Daisy*."

"Well, if they named the movie after the guy that did the driving, then I'd know his name."

"Maybe his name was Watson. Home, Watson!" she commanded again. "Bye, guys; don't fight too much. It's not good for your skin," she advised us, giggling as they departed.

"Let's get you home into a tub," Greg sweet-talked his girlfriend as they faded from earshot.

"Let's get you into a tub," she agreed.

For a moment, silence hung between us.

Just me, Josie, and Beck.

"Spade doesn't know what he was talking about," I apologized to them both.

"Goodnight, Nicolette. See you in the morning," Josie said. Nicolette, who hadn't moved, was surprised to be bid farewell. But she did get the hint. She'd grown so small on her pool chaise I hadn't even remembered she was there.

"Oh. Right. Okay, goodnight."

We watched as she took herself back to her room. When her door had closed, we saw her curtain rustle. It didn't take a genius to know what she was now standing behind. She was still watching. Maybe they all were. As if they hadn't seen enough of the show already.

I felt responsible. I had asked my friends to trust me and in turn to trust my partner, and he had actively tried to betray them. That was my fault.

Even if he wasn't successful.

"Spade's right," Josie said carefully. "We were never a group of four, I hope you know that," she said. "And there are no trios in the High Council."

"No, I know," I agreed. "But he shouldn't have double-crossed you. There was no reason."

She shrugged. "I double-crossed him first. By giving a placebo potion."

"It's a good thing you did," Beck added. "What a snake."

I nodded, but Josie frowned.

"How do you think he feels, seeing his partner always running to someone else's side? Taking another person's hand? Falling into another person's arms? Some *friend* always in the spot he should be holding?"

She asked. She let the questions hang in the air. All these things that applied to Spade applied to her as well. "It doesn't feel good."

"Josie, you have to know that—"

"Mae, stop talking. Don't deny it again. You're only fooling yourself."

"I'm not that person," I blurted out. I could feel that tears were building just above my cheeks.

"We both saw you."

I had been blindly shaking my head, disagreeing with everything she said, but here, I stopped. There was such a thing as objecting too much. Josie and Spade were wrong. It wasn't true; there was nothing there. Beck and I were just friends supporting each other through a strenuous situation, same as I would with her. I had done nothing improper or wrong. There was a line. We hadn't crossed it.

"It was nothing," Beck told his girl, much more even-keeled.

I ignored how his classification of me as *nothing* stung in my heart.

"We were running. In total chaos. Hail, rain... we didn't notice. She just reached out and I caught her. She would have fallen. That's all it was. The rest was a dumb ruse to screen out Anita and Jacob." He stepped closer, handling his girlfriend the way she'd let him handle her so many times before. "You're my girl, Jo. You're my everything. My partner. My person. I'm not going anywhere." He looked her deep in her eyes.

She stared into his, searching for something to hold on to.

Awkwardly, I looked away. In reality, this was their fight, and I shouldn't have been there. But leaving now would be rude. I tried to remind myself that Josie's worries weren't really about me. Her bottom lip trembled. Somewhere in his gaze she found her answer, and her lips folded into a sad smile.

"Come here." He pulled her in and kissed her softly, slowly on her quivering mouth. The first kiss was tentative, but the second one looked surer.

Now I really shouldn't be watching.

"Well... that's my cue." I stood, causing the renewed lovebirds to look over to me.

"Mae, you should know, tomorrow you're on your own," Beck said.

Josie nuzzled into his neck, reclaiming her territory. Beck had talked her down, but he was solely her man. It was important that I know it.

I nodded. I was alone. Of course I was. I'd been alone since I got here.

"Well then, I guess I better make things right with Spade," I agreed.

TWENTY-TWO
A WALK THROUGH THE FOREST

THE NIGHT UNFURLED, but I didn't speak to Spade. I didn't talk to anyone. I went back to my room, closed the door, and slumped down to the floor. I was a mess. What was I going to do tomorrow?

Since arriving here in limbo, I had been to hell and back on the High Council course. Twice. I had interpreted strange dreams. I had lived through the seven trials. I had done it all on my own. Spade stood by my side, sure. But I never fully trusted him. And now I was right back where I started. Fully alone.

Stuck with a parabond I never wanted and zero options to change that scenario.

I was miserable.

I wanted to sink into oblivion.

Only it turned out sulking was pretty impossible when walls were thin and your neighbors were happy paramours. Not even Aunt Abeline's mouse buzzer could dampen the sounds of their fun. I could hear every giggle. Every grunt. Every moan. Greg and Marcy had plenty of pent-up energy to expend, and they were taking it out on our shared walls.

"Give me a break!" I shouted, chucking a shoe at the divider between us.

But their playtime wasn't over. If anything, the moaning and the wild time just got louder. I couldn't stay and wait for nature to take its course. I had to get the hell out of that motel room. I grabbed the sneaker I'd just thrown and stumbled out to the courtyard. I didn't want to sit by the pool. It was the scene of too many recriminations. Plus, there was one thing I knew for certain: there wasn't a single person in limbo with whom I still wanted to have a conversation. I was done talking. I was done with a lot of things.

I simply put one foot in front of the other.

Walking felt exceptional.

I willed myself forward, marching into the darkness on the bumpy gravel road. Retracing the route that Greg had first taken to drive me and Marcy into the High Council.

It should have been a cool night, our calendar now heavily into the fall season. I had grabbed my jean jacket on my way out, but strangely, for whatever meteorological reason, the summer still hadn't gone. The warm weather held on. The pleasant air held me tightly, and I was glad. Let the warmer days reside for as long as they could.

The moonlight filtered down through the trees and speckled the gravel beneath my feet. All around me, the forest was still. It reminded me of my first date with Spade. How I'd enjoyed his company then. He'd taken me out to dinner, and we'd learned so much about each other. We'd talked all night but still had more to say. After steak and salad, it was on to Tucker's Point, the romantic lookout over my family's lake. It was a place I figured he'd taken plenty of chicks before, and, after my conquest, he'd take plenty of women again. The view was great.

Not only that, the scene was perfect.

We had strolled through a moonlit forest and stopped amidst the pine needles. It was all so romantic. He'd kissed me softly, slowly in the semidarkness. Our first kiss. My skin had tingled, and my body expanded. He'd held me so gently with just the right amount of tension, it had felt like a new world had opened and I was free to walk in. But even then, we didn't even make it through that first night without fighting. In fact, we came to a dramatic end. And we'd been fighting ever since.

Spade was right. I'd been acting like I was the victim and he was the monster, but it was a more complicated scene. He had feelings too. And it was true. Ever since our date-gone-wrong, I refused to fully trust him. With good reason, maybe, but also, from that day forward, I'd always had one foot out the door.

Spade wasn't blind.

Of course he'd try to protect himself. I couldn't blame him. But that was the problem, not the solution. Spade and I were just two people fixed on our own self-interests. Worried about our own needs and feelings. Not being considerate of the other. How could we make things better? Was it even possible to become a healthy unit? And if we couldn't, how could we ever parabond?

There was that term.

Parabond.

My paranormal bond.

How much of my future was already predetermined?

And why did I still feel so strongly that it was never supposed to be a forever partnership between myself and Spade? So many of the couples here weren't actually romantic couples. Rick and Hilde acted like siblings. He was the de facto parent in the partnership they'd created. Tej and Sloane never spoke a negative word about the other, but they had virtually no connection. They simply tolerated the other. You could drive a truck through the distance between them. Nothing about their coupling seemed happy or pleasant or fun. It was simply fate-determined. And Vince and Nicolette were a far harsher couple. When Vince and Nicolette spoke to one another, which was already a rare sighting, no one could describe their discourse as kind. So why did I feel so strongly that my parabond should be both loving and fun?

I didn't want to settle.

I wanted a partner I could trust and rely on like I'd seen Greg could with Marcy, or how Josie did with Beck.

Beck.

Spade was right about him too.

I'd arrived at the High Council convinced I was hoping to partner with Josie. When that didn't happen... I didn't want to admit it, but maybe Beck was the next best plan.

I had kept us all together. I had said we were a foursome and that we had to fight the other alliance. I had interpreted my dreams in that manner. But maybe I was just making sure Beck got through to the next round of competition. Maybe I was doing everything I could to help him advance.

Why?

We'd never be partners. I wouldn't do that to Josie.

I *wouldn't*.

Even if that didn't ring true to her, to Spade, to anybody, I meant what I said.

I could never have Beck as my partner.

Yeah, in a dream world, maybe I would. In imaginary town, I'd pick him for sure. From all the guys here at the High Council, Beck was the only one I would actually choose. But that dream world didn't exist. I would never get to live there. Because in that mythical, ideal neighborhood, Josie and her feelings didn't exist.

But here, they did.

They existed.

I would never take him from her. I wasn't that girl. And also, he didn't want me. I wasn't some all-powerful woman who always got to choose. He had made it very clear. Beck wanted Josie. It was always

Josie. Since the first day I met them, Josie was his one and only girl.

We would never be partnered together.

And that was my deal.

I was stuck with one option.

The same option I'd known all along.

Spade. Or nothing.

I looked up in surprise at the sound of a car's engine screaming by. I was mulling and musing about my crap situation for so long, I had reached the end of the drive. I'd arrived at the outside world. Through the final thicket of trees was the highway to town.

Maybe I should just go.

I could leave.

If Spade was so wrong, then I should exit.

I'd come this far; I could just keep walking. No one was stopping me. I made the final turn through the forest and broke out to the road. I'd been so caught up in the High Council duality of choices, but seeing the road now, I realized that was a false bilaterality. It wasn't Spade or *die*. There was a whole world out here. A world of choice.

And I could just leave.

I'd head for home. Home to Aunt Abeline. She never made it to the High Council. She was never invited. But maybe that was fine. It was good. Fate finally figured it out. It had gotten me all wrong. I wasn't a member of the High Council. I was a reject like Aunt Abeline. She turned out fine. Great, even.

My heart lurched.

How I longed to sit with her and mull over her Scrabble, desperate to find the most perfect word for the biggest score. Those were my very best memories. I loved to watch her put her vocabulary to the test, even if she only played the game against herself.

Aunt Abeline would understand my departure. She'd be fine with it. Be true to myself, she'd told me. I could come home at any time. I chuckled to myself. She probably didn't mean at two in the morning. But sometimes one's best choices were made in the middle of the night.

Fate brought me this far. It had walked me right off the property. I should take it as a sign. I wouldn't bond, just like my aunt. All the competition and the trouble and the tribulation at the High Council felt so forced upon me because this wasn't my spot. I was a square peg in a round hole. I was tired of forcing it down.

My mom had made the journey, but now I knew it wasn't for me. I was meant to go home.

Tonight.

This evening.

I would leave the High Council forever. I would go and never return.

Out here on the roadside, everything made perfect sense. I didn't even need my belongings. I'd just head out on my way. I did wish that I'd grabbed my phone instead of this stupid jean jacket. But it didn't matter. I could just keep on walking and find my way home.

I walked on the side of the road in total darkness, only the moon and the stars to guide me. That was fine.

I could see well enough to safely travel. It was actually amazing how in the absence of any man-made glow your eyes adjusted to the dark. But just as I was starting to enjoy my moonlit wander, suddenly oncoming headlights filled the night sky.

The car came over the south hill. Its lights swept over the road and across the side foliage. The engine's roar disrupted the night's quiet sigh.

I moved farther onto the shoulder to let the vehicle pass me safely. But instead of blasting by, the driver slowed down to a crawl. I wasn't interested in hitchhiking. I wanted to leave the High Council, but I didn't have a death wish. I tried to wave them on. No thank you. The car rolled to a stop beside me. Feebly, I tried to ignore them, but the driver rolled down their tinted window.

Thankfully, it wasn't a homicidal murderer.

Unfortunately, it was Lady Mauve.

"Get in," she said.

Did I really have a choice?

"I'M LEAVING THE HIGH COUNCIL," I told her.

"I see that." Lady Mauve reached over from the driver's side and opened the passenger door. "Get in," she repeated. "I'll drive you home. Walking in the dark's not safe."

"Ha. You just spent the last two days inventing a thousand ways to kill me, and now you're worried that something could bring me harm? What a joke." I crossed my arms.

"There," she said, pointing back to limbo, "you learn your depths and test your abilities. This," she said, gesturing to the isolated road, "is a dumb idea from an impulsive kid who's sad and tired and wants to go home. I won't be able to sleep if I think you're run over. So get in the car and I'll drive you home. Then you'll be out of my hair for good."

I frowned. "What about my stuff?"

"What about it?" Lady Mauve could barely contain her contempt.

"I can come back another day with my aunt and retrieve it?"

"No, I want your ripped jeans and gray T-shirts all to myself." She rolled her eyes. "Quit stalling. Unlike you, I've got a busy day ahead."

If there was a catch, I couldn't spot it. "Okay... thanks." I got in the car. The truth was, if I was going to walk home all night, I should have worn sturdier footwear. My heels were already starting to wear against the scratchy backing of my shoes.

As soon as my door was shut, Lady Mauve hit the gas. "Won't your aunt be surprised." She eyed me, then looked back at the road.

"I think she'll understand."

"No, I get it. Your partner doesn't like you, so you quit."

"Spade's not my partner."

"I guess not."

"And he only doesn't like me because I don't like him! Did you ever think of that?!"

"I did..." she agreed, but she didn't seem to care. "Put on your seat belt." Annoyed, I dragged the safety measure across my chest. "I just don't think it matters." Lady Mauve shrugged. "Mae, your feelings don't count."

"Gee, thanks."

"Not in the grand scheme of things. Oh, and while

I'm thinking of it, to make things easier for yourself on your transition out of the coven, you should say to your aunt and anyone else that you failed out of limbo instead of quitting. A loser we can stand, but no one likes a quitter. Watch yourself." As she slowed for a stop sign, she held an arm out across my chest. I was already quite tied in by the seat belt. She threw on her blinker and made a right turn.

"What do you mean, make it easier?"

"Oh, you know. For Abeline's feelings. She was probably hoping you'd learn more about Sierra's death. Carry on the family legacy, that sort of stuff. But don't worry. If you *failed*, not *quit*, Abby knows *that* feeling. Runs in the family too, I guess."

I knew she was trying to get a rise out of me but even knowing what she was doing, Lady Mauve's flippant tone stung. "What could I learn about Sierra?" I asked. My eyes narrowed and I watched for any details, but Lady Mauve didn't respond. When I could see she wouldn't answer, I slouched back.

Why bring up Mom's death? She died of a medical diagnosis, not some mystery illness. Sure, the doctors couldn't specifically isolate exactly what had happened, but that was just what was written on her death certificate. I was so young when it went down, how in-depth with a child were they going to be? I'm sure they told my aunt all about it. She knew all the therapeutic details. It wasn't something that needed exploring... but this was what Lady Mauve wanted, to stir up a thousand new questions in my head.

She just drove. Totally ignoring me. Driving me

crazy. Well, I wouldn't give her the satisfaction of begging for answers. I stared out the window, ignoring her too.

The streets started to look more familiar. I tried my best to focus on the fields and recognizable landmarks, but I couldn't feel relieved about the geography with all the other emotions that were bubbling forward in my head.

Finally, I gave in again. "Did you know my mother?"

Lady Mauve just drove, a little smile on her lips.

The lack of medical diagnosis by those doctors was normal. People died of undiagnosed illness all the time. It was nothing special... unless it was... magical.

"Did you...? Do you know something?" I asked.

Her silence was impossible.

"Tell me!"

Lady Mauve frowned. "You need to get a better handle on your emotions, Mae."

I turned bright red but held my tongue.

She made the next few turns in silence, probably just to punish me, but I had learned my lesson. I didn't snap again. I stayed quiet all the way to my street. But the silence wouldn't give me my answers.

"Please," I finally whispered.

She shot me a look and sighed. In two more turns, she pulled into my driveway. "Mysterious deaths tend to be less mysterious when you cross a witches' coven," she said quietly. She turned off the engine. "You're home."

"So it wasn't..." I trailed off, then cut right to the point. "Who killed her?" I tried to match Lady Mauve's tone. Quiet and deliberate. I stared out the front of the car at my family's lake house frontage. The deck, the screened-in porch, our kitchen window. Home. The only place I'd really belonged. The only place I'd ever felt safe.

It was dark. Of course. Aunt Abeline was asleep in her bed. My arrival in the middle of the night would come as quite a shock. Was it really only a few days since I'd been gone? It felt like a lifetime.

"Who killed Mom?" My voice cracked, betraying all the emotion I was bottling inside. I looked away. Lady Mauve was right. I needed more control.

"I don't know, Mae. I'm not a detective. We've arrived, and you're leaving. Out you go."

The choice was clear.

I could quit. I could head back to the lake house, back to a quiet, simple life with my aunt, happy to have someone in my corner to love and trust. Things would be easy. I could grow old quietly, on my own terms, and never know who I really was, what it all meant to be a witch. I would never explore the coven or learn the truth of what really happened to my mom.

Or I could head back to the High Council with Lady Mauve, fight every step of every struggle on my own, battle them all, trust no one, love no one, and learn all the secrets I wanted to know.

"Who's my dad?" I asked.

Lady Mauve smiled. "Now that's a place to start.

But only for a girl who makes it into the High Council."

I sat back and frowned. "Fine." I tried to pull the door handle to let myself out of the car, but Lady Mauve's lightning quick reflexes snapped the door lock button and stopped me from going.

"Fine, what?" she asked. The door didn't budge. This was the first time a little worry had crept into her voice. It was my turn to smile. Calmly, I unlocked the door once more.

"Fine, I'll join your High Council."

Lady Mauve feigned disinterest, but I could tell she relaxed with this news. She reached out to stop me from leaving once more. "Don't you want me to drive you back?"

I gave her a pitying look. "Why bother? We both know we never left."

I got out of the car.

Before my eyes, the lake house I knew and loved faded away, bringing the motel's ugly old exterior back into sight. The house had been a lie-guard illusion. But as I departed the car, it drifted away, disappearing into the night.

"See you in the morning," I told her.

It was hard to tell because Lady Mauve was incredibly tough to read, but as I departed, I thought I saw a little smile.

TWENTY-FOUR
NEW QUESTIONS ASKED AT BEDTIME

I LAY awake for what felt like hours, replaying that last conversation in my head.

My mother's death may not have been natural?

In the context of all I'd seen since arriving in limbo, that made a lot of sense. After all, I'd witnessed a slew of things that science couldn't explain. But it had never crossed my mind that her death might have been a murder.

Who would want to kill her?

How did they do it?

And what role did my father have in all this?

Good old Dad.

Who was he?

Did Lady Mauve actually know him?

Could she ever introduce me? And if we did cross paths, what on earth would I say? The same questions whirred through my mind over and over, lulling me into a restless sort of sleep. Soon, I was dreaming.

Ahead of me, in my dream, I saw a spectacular dining room filled with a giant table with fabric-adorned chairs to seat twelve. Each seat was covered in a rich black velvet. They were the kind of cushioned, oversized dining chairs you could sit on for hours and still be comfortable in. The legs of each seat were meticulously spindled into delicate tubes, making a chain link of wood pearls from the floor to their thrones. The table itself was a dark-stained oak. It had been cut out of the forest and built into a sturdy structure in the center of the room. There was no way it would have fit out the door from which it came unless it was broken into pieces. It was dramatic and large.

On the table was a beautiful centerpiece of greenery and candles, each one flickering mood lighting into the room. Their wax dripped down their spindles, all in white and in different sizes, a collection of melted sticks. The candlestick stems disappeared into a dramatic collection of woven fruits, flowers, and leaves.

Dinner was already on the table.

It was a turkey dinner dressed up with all the fixings of stuffing and mashed potatoes, hand rolls and squash. There were cooked peas and cranberry sauce for days. But the meal didn't stop at one celebratory menu. There was mac and cheese bubbling with breadcrumbs and a chocolate fountain overflowing with decadence. There were bountiful salads served on oversized platters and a breadbasket topped with an edible swan. Other dishes held asparagus with melting butter, sweet potatoes with marshmallow broiled on top, raw vegetables with every type of ranch dip available, every cheese and cracker you could think of, and six or seven different pies.

The table was an opulent feast.

Around it sat all my friends from the High Council reaping.

No one was eating.

They all sat there in silence.

And upon further detailed inspection, although they were each recognizable, they also looked like a strange group of guests.

Nicolette wasn't sitting at the table. Instead, she held on to a ceiling fan hanging in the rafters of the room. Periodically, she tried to reach down to take a bun. She stretched out her hand and swung the fixture back and forth, but it was no use. Her arm couldn't reach the table. At the head of the feast, Beck and Spade ignored the sustenance altogether and instead they drank wine. They swigged the stuff back like water on a hot day, not really tasting it. Their eyes were glassy from consumption. Neither boy even looked at me. They didn't speak to each other, and neither offered a sip to anyone else who was there. Josie sat beside Spade, balled up under a blanket to keep warm. Tej was beside her wrapped in a sheet like a toga, a pillow under his butt like his chair was his throne. Hilde and Vince were even more strange. It looked like a sack of flour had exploded between them. Both were covered in a fine white dust that stuck in every crack and fold of their skin. Its dramatic white color made their eyes appear black as coal. Vince was piling his plate high with mashed potatoes. Up and up his pile went, far more than a single person could consume. On the other side of the table, Greg and Sloane shivered with the cold. They also seemed to need a blanket or sweater or something. But Josie didn't offer to share her bedding. Greg held his legs into his body in a hug and rocked back and forth. Sloane's bare skin looked blue in the low candlelight, and she couldn't stop her teeth from chattering. She too wrapped her legs into her arms in a bid for body warmth. There they sat, in fetal positions. No one offered to warm them, although the last couple could have. Marcy and Rick were weirdly covered in clothes. Rick seemed to be wearing a person's entire wardrobe. On his head, he sported a whole collection of hats, and Marcy had flaunted every scarf and accessory she could find. Obsessively, she whisked the outermost layers around her neck. Over and over. They would fall to her shoulders, and she would whisk them back once more. She must have worn twenty of them. Everyone appeared sort of miserable in their own unique way.

I wanted to salute, to give a toast, to reach out, to give solace or something. At least I felt I could encourage them to eat the dinner, as I didn't want it to be wasted and left alone. But like Nicolette, I couldn't reach them. I realized I wasn't on their level either. I hung above them, huddled on another light fixture, and I couldn't reach the table, no matter how I twisted my body to and fro. I was trapped there, on the ceiling... until suddenly, things started shifting and I fell right through the floor. I hit the dinner table with full impact, white dishes smashing all around me. Luckily, all the blue glassware on the table was saved.

The impact in my dream jarred me back awake in real life.

I sat up with wide eyes, breathing deeply, touching various bones and flab on my body to assure myself I was, in fact, still totally intact. I hadn't actually smashed into a dinner table full of an opulent feast that none of my compatriots were consuming. It was just a strange dream. Another strange vision with small details to assess and interpret. I dragged myself out of bed and took notes of whatever small pieces I could still remember in hopes they'd help in tomorrow's events.

After that, I drifted back to a restless slumber.

Whatever the morning would bring, I'd be ready.

TWENTY-FIVE
YOU WERE RIGHT. I WANT TO WIN

"YOU WERE RIGHT," I told Spade as soon as he came out of his motel room.

I'd been leaning against the bricks by his door frame for over twenty minutes, waiting for him to come out to breakfast, hoping if I caught him in his doorway, we might eke out a moment just to ourselves.

He was surprised, but not in a good way. He didn't even crack a smile.

"I was wrong," I told him again. "And you were right,"

"I know." He crossed his arms in front of his chest, no longer willing to meet me halfway.

"Can I come in?" I looked behind him. His room was just as shabby and small as mine.

"No."

"Fine. I just thought you might wanna win this thing. But if not..." I shrugged.

His eyes narrowed. He considered his options for a

moment, and seeing he was just as stuck as I was, he shuffled aside to let me inside. I slipped into his space. It smelled like him. Only stronger and more manly. He had probably just sprayed cologne.

"Here's how I see it." I paced. A tick I'd inherited from my aunt when she was nervous. "You don't want to partner with me. I don't want to partner with you. But we're stuck together. Even-steven."

"This couldn't wait 'til after coffee?"

"Spade, I want to get into the High Council. I know you do too." Anger flashed in my eyes.

"Oh..." Spade looked surprised but smiled. "Well, alright." He grinned wider. "Finally. No more stupid alliance?"

I shook my head.

"What gives?" He wasn't yet willing to commit.

"You were right," I said again. "I get it. I had one foot out the door. That sucked for you. It sucked for me too. That's over now. I'm ready. I'm all in." I looked out the window to the rest of the teens and Lady Mauve sweetly playing the piano. I could see I hadn't won him over completely, but I didn't have another card to play. "Look, do you wanna partner or not?"

"I don't know."

"Spade!"

"Okay. Fine." He grinned. "I'm in. I've always been in. Shall we seal it with—"

"If you say *a kiss,* I'll drop-kick you right in the face. We're partners. Just partners. No more trying to get yourself into or out of my pants."

"I never wanted *out* of... fine." He grinned. "Pinky swear. Partners 'til the end. We trust each other completely."

"Partners. Full trust. Completely," I agreed. We twisted our pinky fingers together and nodded.

"Which is good cuz we can work together, but I don't have to kiss you. Try to keep your hands off me," he said, cracking a sparkling grin. There was that charm. I'd missed that.

I shoved him.

"Watch it!" He ticked a finger. "Hands to yourself."

"You watch it," I told him, but we were both smiling now.

"Alright, partner. Let's dig up some breakfast." Spade opened the door for me, and we left his motel room together. Several teens looked up, including Josie and Beck, who raised their eyebrows. To the late arrivals at the pool, it might have appeared that we spent the night together, but I didn't care. I just wanted this trial by fire to be over so I could start to learn about the things that really mattered, starting with the name of my father and what really happened to my mom.

I poured myself a cup of coffee, grabbed a plain bagel, and slumped into the chair beside Sloane. Spade and I had agreed to be partners, but spending too much time together was still a bad plan. He was bound to do something soon that I wholeheartedly disagreed with or something else that was more than I likely could stand. Even on his best behavior, our priorities weren't the same.

"You look different," Sloane noted.

"Fighting for your life will do that," I said.

She shrugged. "It wasn't so bad. We're meant to be here." She eyed Tej. He was chatting with Greg and Marcy. None of them seemed to have a care in the world. "So are you," she added.

"You saw it, didn't you?" I realized. "Today? You know how this all goes down."

She nodded. "First, you're gonna help me. Then you'll help yourself." She readjusted as Hilde came over. The tone of her voice during the message she'd just given was quiet. Instinctually, I knew her words were for me alone. I nodded, then smiled brightly at the younger girl.

"What do you think today's adventure will be?" Hilde asked, sitting down on the cement paver at our feet.

I wanted more details from Sloane, but her body language made it clear that our previous conversation was over. Hilde wasn't privy to those notes. How would I help Sloane? All the alliances were over. I was done putting anyone else's needs above my own. Spade and I were headed full speed towards the finish. Run you down and screw you over, no matter what the task required. For us, there'd be no holding back.

"I bet there'll be fire. I kind of dreamed about it," Hilde added with an air of confidentiality. "I'm a bit of a dream-cast myself." We nodded. But neither Sloane nor I offered any detail of the visions we'd seen in last night's slumber.

"When this is over, who do you think will be out?" I wondered, my eyes floating around the group.

"Josie and Beck," the girls answered in unison.

At my surprised look, Sloane softened. "Well, I would have said you and Spade, but today your energy is strong."

I looked across the pool at Spade, who caught my glance. He winked. "Yeah. Some things changed."

Sloane nodded. "The more things change, the more they stay the same."

"My mom says that," Hilde said.

"It's kind of famous." Sloane shrugged.

"Who said it?" I wondered.

"I don't know," Sloane admitted.

"Well, what does it mean?" Hilde wondered.

"I don't know," Sloane admitted again.

"Then why'd you say it?" I questioned.

"I don't know!" We all answered at once. This made us giggle.

Sloane shrugged. She took a long, slow sip of coffee. "It sounded good in the moment," she said with a smile. "I'm all sorts of sage."

Hilde's eyes narrowed in miscomprehension.

"It means truth-teller," I told her. The younger girl nodded. In the background, the piano playing had stopped, and Lady Mauve and Lady Gray were now expecting our full attention.

"Welcome to round three." Lady Gray introduced

the day with just a touch of dramatic flair. "Five of you couples are about to punch their ticket and become officially part of the High Council. Four in round one, and in the final session, fate will select the final pair. For those not chosen..."

"Don't let the door hit 'cha on the way out." Lady Mauve grinned.

"Similar to yesterday," Lady Gray regained the conversation, "you will awaken, then make your way back to the pool hand in hand with your chosen partner. On arrival, you will leap into these waters. Only, unlike yesterday, that tandem leap of faith will cement your parabond selection. From that point on, the selection will be permanent."

"Be the first eight to get wet and you've completed your task," Lady Mauve agreed.

"I'm big on completion," Greg said. Some of the others laughed.

Marcy swatted his sleeve.

Hilde looked to me, but I just shook my head. That wasn't a joke worth explaining.

"Today's task is no laughing matter," Lady Mauve agreed with me. She gave him a pointed glare. "It'll wipe the smile right off your face," she told him.

But she needn't have worried.

Her tone had already succeeded. Greg wilted in place.

"The rest of the teams will, um..." Lady Gray faltered.

"Our final two pairs will knuckle it out head-to-head in a roulette game of fate where only one team will survive," Lady Mauve said.

That brought us all back to earth. We each had a one-in-six chance of being kicked out of the High Council. Those odds weren't great.

"You should know, if you don't make the cut, it was never a personal failing. Fate sorts us all out, guiding our choices to the proper predeterminations. Fate discerns who truly belongs. If your home isn't here at the High Council, fear not. Another journey awaits. No better, not worse. Merely different," Lady Gray assured us.

"And we don't take losers on our squad," Lady Mauve added. She handed out the little yellow pills. "Bottoms up."

I watched the other teens one by one. They each popped the pill in their mouth, and then they swallowed it down. Across the pool, I caught Josie's eye. She nodded to me and put the pill on her tongue. The early adapters already slumped in their chairs.

I turned to face Lady Mauve. She was watching me closely. I put the pill to my lips and swallowed it down. For a moment, I thought I saw her grin.

Then everything disappeared.

TWENTY-SIX
MAKE YOUR OWN EXIT

WHEN THE DRUGS WORE OFF, I awoke in a hot, stuffy room. My back hurt from lying in an awkward position on a hard surface. Unlike in round one and two, this time I was inside a building. And I wasn't alone.

"Nicolette?" I sat up to see the girl.

She looked up from where she'd been going through the contents of an old wooden chest. "Where are we?" she asked.

"I was just about to ask you." Here we go again, I thought.

The temporary bedding that had been so unkind in its lumbar support while I lay on it turned out to be the wood framing and insulation of an attic. While unconscious, we were stuffed into the rafters of a house.

"It's definitely a cubby," I said.

"Some sort of attic," she said.

"Makes sense."

The ceilings were so low, neither she nor I could stand. And we weren't particularly tall women. I hopped up on bent legs and began examining the boundaries of our undersized room. The foldaway ladder door to the floor below was latched shut with a spinning padlock. To open the device, four slots needed the correct answer from a tumbler on the lock. Each tiny wheel was full of a selection of letters. They were fairly large tumblers. It didn't seem there was a way to crack the code just by luck. The locked door was the only exit. There were no other doors or windows in the tiny space above the house. The attic was cramped and dark. The room was illuminated by only a single bulb light that had been activated by pulling a string. Its on-off switch dangled haphazardly in the middle of the room. Shadows gathered in the corners. It was impossible to tell the time of day. Since both Nicolette and I were short, we didn't have to crouch too much, but there really wasn't any room. Moving about was awkward. We had to be careful where we stepped as there was no solid flooring beneath us. Just a wooden frame of rafters and insulation panels stuffed in rows. Falling off the grid could make you crash down through the ceiling, so we were both careful where we stepped.

The only furniture in the room was the wooden chest that Nicolette had already rifled in, and the only decoration was a single sign hanging above the locked, folded door. It was hand-stitched into a crochet design. It read

. . .

*From biggest to smallest, from first to last. The locked
door beneath you so too you shall pass.*

"Ugh, I hate poetry," Nicolette complained. "It's just
not art."

"I don't think it was meant to be art. It's a clue, like
in an escape room," I said. I had seen these sorts of
games in bigger cities and suburbs. People would pay
money to be locked in a live action board game and try
to use logic to answer clues to escape within a time
limit. "It's got to be the key to decipher the padlock.
We just have to figure it out," I explained. "It says 'biggest to smallest'. Anything of variation in the trunk?"

"Just these hats."

Hats...

I blinked.

Rick had been wearing a bunch of hats in my
dream. He was definitely the biggest body among all
the potential parabonders.

"Try Rick and Hilde. They're the biggest and
smallest," I suggested.

Nicolette nodded. She reached for the lock, but
that wasn't enough.

"There are four letters," she said.

"Okay, *R*, then *H*... who was first and last?" I
wondered.

"Jacob and Anita? They arrived at the High

Council first. At least, they were already on the chaises when I got there. And they came in last in yesterday's race."

"Worth a shot."

Nicolette inputted the letters *R H J A* into the tumblers and tugged at the lock. Nothing happened. She shook her head.

"Okay, well who was the first to cross the finish in round one?" I wondered.

"Tej and Sloane."

We tried *R H T S*.

Still nothing.

"*R H T* and *A*—Anita was last," I suggested. It was no use. I sat back on my heels. "We're missing something. Another clue? There should be some logic in the solving."

"It could be the first one to arrive at the motel..." Nicolette offered an alternative solution.

"Or the first to parabond or kiss or... it could basically be anything!" I snapped. I knew freaking out at the girl wasn't helpful, but Nicolette just took my outburst in stride. "Can you truth serum our way out of here?" I asked her.

"No, but I've got a pocket full of crazy glue," she admitted.

At my look, she shrugged. "It worked for Beck and Josie. What about you? Did you dream about this scenario? Any useful tidbits?"

"Yeah, the hats were on Rick's head in my dream. And we were all present. Actually, I was with you..."

I realized. "And we were *above* the rest of the group..."

"Like up in an attic?"

"Not really... but my dreams are rarely clear. We were above, and Rick had hats... so..." I tried to make meaning, but nothing jumped out. "I don't know."

"Well, what were we doing?"

"Sitting down to dinner. But no one was eating... We were paired off in various clothing..."

"And Rick was the only one with a hat on," Nicolette confirmed.

"Yeah. He and Marcy were covered in clothes. We were above them, and now we're locked in an attic. There might be something there."

"They were covered in clothes, so..."

"Maybe they're locked in a closet below!" I blurted out.

That made sense. All the weird wardrobes the teens wore in my dream could represent the rooms they were trapped in inside the house. *This* house.

"Tej wore a toga, and Josie was huddled in a blanket," I recalled.

"Bedroom," Nicolette said, catching on.

"Spade and Beck were in a wine cellar," I added, interpreting the stain of dark red on their lips, teeth, and clothes for myself. "Greg and Sloane were blue from the cold."

"So a fridge? Or a walk-in freezer? Oh, I wouldn't want to be locked in a freezer."

"Hell no."

"What about Vince?" she asked.

"He's with Hilde. They were covered in white powder."

"Flour?"

"Maybe. He could be baking up a storm." We both grinned at the idea of Vince doing anything other than scowling.

"We know where everyone is!" Nicolette exclaimed. For a moment, we felt really proud of this new knowledge, but then the realization kicked in. "How does that help?"

"I don't know," I admitted.

She just nodded. She tipped the trunk on its back legs to look underneath for a secret, hidden message, but all the relocation did was reveal more of the precarious ceiling joists. If we weren't careful where we stepped, we could fall right through.

Which... I realized, was kind of what happened in my dream! We didn't solve a clue in my vision. I reached out for a bun and fell right down to the table. Maybe that was the key? We could make a hole right in the floor!

"Here, help me with this." I pulled the insulation out of one of the two-by-four wooden frameworks and looked at the drywall below.

"What are you doing?"

"We might not need to answer the puzzle. Maybe we can kick our way out of the room." I looked at the powdery white surface and tested the floor for strength. There was definite give to the material.

"You'll fall right through," Nicolette warned.

"My thoughts exactly." I grinned.

I braced my upper body on the attic floor and stomped my weight down on the lower plasterboard. It shook, but didn't crack. Sturdier than I thought.

"Let me help." Nicolette came in beside me.

We both squished our legs into the same wooden framework, our butts on the two-by-four frame.

"Ready?" I instructed. "Go!" We both kicked at the drywall. It shuddered. "One, two, three!"

On the second try, Nicolette's foot smashed through the floor. I caught her upper body to keep her upright and held on tightly to stop her from barreling through to the floor below. She was much heavier than I expected, but still I held on.

"Thanks." She wiggled her foot out of the cavity she'd made. "Now what?"

"Now... we look." I flipped around to look down into the hole. The crack in the ceiling was a fissure into the bedroom below us. The room was large, and where we'd kicked through the ceiling there was only an empty rug below. There was nothing standing between the broken, caved in ceiling and the flat, barren floor.

It did seem like a viable exit strategy.

In the world below, I could see the door to the bedroom was unlocked and wide open. Farther into the hall, there was a stairway leading out to the lower floor. It dawned on me that unlike running through the giant fields of the last exercise, the goal today would be to find your partner and exit the building together, as quickly as possible. By whatever means available.

But unless Nicolette had amazing upper body strength to lower herself down that I didn't know about, a drop from the ceiling to the floor below us was too high a distance to manage. I sure couldn't do it. I would have to jump, or more likely fall, from the level above. A distance like that would result in a twisted knee, or worse, a broken ankle. Some of the guys and their oversized muscles might have been able to perform a reverse pull-up to lower down to safety, but Nicolette and I with our puny twig arms were out of luck.

"Hello!" I called out to the floor below, but no one answered.

There was no movement in the house.

"What do you see?" Nicolette asked.

"It's a bedroom, I think. And there's definitely an exit. But the ceiling is too high." I shook my head, righting myself back into the attic.

"Well, what if we land on the bed?"

"Nicolette, of course!" Impulsively, I hugged her.

She laughed, happy to be a help, but also self-consciously pulled back.

See, I thought to myself. I don't just hug Beck. I hug a lot. I'm a huggable person.

But there was no one here to see or prove that point.

I ducked back down into the hole and looked around the room once more. She was correct. In the back half of the bedroom, there it was. A soft, cushy bed. The perfect spot to land.

I got my bearings and led us to the correct spot in the beams to break a new hole in the drywall that would put us directly above the bed. "Over here."

We stripped the framing joist of its insulation and looked down at the new patch of drywall that stood in our way.

"Ready?" I asked.

Nicolette nodded. "Go." We both stomped down below. Again Nicolette's foot broke through the crisp, powdery surface, and in the jagged, foot-sized opening, we could see the mattress directly below.

"Yes!"

We both stomped at the drywall, chipping away at its edges, creating a larger and larger hole. Drywall powder and small pieces of sheetrock showered the mattress. Dust kicked up our nostrils, but we stayed busy at work. We carried on at the hole in the ceiling, karate chopping away more and more tiny pieces until we could see we had excavated a fairly large void.

"That should do it." Nicolette looked down.

"You wanna go first?" I offered.

She shook her head no. I didn't blame her. The drop from the ceiling to the bed still looked pretty far. The architecture of the room below us likely had fancy vaulted ceilings, and once you dropped out of the beams, there was no guarantee that the bed below us would be soft or cushy, or that we would even land on its bones.

But the padlocked door wasn't about to magically open. I couldn't see a better option. "I'll go."

The hole was big enough for me to pass through, even if still a bit jagged. I gave Nicolette an encouraging smile, although I didn't know why I was trying to make her feel better as I was the one who was taking the risk. I lowered my legs first, gently sinking down until my lower body hung loose in the air, then I shimmied my waist and stomach out into the opening. I tried to hold on to the beam above me. My plan was to gradually lower myself down until I could gracefully drop the last two or three feet to the bed.

Unfortunately, gravity was much stronger than my triceps.

As soon as my body weight was through the hole, my mass was too much to hold, and I dropped out of the ceiling and smashed onto the bed below me like a rag doll. My arms, legs, neck, and body ricocheted off the mattress and took big awkward bounces, seemingly in every direction. Violently, I flew off the bed with incredible force. I shot through the air, then landed face first in a heap on the floor.

TWENTY-SEVEN
THE RACE IS ON

"OH MY GOD! Mae! Are you alright?" Nicolette called down through the hole.

For a moment I stayed perfectly still. "Yeah," I answered sheepishly. "I think so."

I took stock of my extremities.

Every part of me hurt.

I had bounced off the bed and smashed into a slim wall between two locked doors. Their unforgiving structures, probably necessary for the building's framework, hadn't done anything to soften my landing point. My head had dented the wall. It actually put a little crack in it. A forehead-shaped crack. On impact, I had bitten my tongue. I felt the blood in my teeth. It tasted like tin.

"So much for a soft landing." I rubbed my neck. After a moment or two of testing out my individual bones and ligaments, I was able to stand.

Behind me, something slammed on the backside of the door.

"Jeez!" I jumped back.

Someone was trapped inside the closet. Several someones. They pounded on the door. Four hands at once. A cacophony of sound.

"What's that?" Nicolette asked.

"Someone's in there!" I said.

If this was the master bedroom, that little door was likely a closet or a bathroom. Behind that plywood exit might be Marcy and Rick. They banged even more insistently.

"Hurry," I told Nicolette. "We gotta go. Come on."

"You think I'd still jump after that? After *you*?" Her eyebrows shot up.

"I'm all good. You can do it." The pounding on the closet grew louder. "But you gotta do it now," I told her. I checked over my shoulder. For now we were still alone, but whoever was locked inside that room had been inspired by my crashing around. Of course, they didn't know I was breaking walls with my forehead. But they must have realized that if I'd smashed my way out, they could too. We didn't need to solve the clues to escape. Brute force could work too.

Nicolette shook her head and disappeared.

"Come on. It'll hold," I called up to her, pushing on the bed. "The mattress was padded. I just landed funny. I'll try to catch you, but we gotta go. Now."

Bam. BAM!

The closet banging became more systematic and

forceful. Inside, someone had found a workable rhythm. I could see the paneling on the door was starting to splinter and crack. I guessed that inside the room, someone had picked up some sort of device to use as a weapon.

"I can't." Nicolette shook her head. "I'm too heavy."

"No, you're good."

The wood splintered.

"Now, Nicolette," I said.

"I'm too big!"

"That's it." My eyes lit up. "The biggest and smallest! It's us. And I'm first. You're the last!"

The makeshift battering ram reverberated through the closet. They were coming.

I backed away. "It's us, Nicolette! *N M M N*." I took a few steps. "Try it. But, if you're not gonna jump, I gotta keep moving."

"Okay, I got it. Go. Go!" She disappeared back into the attic.

Bam, BAM!

This time, Rick broke all the way through. For a moment, through the fragments of wood, we locked eyes. He stared me down. I backed away. He reached a hulking arm through the opening he'd cracked. His giant palm tried to reach the doorknob but couldn't quite make it. I turned and fled.

"No. Mae, wait!" He shouted.

"Outta the way," I heard Marcy tell him, then came

another giant crash. She must have smashed through the door with another kind of a weapon. It made a terrible noise, but I didn't stay to see if they'd finally emerge.

The race was on.

I sped into the hallway. I had to get to Spade before the others. The first pairs out of the house were the winners. And I knew right where to look. He would be in a wine cellar.

Aunt Abeline and I usually lived in tiny two-bedroom apartments on the ground floor or in basement apartments, but I knew in fancy mansions, the wine cellar would be located on a lower level, down where it was cold. Usually a basement. At least that was where they were in the movies.

As I made the turn down the stairs, I could see in the same wing, another bedroom door on the floor was burning. Flames crept up the paneling from the ground. Tej and Josie's faces were crammed in the hole by the floor. They were contentedly observing it burn until they saw me race by.

"Damn it, hurry," Tej complained.

"You want me to burn this place down?" Josie asked.

"No, I want you to *hurry*," he said. "Mae, stop!"

I blew right by, descending the stairs as fast as my legs would take me. The lead was mine. I couldn't waste it. My head start through the house would be barely a minute, but based on the dream that I'd envisioned, I felt confident I knew where to go. At the first floor, I skipped the landing and ran straight down to the basement.

I was right. The wine cellar was directly in front of me at the base of the stairs.

The walls were thick glass, with rows and rows of one-of-a-kind bottles, all on their sides so the flavor wouldn't be lost and their corks wouldn't dry out. The racks stood in stoic rows all lined up there for ogling. Just waiting to be opened in their fancy, temperature-controlled apartment. But nothing prepared me for the sight between the shelves.

"Spade!" I rushed forward. "Oh my god! What happened?"

Inside the see-through cage, Spade, Beck, the floors, and even the walls were covered with dark red blood.

TWENTY-EIGHT
THE HOUSE OF MANY HORRORS

"OH MY GOD!" I ran full tilt at the glass, slamming my palms on the panes, but the see-through structure didn't budge. "What are you doing? Stop!" I pummeled the window, headed to the wine cellar door.

"Mae!" Spade ran to the other side of the pane.

Beck ran out of the wine racks. "It's wine. It's just red wine," he assured me, seeing the horror on my face.

Oh, thank god. My color returned.

"We must look terrible," Beck told me.

But Spade didn't care how they looked. "How'd you get out?"

"There was a riddle." I shook my head. "But we broke free through brute smashing."

"We've got a clue too!" Beck ran to grab it.

"You and Josie?" Spade asked.

I shook my head. "Nicolette. I fell through the ceiling. I hit my head." I leaned real close to show him.

Spade smashed a bottle on the wall between us, exactly where my face would have been. It shattered, shooting white wine in every direction. I leapt back, protective, but the impact didn't even scratch the glass. Spade gave a small smirk.

"We tried with force. Nothing works," he told me.

"Well, maybe from this direction?" I took a few steps back, then ran at the wall. I thumped my own bodyweight against the glass door from the outside but merely succeeded in rattling the wall. It hurt me more than the cellar.

Above, there were footsteps.

"Oh, shoot." I looked overhead.

The others were getting closer. We were losing our advantage.

Beck came running back. "Here. Here's the clue. Here's the sign." He held up a hand-crocheted placard like the one I'd seen in the attic. Only theirs was soaked blood red with wine. It read

If time rewinds years as you sleep, how old by year is Cruella DaVeet?

They looked up at me.

"Who the heck is Cruella DaVeet?" Spade asked.

"Check the labels. It's got to be one of them," I offered.

The boys raced around the room.

"Mae." Another voice called from deeper in the basement hall.

I looked around but saw nothing. Distracted, I glanced back to the boys.

Knock, knock.

I'd been so intent on the boys in their glass enclosure at my arrival, I hadn't even looked around the rest of the dingy basement.

"Mae, is that you? It's me, Sloane." The voice floated out again. She was trapped behind a door at the end of the hall.

"What about under there?" I ignored Sloane and tried to direct Spade from my outside perspective. He could barely hear me over his own frantic rush. Both boys contributed to the chaos, tugging bottle after bottle off the shelves. They checked the words on the labels, then smashed all the rejects to bits on the floor.

"Mae. It's me. Sloane. Let me out!"

I looked in her direction, but Beck and Spade beckoned...

"Mae, it's me. You know what to do..."

A moment passed, then she rapped gently on the door. Almost too quiet to hear.

Knock, knock.

Let me out, the tender knocking said. First you help me, then yourself.

Set me free...

Her words tingled in the back of my brain.

I kept watch on the guys, but something drew me to her door.

"No, under that—behind the barrel chest. What's that one over there?!" I called to Spade as I wandered farther back towards her.

He tried all my suggestions, but to no avail. They still hadn't found Cruella DaVeet.

"First me, then yourself," Sloane called softly through the wood shell. "It's time to let us out."

My attention split in two directions. Without really thinking about it, I opened the exterior latch to their cell. The door swung open, letting a very cold Sloane and Greg out into the basement. Their lips were as blue as their skin. They'd been locked in a cold cellar with no exterior access. Another crocheted clue poem was discarded on their floor. The cement room was damp and chilled.

"Holy snot balls, you actually did it," Greg congratulated Sloane, then smirked at me. "Thanks, babe." He laughed as he pushed by me. "Couldn't have done it without you." He patted my back.

"Mae." Sloane smiled. "You did well." They both ran for the stairs.

"You're welcome." I nodded. In a daze, I watched them depart.

"Why'd you do that?!" Spade slammed his fists on the glass, shocking me back to reality.

"What? I... I don't know," I admitted.

"Why'd you help them?"

"It just happened," I cried. "I don't know." I looked down at my hands. It was like they'd had a mind of their own.

"We're fighting for our lives here!" I could tell Spade was about to rip me into a thousand little pieces. He'd have every right to do so. I didn't know what had come over me. Why had I opened the door? They were our direct competition. I knew that. But it had been like a reflex. I wasn't thinking. Sloane's voice was so cool and so calm. She had lured me in. Spade's face boiled red in frustration.

"I know, Spade. I know. I'm sorry. It was dumb. Keep looking for the bottle."

Luckily, Beck saved me from my faux pas. "I got it." He raced back to our sides. "Cruella DaVeet. It's twelve years old." He showed us the precious bottle.

"Enter twelve," Spade instructed.

Beck had already picked up the locked number dial. "1, 2."

"No," I interrupted. "Read the clue. It's twelve minus sleep for each day. How much do we sleep? Eight hours?"

"Give or take," Beck agreed. He followed my logic. "Oh, I get it. We need to take eight out of each twenty-four hours for all the twelve years..."

All three of us studied the numbers, trying to do the math in our heads. But I couldn't concentrate. Now that we'd stopped all the frantic smashing, a new sound in the basement could be heard. Something strange, like a scratching. It was coming from down the hall.

I spun around.

Behind me in the basement, beside the room that Sloane and Greg had left from, there was another doorway. From there, the sounds were building. Something scratching. But it wasn't a door being brutalized. It was something else... something I couldn't put a finger on.

At just that moment, a knife burst through the plaster wall. No, not a knife. Something makeshift and sharp. Maybe a shard of mirror?

It hacked a rugged hole in the wall beside the exit.

Mirror shards were ripping the wall to pieces. The hands that held them chopped and carved. I caught a glimpse of Vince and Hilde. They were slicing their way through the drywall. The panel between the two doorways began to crumble. Two more teens would soon be out. They were dusted and coughing.

I thought back to my vision. It turned out I was wrong. They weren't covered in flour. The white powder was from the splintering sheetrock. It coated their arms and faces as they tried to break through the middle of the wall.

"Guys, we gotta hurry." I brought my focus back to Beck and Spade.

Vince and Hilde only added the pressure.

"How could we possibly do all that math in our heads?! Twelve years of twenty-four hours minus eight? That's too much." Spade rattled the lock.

I tried to see Vince and Hilde's appearance as good news. At least we weren't the only ones still trapped in our cell. "What if there's a simpler calculation?" I asked.

"Yeah, okay." Beck came on board. "It's a percentage. Eight out of twenty-four hours is one third. We sleep one third of the day, so take one third off her total age..."

"Eight!" We both solved it at once.

"That's not it. It's two digits." Spade held up the lock

"Try 0-8," we both shouted.

"Cute party trick," Spade muttered, but he inputted the code. "Zero... eight. It worked!" Spade tugged open the lock. I jumped up and down and headed to their door. The boys came to meet me on the other side.

"Math for the win." Beck raised a hand to give Spade a high five, but when Beck tried to exit the cellar, his partner shoved him back into the room.

"Not for you," Spade said.

Beck fell back, just a step or two, but that was enough. From the ceiling, out of nowhere, iron bars slammed between him and the way out. Spade's hand had dropped into a fist and he balled it up to set the trap and lock Beck in the wine room with a new lie-guard illusion.

"Spade!"

"What the hell!" Beck flung himself at the iron bars, but they held tight.

"What are you doing?" My eyes bugged out of my head.

But with his free hand, Spade just grabbed me and pulled me to come along. "This is the deal you made." He glared at me, daring me to take Beck's side. I wilted. "I bought us some time. Come on!"

There were no teams of three in the High Council.

I glanced back over my shoulder. "Sorry," I mouthed.

Beck's face dropped, but we both knew I couldn't help him.

Spade and I ran up the stairs just as Vince and Hilde's bloody arms burst through the drywall. Their hole was larger too. They would be out of their prison really soon. The space they'd cleared was almost big enough for Hilde, but the shards of raw mirror were taking their toll. They had slashes and gashes in their skin. Blood dripped down both their arms. But the pair didn't care. As they reached through the hole, they splattered crimson handprints on the walls.

"Spade!" Beck rattled his cage.

"Change your perspective," I called back, but even that I regretted. Spade was right. All alliances were over. We'd need every extra second of lead time that we could manage. Hand in hand, Spade and I bounded up to the first floor, taking the stairs two at a time. Suddenly, as we reached the foyer, we heard a desperate cry.

"Ahhh! Tej!"

Spade dug into his heels to stop, and I crashed into his back. We looked at the new scene in surprise. Several others were already watching.

"Sloane, I got you. Hold on!" Tej cried.

I pushed around Spade to see the blonde competitor straddling her slender frame over dramatic holes in the flooring tiles. Several of the porcelain squares from the tile pattern were crumbled and gone. A chasm exposed beneath. The foyer landing was pockmarked with voids. When a tile broke away, there was nothing to stop you from falling. No framing, no subflooring; beneath those thin porcelain tiles was just a deep, cavernous hole. Sloane's tapered hands clutched a blue tile while the rest of her body splayed out across several other slates, all trying to hold. Beneath her, both her long legs dangled into the holes.

Tej laid himself out like one might do on a sheet of cracking river ice in mid-December. He pulled her back out of the void, dragging her body across the foyer, trying to balance the weight beneath them to stop more fissures from opening under their frames.

So this was the next step in our journey.

A floor-length booby trap of danger.

Only the blue-colored tiles in the floor pattern could hold any bodies. The others deteriorated on contact. They crumbled away.

"I got you," Tej told her.

It was the first time I'd ever seen Sloane with even so much as a hair out of place. Tej took his time to guide her back to safety, but their danger was our opportunity. The initial shock over, the rest of us jumped right in.

"Come on." Marcy grabbed Greg's hand, and the pair began the treacherous path across the hall, blue tile by blue tile.

"Where's Beck?" Josie asked. She and Rick had stalled in shock at Sloane's predicament. Now that she was almost safe, they ran past, headed to try to find their partners in the rooms on the lower floor.

"Still trapped," I admitted. But like a chicken, I didn't tell her why. She nodded and raced down to find him. How they would unlock those magic bars together, I had no clue. But they were no longer my concern.

It looked like the analysis we'd all made of the blue tiles was correct. They were holding without further booby traps. Sloane, and Tej were now all back on the floor. It was time to get out there.

"We got this." I grabbed Spade's hand. We followed the blue porcelain footsteps, trying to push ourselves in front of the couple coming from the left while moving safely across the floor.

"Mae!" Nicolette shouted from the staircase. She had just run down the stairs. "Where's Vince?"

"You have to find him!" I called over my shoulder, not looking back. If my basement interaction with Sloane had taught me anything, it was to keep my mind focused on the most pertinent task. One slip up here would result in a dangerous fall. Again I wondered just how far the High Council would go while plumbing the hands of fate. Would we face grave bodily injury? They seemed pretty willing to test the depths of our skills.

Some introduction to the Council.

Greg and Marcy squeaked ahead, but Tej and Sloane didn't let Spade and I pass. We all squeezed down the hallway in a bottleneck, moving from blue square to blue square as quickly as we could.

Suddenly, Vince burst on the scene. "Move," he said without hesitation. He saw the messy scene on the landing and the pattern in front of him, and he knew just what to do. He grabbed Nicolette's hand in his bloody palm, and a fourth couple moved out on the course.

"This is all too close," I muttered.

"Just watch your step," Spade said.

"You're bleeding," Nicolette said in a worried voice behind us.

"It's mostly Hilde's. She cut herself pretty badly," Vince said.

My ears perked at this. My little Hilde? She was injured? Where was she? I looked over my shoulder, but there was no sign of the younger girl. She and Rick were still one floor below. At least I felt sure he would help her. I hoped she was okay. My foot caught the edge of a white tile, and it crumbled below me.

Spade grabbed my arm. "What did I say? Keep your head in the game."

"I got it." I frowned. Again I checked over my shoulder. Still no sign of either partner.

"Stop looking for your boyfriend," Spade snapped.

"I was looking for Hilde. I can have human emotions and still win this game."

"Is that what you think?"

"Damn it!" Tej picked the wrong route and ran out of blue tiles. He had to backtrack to make around the final turn. Spade raised an eyebrow and smiled at this event, but we had no time to celebrate.

"What the hell is that?" Marcy asked. She and Greg arrived at the end of the hallway.

"It's like a real life game of The Floor is Lava," he murmured back to us. "Except look... the floor is seriously full of lava. The room is freakin' on fire. You'd have to be a maniac to cross to that door."

"Whoever created this house is seriously messed." Marcy frowned.

"That way," Greg said. The lovebirds had checked both options available and headed away from the lava-filled room.

"Hilde dreamed of fire," I whispered.

"We can catch 'em," Spade encouraged. He pushed forward even faster.

"Careful!" I noted as a sloppy toehold from him shattered a mix of white tiles underfoot. Their porcelain shards tumbled into the unknown.

Hilde had dreamed of fire and I had dreamed of *this*. This hallway. Sort of. All the white dishes in my dream had shattered, while all the blue ones held firm. That wasn't a coincidence. I was really having visions. I would have to improve at understanding them before they actually happened instead of parsing their details after the knowledge was too late. But that's what the High Council was for. A chance to develop.

As we arrived at the end of the foyer, we too could see the house diverged into two different options. Two different directions with very disparate, dangerous themes in the rooms. To the left was the lava chamber that Greg and Marcy avoided.

We could see their analysis was correct. It was like the children's game The Floor is Lava. There were traditional living room pieces of furniture set up around a room above a floor ablaze with fire. Unlike the kids game, the stakes here weren't imaginary. Over every inch of floor was a melee of flowing, bubbling lava. Even the reflective heat bouncing up from below was intense. It was clear the idea was to travel from furniture piece to furniture piece without ever touching the magma. Because if you did, your skin would scald in a matter of seconds. Every surface in the room licked with fire. The edges of each field of safety bubbled and popped with significant threat. Real heat. Real fire. Real lava. To make this your exit strategy was to seriously risk your life.

But at the far end of the room, there was a doorway.

Did the pool rest behind it? There was only one way to find out.

In the opposite direction, there was a watery option. The second route was a kitchen. A supremely dangerous and sunken kitchen with deep flooded wet floors. Ground to counter, the room was floating with water, but the depth made it clear if you dove in, you wouldn't be touching the bottom. This magical well was cold and deep. The parts of the room above sea level had all the usual counters and tabletops and appliances of a regular kitchen, but unlike in a normal kitchen, there were plenty of things to beware of. The electrical work was rough and unfinished. In several spots, live wires dangled dangerously close to the pool. Electricity and sparks flew on every path you could journey. And we all knew water and live electrical wires were a dangerous duel.

If the exposed wires touched down, anyone in the water would be electrocuted. If that wasn't enough, the walls and counters were covered in traps. There were knives and hot pots. Blades hung down. The heating elements were on, blazing hot. Unsheathed and sharp landings spattered the routes. While this room wasn't hot to the touch, it held similar dangers. If you slipped even a toe in the water, there was a good chance you might be electrocuted, and if you jumped too fast or too far on the counters, you'd get burnt or sliced on the spot.

Like the lava living room beside it, the underwater kitchen also had a doorway. There was no way to tell where that exit might go. We'd have to pick our poison.

"I vote water," Spade said.

I nodded.

We chose as did Greg and Marcy before us. They had a bit of a head start, but we quickly headed out on the course. As he made the first jump, Spade could see he'd need both hands to compete on the obstacles. Whether Josie and Beck had gotten free or not, the illusion in the wine cellar had to go. He released his palm without ceremony. One floor below, Beck was released.

Spade and I were fast, jumping from item to item to get across to the door.

"Watch out for the water," I warned, pointing at the sparks emerging from the element on the stove.

"Oh, no. You can touch it." Greg grinned. "If you like the smell of fried chicken." He laughed.

Spade didn't retort.

"He's calling you chicken, did you get that?" Marcy teased.

"Oh, I get it," Spade told them. "And I'm comin'." Spade's confidence and agility made quick work of their lead.

Greg had taken the more precarious route of climbing up and over the fridge and rock climbing across the upper cabinets, relying mostly on upper body strength to move through the room. Spade and I followed Marcy's more realistic route of chair-to-chair access. With steady feet you could make quick progress through the pathway. And with a little luck and her natural hesitations, our sure-footedness meant we were narrowing in.

"Go the other way," Marcy complained. "I feel crowded." She stalled on a spinning kitchen stool. Around and around the little chair went.

"Not to worry Marce, we'll be out of your way soon." Spade leapt to bypass the chair she was standing on and landed on the next seat in the matching dining collection.

"Sorry," I apologized, but didn't slow down. I held on to his hand and jumped and hopped where he stepped. Our momentum carried us past her. Suddenly, we were in the lead.

"Greg! They're passing!"

Greg's shortcut had brought him only one jump from the exit, but it was a mistake for him to go out there. He needed Marcy to finish with him. He looked back over his shoulder and assessed his other moves. He leapt off the upper cabinets onto a ceiling fan. It shook and slumped with his weight.

"Watch out!" Marcy screamed.

I gasped, but the light fixture held.

"Keep moving," Spade instructed.

I tried to ignore them, but I saw their continued progress out of the corner of my eye. Greg held onto a blade of the fan, which, in its slow rotation, spun him around to the back of the room. He dropped down on the counter behind the kitchen table.

"Go." I pushed Spade forward. From his new spot, Greg had an easier track to the exit, but it was a tough route for Marcy to claim.

"You got this baby." Greg held out his arms. "Make the jump. You know I'll catch you."

Spade and I snaked forward, chair by chair, in all, six to cover. Him taking the risks, and me bringing up the rear. Behind us, Nicolette and Vince entered the kitchen. On the tile routes in the hallway, Tej and Sloane must have further stalled.

No one wanted to tackle the lava.

Once again, Vince's climbing experience came in handy. He could scale any item. The boy had no fear.

He climbed over the appliances in the same route that Greg had taken, but he could move at an incredible pace. Left on her own, Nicolette floundered. She tentatively reached out to make her first move.

"We gotta go," I muttered. "I'm right behind you," I assured Spade.

"Big jump, babe," Greg coaxed Marcy. "You got this."

Marcy could see their only chance to pass us was to leap across the room. It was a daring jump from a small bench to the oversized counter where Greg stood waiting. She wouldn't get much lead but they didn't have another choice. She took a moment to gather her courage, her hands balled at her side, then she went to the far side of the chair, turned, and ran towards her man.

She leapt over the water, arms outstretched. I couldn't help but gasp. She wasn't going to make it. Her eyes widened, as she fell! But suddenly, a giant hawk swooped into the room. Its talons snatched her clothing, and its strong feathers pumped their wingspan to give the two a lift. The mighty bird raised her an inch or two forward, then released its giant claws. Marcy dropped to the other counter and it was just the height they'd need. Greg snatched her from the air. He pulled her to the safety of his counter.

As quickly as the hawk appeared, already it was gone. Had it ever really been there?

I wasn't sure. But Marcy made it.

From there, the path to the door was smooth sailing. They had only one more small jump down onto a cement riser in front of the door. Greg yanked open the handle. Blinding sunlight burst into the room.

"Sunlight!" Nicolette yelled.

We could all see that the door led to the backyard. Just where we wanted to go.

Greg and Marcy cheered with each other, ran right through the opening, and slammed shut the door. They had beaten us by mere seconds to victory.

"Come on!" Spade called as he made the final jump.

I reached out a hand and landed beside him. Over my shoulder, I flashed an excited smile at Vince and Nicolette. They were also almost there as well. Tej and Sloane had also finally appeared. Since they were the fourth couple to stand in the opening of the two foyer options, I realized that meant the bottom two teams would be Rick and Hilde, and Josie and Beck. That was sad because I had grown to love all four of those competitors. It was crazy to think they would have to compete head-to-head. But that wasn't something I could control. It was up to the hands of fate. I was in this now. I'd given my full allegiance to Spade.

I'd pinky sworn. But we hadn't yet finished.

"Ready?" Spade smiled.

I nodded. "Let's do this."

He cranked the handle on the door, but the exit didn't budge. "No." He dropped his smile and wrenched the knob with both hands, but the extra grip didn't help. The hardware didn't budge.

"What are you doing? What happened?" I too cranked the handle, but the doorway didn't open. I pushed on several spots on the door, but it was no use. We were still trapped.

"The portal closed!" Tej told Sloane.

Still closest to the foyer, the taller pair spun and backtracked across the blue tiles to make it through to the other exit choice—the path across the lava.

"Damn it!" Spade kicked the door. Now he and I were at the back of the pack.

"Turn around, go!" Vince instructed.

Harried, Nicolette turned around and remade the jump she'd just completed. For his part, instead of going back up over the refrigerator, Vince solidified his handhold on the freezer door then cranked it open, swinging himself across the floor length on the hinges of the door. It was a smart move. He quickly swung all the way back to Nicolette.

Tej and Sloane were getting away! Vince and Nicolette were too.

I realized there was no way we could make it back across all those kitchen chairs in time to compete for the other exit. "We gotta swim," I told Spade, coming to the only conclusion.

"What about the short circuits?"

"It's a risk," I admitted. "But I don't believe they would electrocute us. That's how a lie-guard loses power, right? If they can't convince us that it's true?"

Spade wasn't sure. "Really?"

No, I have no clue what I'm doing.

"For sure," I told him.

"Whoa!" Nicolette screamed as the tiny high chair she was balanced on buckled under her weight.

"I got you!" Vince grabbed his partner. If we were going to catch them, this would be our only opportunity.

"Okay. I say we do it," Spade said. He could see that I was right. It was our only chance.

"On three," I told him, changing my stance into a dive position. "One, two..."

Spade braced his body for watery impact. "Three."

We both leapt.

I half-expected a lightning bolt to jolt through my system, but only the vibrant shock of cold water hit my skin. We were both strong swimmers, and the speed and trajectory of our dives brought us back to the foyer quite quickly.

I was right. That watery risk put us back in front of Vince and Nicolette. They had stalled. She didn't want to let go of the high chair, but she also didn't trust it to hold her.

Unfortunately, they weren't the only ones to worry about. There was even more competition in the hall. Rick and Hilde had finally arrived on the stairs. Both her wrists were wrapped in bandages made up of strips of Rick's missing T-shirt. He stood bare chested and her hands were covered to her elbows in the makeshift gauze. There was no way to see how bad the injuries were, but the fabric they'd used to blot them had already turned a deep crimson red. They were starting to cross down the tiles. I hoped she would finish the course quickly to get some proper medical attention as well.

Farther in the background, Josie and Beck came also.

Our early cohort lead had disappeared. This would be a race between all of us of only one or two moves.

It was easy for the late arrival couples to discern the pattern of safe travel on the blue-tiled hallway, as most of the white tiles had already crumbled into oblivion. For them, it was clear game of hopscotch. But I couldn't focus on their journeys. Spade and I had to get out of the water and across a room full of lava before the portal closed once more.

Tej and Sloane worked their way across the living room furniture ahead of us. With the threat of electric shock in the kitchen diminished, this path to exit seemed much, much worse. There was no room for even the smallest of errors. The floor was so hot it would scorch your extremities even on contact, so any move between the furniture had to be precise. But the magma was also flowing, flooding over its own molten hot lava, sometimes bursting to the surface, sputtering burning material and steam. You couldn't risk a wrong move. There was no way we could catch Tej and Sloane before they reached that exterior door. With our upper arms, both Spade and I lifted ourselves out of the kitchen water and onto the ledge of the foyer. But it was already too late. We saw the flash of sunlight as Sloane and Tej successfully exited out of the living room door.

"Come on." Spade held out a hand. If we hurried, we were still in a good position to make the next exit. But I stopped.

"What if the exit portal ricochets back and forth?" I whispered. "One door, then the other."

Spade looked at the door we'd just left. "Damn it. You're right."

There was no time to discuss it further. If we wanted to be one of the top four couples, there was only time to act. We dove along the route we'd just come through, plunging back into the water. My body cut through the liquid quickly, Spade right beside me. We made a beeline for the door. Only we couldn't swim there.

Suddenly, from nowhere, a tremendous current built underwater. It sloshed us out of the middle of the room and tossed our bodies over to the broken appliances at the side.

"Spade!" I shouted, gasping in water. The current dragged me down, kicked me around in a whirlpool. I kicked with all my might to resurface, no longer sure which way was actually up.

Luckily, a hand grabbed my arm and yanked me to the surface. As my face breached the surface, I choked and gasped.

"Hold on!" Spade yelled. He grabbed a cupboard door and pulled me to him. He helped me put my hands on the particle board door. The current thrashed the cabinet short. There was no way to swim through the kitchen waters because this unrelenting current wasn't found in physics or science. The typhoon that had gripped and thrown us had come from a magical source.

Vince.

He had his hand held to his side and his face twisted in concentration. He used his energy to split the kitchen water into two parts just like we'd seen at the quarry, only here, in such a small body of water, that harnessing power created savage currents for anyone else in the pool. He and Nicolette ran across the open floor, climbed up the cement risers, and turned our the kitchen door.

It opened.

They disappeared into sunlight.

"Damn it!" Spade smacked the water.

Without Vince to hold the waves in check, they crashed back to the floor. We held on to the cupboard through the initial throttling of currents, but the second it was calm enough, we both dove for the foyer floor. We knew immediately what to do. There was only one option.

"Come on!" Spade encouraged as we clamored back to the foyer.

"Next one's through the lava," I told him.

"Next and last," he agreed.

We were able to cross the foyer to the living room just as the other couples arrived. Their eyes went wide at the scenery.

"Hold my arm!" I didn't even hesitate; we had to get onto the pathway first. As Spade grabbed my hand, I swung a leg over the popping lava bubbles, trying to reach the first sofa end table in the journey. The reach was a stretch, but there wasn't time to be scared. I danced my tippy-toes onto its surface, then made the lunge. I landed the first step safely, letting out all the breath I didn't even realize I'd been holding. Next, I spun round. To make the route clearer for Spade to jump, I kicked a decorative globe off the table surface. The paperweight bounced onto the sputtering lava's, and the heat from the magma liquified all the countries of the world. We couldn't help but watch it boil to nothing, then disappear forever into the burning hot ground. One wrong step and that would be one of our appendages. Spade and I glanced at each other. The danger here in the living room wasn't pretend.

"We can do this," he told me. I nodded as he jumped to meet me on the small table.

Beside us, Rick and Hilde had also entered the field. They realized they couldn't simply follow or pass us, so they picked the more dangerous route to journey that would require hanging from draperies and taking bigger chances—a scary choice for anyone, but especially frightening for someone with sliced fingers and arms. But they weren't wrong. It was their only chance. Maybe if it got too dicey, they were counting on Rick's giant wingspan to carry them through.

The race was on.

Spade and I hopped our way across the next sofa,

then we stopped on the farther arm rest to plan our next route.

"Stop!" Josie shrieked. "I have a glue bomb, and I'll use it."

From the entrance to the lava, she held up a sock bomb, like the kind she'd used on Jacob and Anita. This time, she shook the initial ingredients and the reactive chemicals into one bomb. We all froze for a moment while Josie wildly looked on.

"Go!" Spade shouted. "A moving target it harder."

I took the first plunge, stepping out onto the table I'd just cleared. Spade followed. We were too far on the course for her to be assured of a direct hit, especially since she only had one bullet.

Hilde and Rick also picked up their pace. Their route choices seemed to get wilder and wilder, but maybe they were just trying to make themselves harder to reach. Josie resealed her sock full of chemicals, mixed and primed and ready to go. There were two teams to immobilize. But she could stop only one. They whispered a plan to one another. Who would they pick?

Surely we'd be toast.

Spade and I had crossed and recrossed them. In fact, he'd already double-crossed Beck earlier this round. Our only hope was to create a difficult moving target. Josie took aim. She grunted and threw the glue bomb. I peeked over my shoulder and prepared for impact.

But I was wrong.

The projectile wasn't coming for Spade and me.

She hurled it at Hilde and Rick. But they were ready for it. In her own defense, Hilde dropped both her arms and harnessed a huge gust of wind. Just like we'd seen her do with the water by the pool. This time, instead of liquid, she blew the chemical bomb back onto the foyer, where it burst on its deployers, covering both Josie and Beck.

"No!" Josie screamed as their limbs stuck together.

"What the hell," Beck complained.

Spade and I could only watch with horror, then relief that we hadn't been caught in the cross-fire. Also, we both realized Hilde was a lot more powerful than anyone had given her credit.

"I thought you said she was a dream-cast," Spade whispered, frowning.

"Well, yeah. That's what she said. But remember at the pool? With the wind? I forgot she did that." My eyes widened. "Holy crap. Hilde has two powers," I realized.

"Maybe more," Spade agreed. "No wonder she was inducted so young."

I made the jump to the coffee table on the route to the reclining armchair. "What did Sloane call them?" I tried to remember. "A twofer? No, that's not it."

"Whatever she is, we've still got to beat them. It's us versus them. Quickest now to the door."

We were following the successful path we'd seen Sloane and Tej take a little earlier. It was clearly the smartest route. Hilde and Rick had seemed to paint themselves into a corner. I wasn't even sure from where they'd journeyed, what other path to the door they could take. All the furniture seemed to dead end in their direction. But, when I peered over my shoulder to see how close Rick and Hilde had moved behind us, I was surprised to see they weren't jumping from thing to thing. They had stopped.

"Spade…" I pointed. Rick was slathering some sort of concoction on their feet. "He's a chemist…" I remembered. "She knew there'd be fire. Oh, damn. They must have found a spell. You've got to use an illusion to stop them. It's the only way to level the field," I warned Spade.

"Just go. Just hurry." He pushed me forward.

I made the next jump, but as soon as I landed, I peeked back again. Rick was testing it out his concoction. Whatever was on the bottoms of his feet, it held safe against the fire. He could stand and walk on lava.

"Go, move!" Spade was running at full force. He didn't wait for me to invite him across.

"Do something to slow them down."

"Keep moving."

"Spade! Do something!"

"I *can't*." He frowned. "I can't, okay? I used up all my power."

"What? When?"

"Stopping Beck."

"Are you for real? In the wine cellar? What a waste."

"Well, I didn't know his partner was going to glue them in the foyer," he snarled. "Now keep moving."

"We got this, Jo," Beck encouraged Josie in the foyer.

"No, we don't. Stop saying that." I couldn't see her face, but frustration showed in her voice. "We're at the back of the pack as usual!" Even though Josie had brought another antidote with her, they knew they'd never catch Hilde or Rick. Whatever mixture Rick was able to coat on their feet, it salved their skin and dulled their senses. Hilde tested it next, precarious at first, but she too grew more confident. The mixture held. Even on lava, their feet didn't burn. They practically skated to the door. With bloody sleeves and slick feet, the final couple leapfrogged past Spade and I and yanked open the exit.

Sunshine poured in.

The twosome raced out. They disappeared from view, and the door slammed shut. Darkness engulfed us. We were in the bottom four.

TWENTY-NINE

FOUR OF US LEFT, TWO SPOTS
TO FILL

I AWOKE to the familiar hum of the mouse deterrent buzzer. I was back.

In my motel room.

In my bed.

Tucked under the covers, like I'd been after all the other events. Even teamed up and fully committed, Spade and I had failed to pass the test. Again. The other four teams in the original defunct alliance had all found their way through to the High Council. Their parabonds were reinstated. Leaving the four of us left, with only two spots to fill.

Me and Spade.

Or Josie and Beck.

Four beats two, I muttered to myself.

This, I realized, could have been what my card playing dream referenced. In fact, any stage of what had happened in the last few days could have been part of the interpretation of the game in my dreams.

Maybe Spade was right, and I was never meant to help Josie and Beck in the early tasks. I'd just misread my dream's purpose. There were too many ways to interpret each and every thing in my visions I'd seen.

But the dreams were the only power I had, so I went over the details once more.

I stared down at the papers where I'd accounted for both visions in great detail. Card games, tumbling tapestries, the suicide king, a giant duck waddling in. Some of these things had happened. Others were subconscious rivers of information, dribbling down the page. It was impossible to know which scratches of the pencil held incoherent musings and which were the true guides that could help bring a victory. They were like clues or hints, never answers. I sighed and wished again that my witch powers gave me a more concrete skill or task.

My head hurt.

I sat back and thought things over.

I didn't know when the last round of competition would start, and I didn't really care. Whenever it was, I'd be ready. It was a fight I had to win—at direct cost to Josie and Beck, the two I'd sworn were my closest friends. Could I really turn my back on them and destroy their destiny?

I couldn't see another path.

If I didn't ascend to the High Council, the truth about my family would never be discovered. My father's identity... my mother's mysterious illness... her *murder*? That word was still too fresh to say out loud. It seemed crazy to think there was someone out there who had wanted to kill Sierra. Who succeeded! But why? What did she do? I couldn't give up now. I had to learn the truth.

Our only strategy would be to employ Spade's skills at the last possible moment and wait and to see our advantage, where an illusion would work, where it could drive the biggest impact. But Josie and Beck would bring it too. Their very best. Their battle ready. I'd expect nothing less. In her heart, she'd always known I was her ultimate competition. For so long, I hadn't believed it. Now I knew that it was fact.

Fate could be so cruel.

I scanned over the paper recollections. Two kings and two queens. Then one would fold.

I sat back on the bed.

Maybe that's what it meant. It was time to fold on all the things I'd held dear. The promises I'd made to myself and to others. To turn them away. To think only of myself and of my battle. I would cling to this inten- tion. I would fight and claw my way into the High Council. Josie could have her partner. But she couldn't have my spot.

I slipped out of my grubby clothes and bathed my sore muscles in a hot, soapy shower.

This journey's rough-and-tumble edges had made small and large appearances all over my aching body. Knicks and cuts imprinted my skin. The place where I'd bounced off the mattress and smacked my head into the wall was blossoming into an ugly yellow bruise with an inky purple center. Along with the bump on my forehead, a second bruise threatened to spread from my hip all the way down my thigh. It was tender to the touch.

I took my time in the hot water.

I cupped batches of liquid in my hands, then dashed them down my body in an extra rush of muscle salve. Over and over, I flooded my skin in the continuous flow from the shower. I turned and faced the taps, leaning forward, letting the gush drip through my hair and run over my forehead, down my cheeks and nose. It accumulated over my lips. I sputtered and blew out, not consuming the water, but giving in to the downward gush. It flooded my outsides with warm rushes of love.

I closed my eyes and meditated.

I stayed there, still in that shower until the hot water heater emptied and the temperature grew warm.

Then cool.

Then cold.

Finally, the coldest waters spattered my body and harshly instructed, it was time to move on. I patted my skin down with a fluffy towel. Then I took the time to fully blow-dry my hair. I smoothed each layer, staring at my reflection in the mirror. Since this was the last time I might even be here, my very last day at the cusp of the High Council, it felt only right to give my appearance my all.

I coated my lashes in mascara and laid out my nicest clothes on the bed. I stuck with the usual dark khakis, but instead of a typical gray T-shirt, I laid out the pineapple tee from my aunt. The brand-new fruit motif brightly shimmered. I grinned and pulled the little gift over my head. I smoothed it over my shoulders, down my body. It fit perfectly, as my aunt knew it would. A warm fabric hug from my biggest supporter. Now Aunt Abeline was with me. I was ready to go.

This was the final battle.

Whether I won or lost, I would go out as my true self. My very best version. I clasped my grandma Mim's moon charm necklace around my neck, and looked in the mirror. I smiled. If this was the whole package, I could live with it. I'd put it all out on the table. Live or die by the sword. It was time to learn my destiny. These bonds were predestined. I was ready to go.

I left my motel room and looked around for some people to join. Maybe find Spade to tell him I was ready or locate Beck and Josie and wish them best of luck on the course. I wasn't worried about hard feelings. It was winner take all for every one of us.

But... as I came onto the cement concourse, there was already something happening poolside. The other teens were all there, and there was plenty of whispering. In the midst of them stood Lady Mauve and Lady Gray. As I neared, I realized I was the last to join the gang. Josie, Beck, and Spade were already present. People grew silent as I approached.

"Oh good, you're with us," Lady Gray noticed.

"Did I miss the call?" I wondered.

"No, no. The final round will begin in a moment," she assured me with an overly false pleasant demeanor.

"In your fiercest battle clothes." Lady Mauve sneered at my sunny wardrobe, but I didn't care. I wouldn't be shamed. This was who I was. Take it or leave it.

"I think you look nice." Josie smiled. "Doesn't she, Beck?"

Beck looked over at me and nodded dumbly, but he didn't see me or my pineapple shirt. He didn't see anything. He looked totally shell-shocked.

"Don't talk to my partner," Spade growled, stepping between us.

"What's going on?" I wondered.

"Blah, blah, blah. Let's keep it for the course," Lady Mauve said. She aggressively shook the pill bottle, trying to rush us all forward.

"Wait... what?" I looked at the others.

"Let's do this!" Spade said, pumping himself up, offering me his pinky swear.

"Oh... kay." I looked between their faces, then tied my pinky around his. We did the miniature swear. The energy between the group was disconcerting. Not just Beck, but all the others. This was definitely weird.

"Let's do this!" Lady Mauve cheered, trying to scoop us all forward.

I let myself be gathered in her wingspan. I had no clue where we were going, but I was willing to let her take me away. I was in. I would fight with every instinct to get through to the High Council. Even scared and uneasy, I was still in command.

I hoped Beck and Josie knew that there would be no hard feelings. They should come at me with their all, as I would bring my all to them.

"Mae." Josie reached out and touched my arm. A shock ran through me. Her fingers barely grazed me. "There's something I have to tell you."

"What?" I had to look over my shoulder as I was being taken away by the momentum, the others all cheering and talking around me. But the second I did, I stopped in my tracks. Josie wasn't coming.

Everybody else stopped with me. But, I gave her my full attention.

She sighed. "Before you start the last round, you should know... I won't be joining you there."

THIRTY

COURSE CORRECTION

"YOU QUIT? YOU CAN'T QUIT!" I dragged Josie away from the group. "What do you mean? It's the final battle. The battle of the fittest. Fate will show us the right thing to do."

"I'm glad you said that." She nodded. "It already has. Fate made it clear. I should never have bonded with Beck."

"I don't…"

"He isn't mine," she said.

"Whose is he?" I asked, but she just stared me down. "Me? Oh no. You're wrong."

"I was. But I'm course correcting. You and Beck are the true match. That's been real since day one."

"No."

Josie sighed. "You've been a good friend. Probably better than I've deserved."

"Don't say that."

"I didn't even text to warn you we were coming." She frowned.

"I didn't text you either," I countered. But we both knew that the level of culpability was higher on her side. "I was freaked about Spade at first, but I've come to terms with my position. Everything's okay. I'm part-nered with him. Beck's not my guy. He's yours. He's always been yours."

She just shook her head. "All the signs were there... the truth serum... he didn't even notice Anita had taken my place. *You* noticed. He didn't notice."

"Josie..."

"I'm not done. He told me about how you two beat the system and spent time on the beach during the seven trials. It was his only moment of peace... Mae, since you got here, I've felt uneasy. You know that I felt it. There was this rabid tension and I tried to fight it off... so many denials..."

"But the denials were good. Because it's not true. None of it."

"Now I know why I felt what I felt. I should have listened sooner." She shrugged. "I didn't see it once, you know? Years ago with him." Her eyes flitted to my partner. "I was stupid. But now I get it. I'm very open to it now. The signs. It's obvious, Mae. To me, to Spade, to everyone else."

I glanced around. The others were nodding. Sloane offered a terse smile. Beck stared dully into the distance. Spade just scowled and glared.

"You and Beck will be an excellent partnership," she told me.

I pulled her farther away under the guise of more privacy, then dropped my voice to a whisper. "If that were true, he could have just found my necklace. He would have. He had multiple chances."

Josie peeked back at the crowd. "I've thought about that. All this extra time... these extra events, all these extra chances... I think that was for me. Fate was giving me the time I would need. Time to release. Time to be free. If you'd bonded at the school, on that first or second morning... if fate had just handed him over, it would have felt like a knife in the back. By you. By him. An act on all accounts that I would have never been able to get over. But now I can. Now I know this isn't my bond to make. It never was. I see that so clearly. This is the way things should be. It's the way that things *are*. It's not my spot. So I'm done. I won't be joining the High Council." She seemed so certain. For a moment, I didn't know what to say.

"Josie..." I started with her name, hoping more elegant words would come.

"Have you talked her out of it?" Beck had finally come to his senses and joined us.

"No."

"She can't and she won't. I've made up my mind," Josie said. But that didn't mean she'd convinced the other two parties involved. "Look, if you can peer into each other's eyes and tell the other honestly that you've never considered what it'd be like to be partners..."

I peeked at Beck. I held his gaze for only a moment. The look was too intense. We both flinched and looked away. I couldn't prove she was wrong. Neither could Beck.

But that didn't mean she was right.

"That's what I thought." She nodded.

"Jo, I'll never betray you," Beck told her.

"I know." She smiled and gently brushed the hair from his face. "Thank you. That loyalty is incredible, but I want more." She stepped back from us both. "This isn't my spot," she said. "So I quit."

Lady Mauve, who'd been hovering nearby, put an embracing arm around both my and Beck's shoulders. "Well put, Josie. Well put." She physically steered us away from the girl. "Now, if you don't mind, I'd like to get the rest of this rolling. Some of us have places to be." She released Beck but continued to drag me forward. I wanted to object, draw the conversation out, find another argument, but what more was there to say? I looked over my shoulder as Lady Mauve marched me out of their vicinity.

"I'll quit too," Beck told his girl. He put a hand on each of her shoulders as if he was willing her to reconcile. Josie shook her head.

"If you're saying or doing that for me, Beck, it's not what I want. What I want, what I *really* want, is for you to be happy. To bond with Mae. To go to the High Council. That would make me so glad. Wouldn't that make you so happy?"

"I don't know." Tears spilled from his eyes. His tall shoulders started to heave.

"Yes, you do," she said quietly. Beck couldn't hold it together any longer. He cried in mournful heaves, his whole body shaking. Tears crowded Josie's lashes and tumbled down her cheeks, but she never stopped smiling. "Beck, I'm setting you free. I'll always love you, and because I love you as much as you love me, I know... this is the right thing."

"But..." he defended again, trying to stifle the emotion.

"Shhh, stop talking. Those are just words," she said. "Once you've said all you can say, we both know what will happen next. You'll go to her. You'll be happy. I won't be your parabond in the High Council. And that's okay. I release you." Josie wrapped him in a final embrace. His ugly cry was over. Beck wrapped her in his arms and buried his head. She whispered final, comforting things in his ear.

Their last words as a couple were left for the two of them alone.

I pulled my eyes forward to give them their privacy. Josie was really leaving. She was sure that Beck and I were meant to parabond. That our connection was predetermined. It was something I'd sometimes wondered too, in the hidden recesses of my mind. Something I'd never have acted on because Beck was deeply off limits. Only now... he wasn't. But what about Spade?

"Are you okay?" Sloane asked.

Lady Mauve let me go to ready the proceedings and as soon as she did, Sloane and the other girls surrounded me. I realized I must look as shell-shocked as Beck had at first. I had been crying without even realizing it.

"I'm fine," I said, wiping the wetness from my own eyes.

"What happens now?" Hilde wondered.

Sloane and I looked at each other, then to Nicolette and Marcy.

Nobody knew.

"Maybe you pick your partner?" Hilde suggested.

"The parabonds are chosen by fate," Sloane disagreed.

But suddenly, none of us knew what that meant.

"Choose Spade," Hilde said. "I mean, if you're picking."

The others seemed surprised, but I knew immediately where she was coming from. Spade and Rick had come to her rescue. He had helped remove her from Jacob's grip. And Beck and Josie had launched an unsuccessful blitz attack on her and her partner. Of course she'd pick him.

"Hilde, it's not that easy," I tried to explain. "There's a history of mistrust and—"

"Then choose Beck," Nicolette demanded.

I was actually glad for the interruption, as I didn't really want to explain the darker ways the world worked to someone so young and naive. Unfortunately, Hilde would find out soon enough for herself.

"Why?"

She shrugged. "He's always known you were his partner. Remember? He didn't want Josie. The truth serum gave him away."

Marcy nodded. "But don't forget, he also said he has a crooked package." The rest of us groaned. "What! Not for nothing." She winked. "It's just a good little tidbit. You get what you pay for."

I glanced at Sloane. She was about to say her two cents, but I threw up my hand. "Don't," I told her. "You already manipulated me enough. In the last round? With the unlocking? I don't want you in my head." She smiled, put her hand to her lips, and mimed zipping it shut.

"Alright," Lady Gray called us back once again. "Come and join us."

We gathered poolside.

"Any other surprises?" Lady Mauve raised an eyebrow and looked me up and down. When I didn't flinch, she checked in with both Spade and Beck.

"I'm not quitting," Spade said loudly. "Mae is my partner," he added. "She gave me her word." He gave me a pointed look. "We both pinky swore."

I know.

He didn't have to remind me. I promised I would trust him. We'd be paired until the end.

"I'm not quitting either." Beck had recovered. "It's Josie's last wish," he said, then looked at me shyly. "And I want it too," he added quietly. "Mae is my parabond."

We locked eyes as he said the words out loud. Inside, my stomach fluttered. But this was all so fresh. How could I be certain he really meant what he said?

"And you, Little Ms. Pineapple? You wanna quit?" Lady Mauve asked sweetly. She was no doubt thinking of my secret escape from the compound only one night before. All eyes were on me.

"I'm not quitting," I said.

Lady Gray looked relieved, but Lady Mauve didn't show any emotion. She simply picked up her little bottle and shook the pills from side to side.

"Then it's time for the final battle."

FOR A MOMENT, nobody moved.

"Come get your pills," Lady Mauve said, her impatience showing. "You know the drill."

Spade, Beck, and I all came forward.

"You gave me your word," Spade told me.

"When she made that promise, she couldn't possibly have known—" Beck tried to interrupt.

"That you were all in on some other girl?" Spade spit. "I think that fact was pretty clear."

"Okay, guys." I sighed.

"She's been tryna shake you since day one," Beck fired back.

"Stop."

"And we have talked about that issue. We *communicate*." Spade enunciated each syllable.

"Long term, Mae knows. I'll be the loyal partner," Beck said quietly.

"Tell that to her friend." Spade bitterly laughed.

"Her name is *Josie,*" Beck defended.

Spade pointed at me. "And *her* name is Mae. Or did you forget that already."

"Okay! Enough. I can speak for myself," I told them. "Just stop bickering."

"You want this to stop? Then choose. Tell him. Who's it gonna be?" Spade asked.

"Who do you want?" Beck asked.

They both stared at me. Every person around the pool was on lock with my face. They all waited for me to decide. But how could I?

My relationship with Spade was a mess. He couldn't trust me. I couldn't trust him. There were times we barely liked each other, and other times the passions were on fire. He was a bully, and he was impulsive, and he rarely acted kindly. But he always had my back when it counted. He tried to manipulate or manufacture intimacy. But we were actually able to get across to each other all the complicated, ugly things we were feeling. And for the most part, we understood why the other always acted the way that they did. Or at least we did in hindsight. Even if we didn't agree with each other's decisions, with Spade I never had to put on any airs. I was always myself. The good, the bad, and the ugly. And I had given him my word.

Then there was Beck.

That boy was thoughtful and stoic and loyal to a fault. I had always liked him, even felt a deep attraction. But who could know how he truly felt? Only moments ago, he was professing his ultimate bond with Josie. We all knew his heart was still entwined with another girl. How could it be free? Even partnering with me now would also fulfill a bond to her. After all, it's what Josie wanted. He and I to combine. That's the result she decided. Parabonding with Beck would make me the ultimate rebound. Even if he really, really wanted a new relationship with me, the genesis of that bond was super awkward. We solved problems well, and I could trust him with my feelings. He seemed thoughtful and empathetic, and offered insight in discussions. It wasn't passionate or very heated, but we worked pleasantly on the same frequency and wavelength. We had fun and enjoyed spending time together, at least the little time that we'd had. But what would happen if Josie changed her mind? Would Beck toss me aside? It was impossible to tell.

I couldn't make a quick decision, especially under the heat of everyone's glare. Not a lifetime choice selection. But maybe, I didn't have to. As Sloane had said, perhaps it wasn't up to me. That was why the High Council built this entire process. It was best to let the fates decide.

"I will trust the results of the High Council process," I announced, careful to look both men in the eyes. I didn't flinch. With that, I picked up my final little yellow pill from Lady Mauve's bottle and swallowed it down. The boys took theirs too, fire in their eyes.

"May the best man win." Beck offered a hand-shake, but Spade ignored his outstretched palm.

"Eat rocks," he told him.

With that, the final battle began.

THIRTY-TWO
THE FINAL BATTLE

I AWOKE to the sound of quacking. What? Ducks? But as I opened my eyes and shook off the effects of the drugs, I realized those squawking noises might have been in my thoughts. There weren't any waterfowl in sight. I sat up, still dressed in my pineapple T-shirt. For a moment, I reflexively touched my grandmother's necklace where it dangled. I didn't want it to be destroyed in the final High Council battle. I had meant to ask Hilde to hold on to it. But I needn't have worried. For me, there was no battle to be won. I was already outside of the house that we had to escape in the final round.

I sat up and propped myself up against the red brick exterior wall, looking around.

"Mae's awake," I heard somebody whisper. Probably Marcy. They were all watching from the pool.

I stumbled to my feet. The drugs making my head a little woozy.

Since we hadn't succeeded in the earlier heat, I had never been outside of the home on the course. But I felt sure where I was. At the far end of a lawn waited the pool and the rest of the class. I looked all around. The wall I woke up beside was definitely exterior. The red brick travelled all the way up to the chimney. On the top floor, there were windows. On my level, the first floor, I could see the exteriors of the two doors I'd seen in the living room and kitchen. On this side of the wall, there were no handles to hold on to. They'd been removed and filled in with putty. Gray slabs that refused to open.

"Look!" Tej yelled. He pointed up in the air. The others followed his gesture. "Black smoke."

"It's on fire!" Hilde squealed.

"Do you think someone set it on purpose?" Marcy wondered

"No, they just knocked over a candlestick," Vince snapped.

"Okay, geez, relax," she snapped right back.

Holding my head, still shaking out the cobwebs, I walked backwards to get a better view and to witness. The others were right. There were indeed large plumes of black smoke coming out of vents at the top of the home. I took a couple farther steps back from the bricks to get a better vantage point and tumbled head over feet across a barrier I hadn't seen on the ground.

"Mae, look out!" Nicolette warned me, far too late.

I fell flat on my back. "Right." I looked around.

The field between the house and the pool looked

wide open, but now that I focused, I could see there was actually a glass maze with high and low blockades. I'd have to weave my way through to finish the course. I decided to make my way now.

The smoke in the house was getting thicker. It had seeped into the atmosphere over all our heads, even floating by the pool. I turned back and looked at the house. I hoped that the boys had escaped from their prisons. They must be almost out of the building by now. At least I hoped. Were they? I had no new information. Not knowing was hard.

I climbed up, over, under, and around the sheets of glass barriers until finally, I made my journey all the way up to the pool.

"Who you gonna pick, Mae?" Marcy shouted.

"Beck's a speck!" Greg laughed.

"Spade's shady," Nicolette countered.

"Don't get involved," Vince scolded.

Immediately, she wilted.

"Let her say what she wants," Tej scolded right back.

Nicolette sat a little taller in her seat but didn't dare say anything more.

"The fates will decide," I called back. "And I trust them completely." I said it so confidently. If only I could believe it myself.

"That's not a risk that I'd take," Marcy muttered, but I still heard her.

I looked between house doorways. *It was a risk.* She was right about that. But, if my partner was as predetermined as everyone claimed, then fate would pull through for me now. The only question was, who would it be?

There were two possible exits.

Two possible champions.

Still, I didn't feel certain. Why put them through this? Test Spade and Beck's resolve in a final battle, leaving my future so uncertain? Shouldn't I know who my partner truly was, deep down in my heart? Why couldn't I just choose him?

"Still want me to remain silent?" Sloane asked. She had approached from the far side of the forcefield that separated the competitors from the spectators. We both stared up at the wall where the smoke continued to puff. It had been pouring out for quite a while. The danger inside could only be mounting. What I really wanted was for someone on the inside to make their way out.

Nothing on the exterior of the house could give us a clue as to the battle underway inside. They could be suffering. They could be dying. Any pain they experienced today was directly my fault.

I peeked over my shoulder. Sloane smiled. She looked so serene with the long blonde hair falling over her shoulders. She'd become a bit of a guide through this process. So it was nice that she wanted to help, but I had another question.

"How did you know that telling me that I'd help you would manipulate me into helping?" I asked.

"Is that what you think?" Sloane chuckled. "Mae,

what I said wasn't a trick. It was fact. In my dream, I saw you help. I only said it because I knew you'd help me. I believed in my heart."

"Because you dreamed it?"

"No."

"Because of your manipulation?"

"Because you're a good and helpful person."

"Who you manipulated into helping," I emphasized again.

"It's not just my need or your desire, Mae. Sometimes one action can satisfy both. Sometimes you satisfy neither." I could tell the theme of this chat was veering over to my current situation. She smiled again. "Is it time for my two cents?"

"Sure. Whaddaya got?" I asked.

"Here it is. You don't owe either of these guys a thing." Already, I shook my head and started to reject her, but she held my gaze and carried on. "You owe *yourself*. It's your life and your partnership. You do you, and what you know is right."

"But right where?" I wondered. It wasn't really a question for her. "In my word or in my heart?"

"That's not much of a question," she said. "Don't be afraid. Fate requires action. Even now. Even head-to-head."

"Come now." Lady Gray shepherded Sloane away. "This is Mae's battle." She patted the girl's shoulders, led her away, then stayed put to guard the unseen wall between audience and competitors. Lady Mauve took up the role of guardian on the other side of the pool.

Their sentry guard purposely ostracized me from the rest of the group.

This was my future. Up to me alone.

I coughed at the black haze that was building in the air around us. What was taking so long? Someone should have been through the door by now. Was Spade lying unconscious in the attic? Or Beck in the basement? Did one of them succumb to smoke inhalation? If something happened to Beck before he could finish this process, Josie would never forgive me, I knew. But there was no way to check on their progress. The doors into the living room and kitchen were locked tight. All I could do was wait.

Suddenly, a door smashed open, and a beaten and battered boy emerged in a cloud of black smoke. If the layout of the house hadn't changed, the door that had opened was the door that led out to the yard from the kitchen. The kitchen was to my right, and the lava-filled living room was on the left. Spade was such a strong swimmer; he was bound to have gone in that direction.

But it wasn't Spade. It was Beck!

The fates had chosen Beck! My heart leapt. Deep down, I knew it was true. There wasn't a question. Beck was always the partner with whom I wanted to bond. Josie was right. For us to come together, we needed the extra time we'd been given in limbo.

For him, it was time to see the truth.

For her, it was time to say goodbye.

For me, it was time to commit to this hard new

magical life. To have the courage to live a life I truly wanted. A life at the High Council. A life as a witch. With Beck.

As my friend.

As my parabond.

As my partner.

He'd needed this too. To depart from his previous obligations.

Why hadn't I immediately announced it from the rooftops? It seemed so obvious now. I felt so guilty for putting him through this last battle. One more ordeal. I could see he was exhausted. He slammed the door behind him and bowled over on hands and knees, sucking fresh air into his lungs. I was about to cheer him on and beckon him closer when the other door to the field burst open.

Spade spit himself out of the door and fell on the grass in front of the red brick building.

What was happening?

Both boys were covered in soot and scrapes and bruises. They clearly had some sort of fist fight or battle inside. Neither could scrape together enough oxygen in their lungs to pick themselves up and run forward.

But was I wrong?

All the certainty of the fates I'd felt a moment previous had twisted itself in knots. If Spade had battled this far and this hard to be my partner, there was a reason I had given him my word.

"Come on." I heard myself will one of them to

stand up. "Come on," I said a little louder now, cheering the right boy to get to his feet.

The others took it up as well.

"You're almost there!" Greg shouted behind me. "Get on it!"

"You've got this," Nicolette encouraged.

"You can do it, my crooked friend!" Marcy giggled.

Beck started rising slowly. Spade stirred and in great agony, he started to stand.

"RUN!" Hilde screamed.

This awoke them both. Using every ounce of strength, the boys realized they were neck and neck with the other. They started running. Their gaits lurched and stumbled, covering the ground between the house and the field. But they weren't moving in rational directions. There was no way, I realized, through the smoke and the haze to see the walls of glass or the sharp turns that were waiting mere steps away at the start of the maze. They were going to smash right into it.

Quack, quack.

Distant quacking noises echoed in the back of my head.

Fate required action.

My dream.

I was supposed to warn them. The waterfowl. The quacking... I was supposed to do something.

"Spade... DUCK!"

Beck dropped to the ground and rolled under the first partition, but Spade didn't have time to react. He smashed headfirst into the glass barricade at full speed. It immediately shattered. Shards of glass flew everywhere.

As a group, the pool collective gasped.

"Spade!" I shouted.

"No!" Hilde added.

Why hadn't he listened? From the blast of glass, Spade was covered in fresh gashes. Blood oozed from his wounds. In defeat, he lowered his hands. But Beck wasn't doing that much better. He couldn't see where he was going. Although he'd taken my initial warning and ducked the first obstacle, a shard of glass that Spade had broken now seemed to bounce a strange reflection into Beck's eyes. It blinded him. Beck held up his hands trying to block it, but the sun's bright rays blasted into his face. He yelped and squinted, but it was no use. He couldn't see where he was going and desperate to hurry, he smashed into another pane of glass. It shattered to pieces.

Both boys were an ugly mix of soot, blood, and splinters. But neither stopped to remove the shards. They just kept coming. It was a battle right to the finish. Up and over they maneuvered the maze partitions. Spade crawled and limped towards me, blood gushing from a gash below his left eye. His one ankle contorted and twisted behind him. Beck could no longer use his left shoulder; it had fallen out of the socket. He was doubled in pain, gingerly holding the limp appendage, but still he kept up his pace.

"What have I done?" I murmured.

They were a bloody, gnarly disaster.

I had asked fate to give me its answer, but here they were, beaten and battered, so close to broken, and the guys were just as head-to-head in battle as they'd been since limbo began.

Only... something was different.

Beck had kept his hands balled since he'd exited the building... and now, Spade dropped his hands again. I thought he might rest a moment, but that wasn't it. It wasn't a defeatist posture. It was a harness. He was attempting to guide the sun.

The wild glare of nature blinded Beck again. He tumbled. When the boy's chest hit the ground, he howled in pain. At the effort, Spade also stumbled, spent and exhausted, no longer able to stand. They each crawled the last few feet towards me, over the final plain.

I waited at the ready, arms outstretched to see which guy would reach me.

But... there was something off about them.

The nagging question niggled at the base of my brain.

Spade couldn't harness the weather. That was Beck. We'd even talked about harnessing sunlight. And, when I'd shouted directions to Spade, Beck had been the one to act. Beck ducked in time. It was Spade who had suffered the consequences.

Ahh.

That was it.

Of course. That was the difference. Once I figured

it out, it was obvious and clear. But more than that, it was the one true answer. Once I saw what Spade had done, my final choice became unmistakable. I knew once and for all which man was my parabond.

All that was left was to act.

Both guys had given every inch of final effort, but they couldn't complete the task without me. They each collapsed mere feet from the line. Spade and Beck both reached out their hands for mine. Fate again left the choice directly in my person. Neither boy was strong enough to finish without my direct action. It was my choice to make. Who would I carry across the finish line?

First, I walked to Beck's side.

"Hi." I gave him a sad, sweet smile. He looked up at me through swollen, bloodshot eyes. I gently brushed the hair off his forehead. He could barely raise his face. "You put up a valiant fight and made this choice incredibly close," I told him. I kissed his forehead. A smile cracked on his puffy lip. I took a deep breath. My decision was made. "But you should have known, I'm a girl of her word," I told him. "I made a promise to trust Spade. I expected that trust in return." I looked deep in his eyes to be sure *he* knew I knew who he *really was*, then slowly shook my head. "You broke your word."

His mouth fell open. He tried to call me back, but I was already on my way. I stood and walked to the other boy's side.

"Hi," I said, giving him a sad, sweet smile.

"Hey," he replied through cracked, bloody lips.

I gently brushed the hair off his forehead. He could barely lift his face. "Can you stand?"

"Sort of."

"I got you." I helped put his arm around my shoulder and guided him to put weight on his good leg. He balanced the injured limb behind him. We hobbled the final couple of steps forward and stood on the precipice of the pool. None of the other teens said a word.

The boy in my arms looked exactly like Spade, but in my heart, I knew that was false.

It was an illusion. A creation of Spade's imagination.

In this final round, Spade had used his lie-guard skills to try to trick me. A final attempt to manipulate me into doing the things he wanted. The real Spade wasn't my partner.

He couldn't trust me. He couldn't be trusted.

I could never parabond with him. In this final deception, he'd truly shown me.

My parabond was Beck.

It had always been Beck.

I didn't know why it took me so long to see or admit.

It didn't matter that he didn't look like himself. In my heart, I knew this bloody, battered version of Spade, was actually my man.

"Are you sure this is what you want?" he asked me.

"I'm sure." I smiled. "I'm so sure."

And for the first time, I meant it. Fate had provided me with the partner I'd always wanted. It was more than I ever could have hoped for.

"Are *you* sure?" I asked.

He grinned. "I just went through hell and back. I've never been so sure of anything in my life. Ready?"

"I'm ready."

He put out his hand, and I slid mine in his. The grip between our fingers was soft and warm and right. We smiled one last time, completely in sync, and together, we jumped into the pool.

THIRTY-THREE
A NEW BEGINNING

THE WATER FELT sharp and refreshing as we swirled in the wake of our jump into the future. The illusion of Spade being my partner vanished on contact with the water, and underneath the liquid, through the huge array of bubbles we stirred up between us, both Beck and I grinned at each other. Our partnership was forged through fire, but at last, the choice was complete.

The parabond process was now final.

We pushed off the bottom and resurfaced as newly minted partners, but before I could suck even one breath of fresh air, the water came alive with a million other arms and legs. The other teens in our cohort had leapt into the pool to join us. It was time for celebration! The five High Council couples had been selected.

Hilde tackled me in the water while Sloane knowingly grinned. She gave a small wink. I smiled back. Some teens were surprised to discover it was Beck in the water, not Spade, but to others, the final illusion had been obvious. I hugged every last friend in the group, a giant weight having lifted from my shoulders. This was the calmest, safest, and happiest I'd felt since I arrived in the small town of Plumpkin... or maybe ever... and I wanted to drink it in.

But there was one last moment of reckoning to deal with.

I turned around to face Spade, knowing I'd have to defend my choice and acknowledge the hurt that I'd caused. But to my surprise, he was already gone, along with the house and the obstacles and the maze that had ultimately caused him to lose. All the evidence of the final battle had been whisked away, and instead, there was a sense of joy and celebration. Even Beck's injuries had magically healed. He made his way over to me in the pool. All around us the teens frolicked. We both smiled.

"You're up and walking," I noted. "How's your ankle?"

"It's a little tender," he admitted.

"Sorry to put you through that." I frowned.

"Kiss it better!" Marcy squealed, kicking right through. We just rolled our eyes.

Beck grinned, then softened. "I keep looking over my shoulder thinking Josie will soon be joining." He shrugged, a little shy now that some of the rush of adrenaline had drained away.

"She really got us here," I agreed, thinking a

million other thoughts I was too chicken to say. "I'm really grateful."

"To Josie." Beck offered an imaginary toast, pretending to hold a glass in the air.

"To Josie."

We clinked hypothetical champagne flutes in an imaginary cheers.

Beck and I grinned at each other.

"Cannonball!" Greg shouted, leaping over us and landing inches from our heads, a tidal wave knocking everyone apart in the pool. But no one was mad or even a little annoyed with his antics. After all, we'd worked so hard to finally get here. To arrive at the celebration.

It was over.

It was finished.

We deserved a little fun.

THIRTY-FOUR

WELCOME TO THE HIGH COUNCIL

"WE WILL MEET BACK HERE at nine for a little induction ceremony," Lady Mauve told us after we had been suitably fed and dried off. I hadn't even realized how famished I was until the arrival of dinner. It felt like I'd been surviving on adrenaline alone for days.

"And dress warmly. The nights can get chilly," Lady Gray warned us.

We dutifully went back to our rooms to prepare.

I'd sent my nicest, cutest shirt to the bottom of the swimming pool in that final round of battle, but I dug around in the depths of my suitcase until I found another thing to wear. The grays seemed too drab for the celebration, so I was about to settle on white, but something at the very bottom of the case caught my eye. A blue T-shirt. I fingered the fabric. Aunt Abeline had prodded me into taking it, I remembered, to add a little spark, but it was still one of my T-shirts. She had said the color brought out my eyes. I laid my pineapple shirt over the edge of the bathtub to dry. My aunt was right before. Her crazy fruit fabric had brought me nothing but joy. I laid the blue shirt out on the bed.

I washed and blow-dried my hair. I wanted to look nice, not only for our entry into the High Council, but also for the other new things that were starting. A new friendship between me and Beck. We were friendly before, but almost in secret. Now things were different. We had both made a huge choice. We made a wild commitment to ourselves and to each other. But when he caught my eye in the pool, I realized there was so much unspoken subtext about our parabond that I still didn't know. Like how to feel. I liked and respected Beck so much, but he was always Josie's boyfriend, so there had been a safety barrier. There was a whole realm of words and emotions and things that we didn't say or feel or do. Would those words and actions be available between us now? Would those feelings? Did I want them? Was he ready to move on? Was I open to that next step?

A wave of goose bumps shivered down my arms.

I blushed at the thought of his hand in mine as we'd made the final connection. Together, we had jumped into the pool. There was hope and there was joy. But it would take some time to figure out the extent of those emotions.

Okay, I decided. Blue shirt it was.

I pulled it on over my head, flattening some of the bounce I'd managed to build in my hair as I tugged, but once my head was through, the result was still pretty great. I looked good. I looked happy. I looked like myself, and Aunt Abeline was right, it did bring out my eyes. I didn't feel any worry that I was trying too hard to fit in.

I fit.

I fit completely.

I swiped some lip gloss on my lips and tucked my jean jacket under my arm as I left my motel room, wondering what would come next as I joined the other nine by the pool. The chaise lounges and the piano were gone. We bunched together, waiting. Hilde leaned on me, and I patted her head. The glow of winning bestowed a pleasant bloom on all of our heads. Tonight, even Vince looked nice.

Lady Gray and Lady Mauve walked around the side of the motel together like they did on our first day in limbo.

"This is it." Marcy squeezed my hand like she had in our ride up to the motel. I squeezed her palm right back.

The women's arrival silenced the chatter. Again they stood at the head of the pool and waited for us to quiet before they addressed us. We awkwardly stood in a row.

"Each year, the High Council chooses seven potential parabonds, then whittles them down. The strongest five, the five couples with the most potential, are welcomed inside. This year, through a very messy reaping period, the High Council welcomed fourteen candidates to its front doors. With the mandate, like always, that only the ten most worthy would one day enter, we built the strongest tests the Council could think of to allow your truest energies to shine. Then fate made its selections." Lady Gray took a deep breath. Her eyes shone. So proud. "Congratulations to the ten of you. This is the first time in the history of the High Council that we can claim that fate required you to earn your spot. Twice."

The two women waved their arms.

They swung their hands over the pool and the motel and the property.

As their fingers danced by, the grounds began to change before our very eyes. The pool became a magnificent fountain, with jets of water shooting spouts of waterfalls. Behind the fountain, the motel transformed into a magnificent castle on epic grounds of lush green plants. The magnificent home looked both ancient in beauty and slickly modern, with turrets and dormers rising several stories from the grounds where we stood. On its southern face were a thousand windows. Delicate stonework with expressive balconies dotted each floor. And in the center of the estate, an impressive oversized atrium of bay windows extended up and up, three floors into the air. It was stately and noble.

Then they gestured to the right, and a cold wind blew in from the north.

The fall season returned all at once, and I realized the ladies had been holding the warmer weather until the end of limbo. I slipped on the little jacket I'd been carrying. The breeze was chilly. We gathered closer together. Winter was coming. The summer was gone.

I snuck a glance at Beck and discovered he was also looking in my direction. Instead of dodging my eye line or becoming shy, he playfully raised an eyebrow. I smiled and wiggled mine as well. We shared a private smile. Big changes were coming.

"Ladies and gentlemen..." Lady Mauve regained our attention. The illusion around us was fully dissipated. She threw our focus back to the expansive castle. "Welcome to the High Council."

WHAT NOW?

Want to dig into sneak peeks, learn about the next releases and find all the other freebies and literary goodies? Join my newsletter at www.juliecatherineau thor.com.

Xo

Julie

ACKNOWLEDGMENTS

We did it! We made it into the High Council! I hope you've enjoyed the journey thus far. This second book in the series was so much fun to write as I discovered the details of the world and the other potential bonds Mae would meet. What a challenge!

Thank you to my editor, Katie Wolf. It's so nice to have a trusted source to look things over and point out things that aren't clear. I truly value your input.

Thanks to David Guthrie and Allana Giesbrecht for being my first looks in the High Council world.

My goal writing book two was to open the world of the High Council a little wider and start to build the magic systems as they appear. I hope you're finding Mae's story exciting, unexpected and just a tiny bit magical.

Have no fear, Mae's adventures are only beginning, and I hope to see you for the first day of school in book 3 of the series, *Poisoned Bonds*. Not to worry, things are never as they seem. See you there!

Xo
Julie

The High Council Witch Chronicles

Paranormal Bonds

Predetermined Bonds

Poisoned Bonds

Planted Bonds

Paternal Bonds

The High Council Witch Chronicles prequels

Enchanted Bonds (a prequel novella)

GRAB

your free ebook copy

a prequel novella

get yours at
www.juliecatherineauthor.com